Before I came to be ~~in the service of~~ the wizard Ebenezum, greatest mage in the Western Kingdoms, I sometimes thought of life as nothing but confusion, with the world a whirling ball of chaos in which anything could happen to you and, given sufficient time, probably would. Since I have become an apprentice, however, I have revised my views, and now consider my earlier worries and fears nothing more than a glimpse at everyday reality.

– from SOME THOUGHTS ON
APPRENTICESHIP
by Wuntvor, apprentice to Ebenezum,
greatest mage in the Western Kingdoms
(a work in progress)

'Gardner skewers all the cliches of quest-fantasy with wit, style, mordant irony and great glee – this series could have been serialised in *National Lampoon*, or filmed by one of the Pythons!'

– Spider Robinson

'The field needs more humorists of this calibre!'

– Robert Asprin

'Gardner has a fine sense of just when to deflate an apparent threat into slapstick.'

– *Newsday*

A Difficulty with Dwarves

Craig Shaw Gardner

HEADLINE

Copyright © 1987 Craig Shaw Gardner

First published in Great Britain in 1989
by HEADLINE BOOK PUBLISHING PLC

10 9 8 7 6 5 4 3

All rights reserved. No part of this publication may be
reproduced, stored in a retrieval system, or transmitted,
in any form or by any means without the prior written
permission of the publisher, nor be otherwise circulated
in any form of binding or cover other than that in which
it is published and without a similar condition being
imposed on the subsequent purchaser.

All characters in this publication are fictitious
and any resemblance to real persons, living or dead,
is purely coincidental.

ISBN 0 7472 3213 X

Typeset in 10/11¾ pt English Times
by Colset Private Limited, Singapore

Printed and bound in Great Britain by
Collins, Glasgow

HEADLINE BOOK PUBLISHING PLC
Headline House
79 Great Titchfield Street
London W1P 7FN

This one's for
Anne
a.k.a. Supersister

ONE

'Even wizards sometimes have bad days. I shall give you an all-too-common example:

'The magician, about to begin a spell of great importance, discovers that all his duckwort has gone bad and he is completely out of eye of newt. And it gets no better! The sorcerer quickly dons his walking robes and strolls down to the corner alchemist, only to discover they've had duckwort back ordered for months, and what newt eyes they have in stock are far too small and altogether of the wrong color.

'Well, the good magician is far too resourceful to let a couple of missing ingredients spoil a perfectly good spell. The mage quickly returns to his eyrie, and attempts some prudent substitutions, say batwing and dried salamander's blood, with perhaps some chives tossed in to give the whole thing color. And the potion looks correct at last! The sorcerer begins to chant the spell that will bring his day's work to fruition. But wait! The pot is burbling when it should be boiling! What could be wrong? (See footnote)

'The mage quickly checks a nearby reference work, perhaps the forty-six volume Universal Guide to Magic, *or my own much more concise* When Bad

---

Footnote: The apt student would have known instantly that our sorcerer should have used parsley instead of chives for coloration.

Spells Happen to Good Wizards. *There, to his horror, the magician sees that, through an almost infinitesimal error, he has transformed a simple weather-predicting spell into a conjuration that will destroy himself, his loved ones, and every other living thing in this hemisphere!*

'*The wizard somehow manages to stop the spell in time, but ruins a perfectly good pair of boots in the process. By now the wise magician will have faced up to one inevitable conclusion: That this day will be one of misfortune, not only for the wizard, but for all those with whom he comes in contact.*

'*But the resourceful mage should not despair that the fates conspire against him! Rather, the prudent sorcerer should take what small advantage of the situation still remains available, and spend the remainder of the day visiting one's mother-in-law or insisting upon an immediate audit by the royal tax collectors.*'

–Ebenezum, greatest magician in all the
Western Kingdoms,
MAGIC FOR THE MILLIONS:
A HOME STUDY COURSE
(fourth edition), General Introduction

It seemed like everybody was sneezing.

'Oh, Wuntvor,' Norei whispered. Her beautiful green eyes looked deep into mine. 'Isn't it terrible?'

The sound echoed through the Great Hall in which we stood, perhaps a hundred different wizards sneezing as one; high sneezes, low sneezes, short little shushing sounds, and huge, long nasal blasts. As difficult as it was to tear my eyes away from the beautiful young witch by my side, this true love that I had found at last, the nasal avalanche was far too overwhelming. With great trepidation I turned away from my beloved and looked down to the far end of the hall.

My worst fears were confirmed. The great oak door, behind which the wizards had conferred in order to find a cure for my master Ebenezum, had been flung open. The sorcerers, so noble and grand when they had entered that room some hours before, now staggered out of it one by one, their once-fine robes askew and torn.

But wait! One man strode through the wizard's ragged ranks, a look of grim determination on his dark-skinned face. Two arms clad in brilliant silver rose above the sneezing mass as this magnificent wizard, this mage among mages, cried 'Enough!'

The wizards nearby held their noses and turned to watch their fellow.

'This will happen no more!' The silver-clad wizard cried in a voice as deep as the farthest depths of the Inland Sea. 'I will banish this curse, as I call upon the spirits!'

His hands wove a pattern through the air too fast for the eye to see. 'Come forth, oh mighty waa . . .' He paused. 'Come forth, oh mighty waa . . . waa . . . WAAAA . . . .' His voice seemed to rise with every word. He stopped and swallowed, his dark brows furrowed in concentration.

'Enough!' he began again. 'This will happen no . . . WAAAACHOOO!'

His sneeze tore his silver robes in half as the multitude of mages about him answered in kind. The entirety of the Great Hall trembled with their distress. The silver wizard was soon lost beneath the sneezing mass.

Something must have gone horribly wrong. My master

and I had traveled here, to far and fabled Vushta, the city of a thousand forbidden delights, in hopes of ending our quest – a quest that began when my master was forced into battle with the dread rhyming demon Guxx Unfufadoo! My master won that first battle, but discovered that he suffered from a sinister aftereffect. From that moment onwards, whenever the wizard Ebenezum was even in the presence of magic, he would begin to sneeze uncontrollably!

Now, a malady of this sort might have driven a lesser magician to despair, but not my master! Ebenezum set out to find a cure, even if it meant traveling to far and fabled Vushta, seat of wizardly learning for all the Western and Central Kingdoms!

So travel to Vushta we did, learning on our way of a sinister plot by the forces of the Netherhells led by the dread rhyming Guxx! We redoubled our efforts to reach our destination, only to discover that the demons had spirited away the very city that was our goal and hidden it deep within their dwelling place beneath the earth, the dreaded Netherhells!

Well, there was nothing to do then but rescue Vushta as well. Since there was no legitimate hero handy, I was sent in the hero's stead, and with the help of good luck and noble companions, Vushta was rescued at last. In return for my service, the greatest wizards of the greatest city on the face of the globe had gathered together, all for the sake of Ebenezum. Now my master's malady would be cured, and all set right with the world.

Or would it?

Wizards were still emerging from the room at the far end of the hall, climbing over the bodies of their fallen comrades, the latter now convulsed with sneezing fits. It was a gruesome sight. I swallowed hard and turned back to my beloved.

'Yes,' I replied, looking once again deep into Norei's eyes.

'It is truly –'

'Terrible!' The old wizard Snorphosio called as he approached us, carefully stepping around or over the prone wizards in his path. 'Instead of curing Ebenezum's malady, he has given it to all of them. I knew this would happen!' He coughed nervously into a thin, almost birdlike hand.

'They took too direct an approach! I knew it! Something of this magnitude needs to be studied for weeks at least. Sometimes even years!' Snorphosio mopped his brow with a gray scholar's sleeve. 'Everyone knows that sorcery is an elusive art. Well' – he paused and took a breath – 'perhaps everyone doesn't know that, but at least wizards do . . . well, good wizards know the truth of what I'm saying.' He glanced distractedly at the roomful of sneezing sorcerers. 'Well, good wizards *should* know the truth I speak. But then again, what is the nature of truth? And how do wizards approach that nature? For that matter, how does nature approach wizards? In fact, is there truth in natural wizardry, or is there rather –'

'Indeed,' I replied in an attempt to cut short the learned sorcerer's musings. At least Snorphosio seemed to be calming down. Before, he had been so upset that he had actually managed to talk in short, coherent sentences. Now, however, the never-ending theorist deep in his soul seemed to be reasserting itself.

'Yes, you are quite right,' Snorphosio replied to my surprise. 'This is no time for theory. It is time for action. I say there!' His voice rose above the collective sneezing. 'Fellow wizards! Can any of you catch your breath long enough to tell me what happened in the other room?'

Half a dozen wizards tried to speak at once. None of them uttered more than a phrase before they rejoined their sneezing comrades.

'This is even more serious than I imagined!' Snorphosio exclaimed. 'But then, who is to say how truly serious a situation can be? And who can put a limit on imagination? And exactly how serious is imagination, anyway? Or how imaginary is the limit of seriousness –'

The theoretical wizard's body shook with an effort of will. 'No! I have no time for these musings. It is time to act!' He paused. 'But, is not musing in itself an action? And what if you act on musing? Is that not –'

Snorphosio shook himself again, clenching his fists. 'Action!' He looked again at the mass of ailing wizards. 'Colleagues!' he called. 'Please, hold your breath for but a moment. I will perform a short magic eradication spell, after which we may talk in peace.'

The noise level dropped considerably as the sorcerers attempted to comply. Snorphosio got halfway through his spell before he, too, began to sneeze.

'Hold!' came a clear voice from the room in which the wizards had conferred. 'Go no further!'

Norei and I turned to look across the disabled wizards, at the meeting room where this had all begun.

One more wizard strode boldly from the room, also seemingly unaffected by the magical malady. The large mass of sneezing wizards filling the hallway about us had raised a great deal of dust. It was difficult to see clearly. Still, there was something familiar about the way the man carried himself, his long, white beard, and dark blue robes.

The mage paused at the edge of the sneezing mass of sorcerers. 'Indeed,' he intoned.

With that word, I knew. It was my master, the greatest wizard in all the Western Kingdoms, Ebenezum!

'Master!' I called, delighted to see him so self-possessed in the midst of this chaos. 'Did the wizards succeed? Are you cured?'

The mage frowned at the mass of magicians before him. He pulled absently at his beard, then turned his gaze from the shuddering mass to look at me.

'Alas, no.' He sniffed delicately into a sleeve threaded with silver. 'I have but had the malady somewhat longer than these others, and thus have learned to control it better.' He shook his head. ''Tis a sorry sight, to see the amassed wisdom of Vushta brought to such a pass.'

'Pardon me, good wizard,' Norei interjected, 'but how could such a thing have happened?'

'Indeed,' Ebenezum replied as he wove through the disabled mages. 'Perhaps if I got a bit closer, we would no longer need to shout.' He moved as quickly as he could through the sneeze-wracked horde. The very sight of the tastefully inlaid silver moons and stars on his wizard's robe seemed to send those crouched nearby into redoubled nasal attacks. Finally he reached the end of the hallway in which we stood, the flagstones here still relatively free of incapacitated sorcerers.

Ebenezum looked back over the trembling sea of wizard flesh. 'It seems that we face new difficulties. It appears that the machinations of the Netherhells were even more insidious than we first thought. By dragging the city of Vushta down within their noxious domain, the demons have somehow subtly changed it. I fear this change may affect everything within the city. We have already seen how it affects the use of magic.'

'This is all the doing of demons?' Norei asked. 'Then that means we haven't defeated them as thoroughly as we thought!'

'Alas, no.' My master scratched absently at the thick white hair beneath his wizard's cap. 'I fear that our victory celebrations are premature. It appears that we have won but the first battle. Vushta and the Netherhells are still at war.'

'But this is terrible!' I shuddered at the very thought of these underhanded Netherhells' schemes. 'What can we do?'

'The first thing is not to panic.' He nodded at the still sneezing mass. 'The enemy has, temporarily, taken us by surprise. They have a slight advantage over us now, but it will not last for long. Already the wizards around us are learning to control their disability.'

It was true. There were far fewer sneezes than there had been but a moment before. Perhaps my master was right. There was cause for hope after all.

'Indeed,' my master continued, 'we must now plan for the long run. As long as we can keep our heads –'

There was an explosion in the middle of the room.

'Hi, guys!' a tiny voice exclaimed. 'I'm back!'

I knew who it was even before the smoke had cleared. Only one creature I knew had a voice as squeakily high and relentlessly cheerful as that.

'Talk about Brownie Power!' the voice added.

There was no doubting it now. A small, brown figure jumped merrily up and down on a pile of sneezing wizards. It had to be Tap the Brownie.

'Boy, is it great to be back!' Tap continued. 'I had a hard time leaving you before, let me tell you. I mean, who wants to go back to making shoes when you could visit Vushta, the city of a thousand forbidden delights! But now I can do all the visiting I want. That is, once I deliver my message!'

Tap unfolded a piece of brown parchment which had been stuck in his belt. 'This is an official proclamation from his Brownieship,' he began.

Tap paused to clear his throat, then spoke in a clear, high voice above the constant sneezing: 'Three hundred twenty pairs of laces; two thousand two hundred four buckles; four hundred twelve yards of –'

His tiny voice died in his throat. 'This appears to be an inventory list,' he remarked as he rapidly searched beneath the rest of his belt. 'Oh, dear, I must have left the proclamation in my other suit. Well, never mind. We'll get it later. Let me just say that, from what our superior Brownie Intelligence has gathered, you folks are in a lot of trouble. Yes, even more than before!'

Only now did he seem to notice the roomful of sneezing wizards. The Brownie whistled. 'Looks like I didn't get here a moment too early! With what's going to happen, you're going to need all the Brownie Power you can get!'

What did this all mean? I turned to my master, to ask him what to do. But the Brownie's arrival had been too much for his malady. Now Ebenezum, like all the dozens of other wizards in this great hallway, was sneezing uncontrollably.

TWO

*'The sages say that "You cannot have too many
friends," and for a change, the sages are largely correct in their sagacity. Anyone can see, for example,
that the friendlier a crowd, the better a wizard's
chances for survival after his spell has gone seriously
awry.*

*'However, there are some circumstances when even
friends can become burdensome to the working sorcerer. Wizards, after all, need their privacy, especially
when involved in extremely complicated and delicate
conjurations of powerful magical forces, or when
dealing in spells concerning the concealment of large
sums of money.*

*'But friends do form a very important part of a
wizard's life, especially when said mage must go on a
fearsome quest far from his native land and thus
needs someone at home to take care of his cat.'*

– THE TEACHINGS OF EBENEZUM,
Volume XXVII

The door that led from the Great Hall outside crashed
inwards then smashed against the floor, its hinges ripped
from the wall with the force of its opening.

'Doom!' the immense warrior Hendrek intoned. His
bulk filled the large doorway, a huge shadow that blotted

out the late summer sun. He held the doomed warclub Headbasher in one immense hand, the club no man could own, but could only rent. The winged helmet atop his head turned as he surveyed the room.

'Doom!' Hendrek repeated. 'Something is amiss!'

'That's what I like about you, big fellow,' a higher, infinitely more grating voice replied. 'You're always able to point out any problem, no matter how obvious it is to those around you.' The truth-telling demon Snarks poked his small, green head around the warrior's belly. 'What have we here? It looks like an influenza convention.'

'It's terrible!' I explained. 'Ebenezum's malady has spread to every other wizard in Vushta!'

'Doom!' the warrior responded with instant understanding.

' 'Tis another foul plot by the Netherhells!'

Snarks whistled. 'It looks like they've come up with a winner this time.' The demon flinched as the warrior growled above him. 'Okay, okay, maybe it's inappropriate to compliment the Netherhells at a time like this.' Snarks got a faraway look in his eye. 'Still, one has to have some feelings about the place one was born. I still remember it all: The smell of the slime pits, the gooey feel of fungus on the walls of my nursery, the special way those swamp gases would get into your eyes.' The demon sighed. 'It gave one a real sense of revulsion, let me tell you.'

Allowances had to be made for Snarks. His mother had been frightened by demon politicians shortly before he was born, a misfortune that led to Snarks growing into a demon that could tell nothing but the truth, especially the unpleasant truth, the more unpleasant the better. This truth-telling tendency had gotten him banished from the Netherhells, but that same extreme honesty had made him a trustworthy companion in our battles with his former home.

'Doom,' Hendrek said again as the sneezing continued unabated.

'What have we been thinking of?' Norei demanded. 'We have to get these wizards out in the open, away from this sorcery-tainted air!'

My beloved was right! I fought down a momentary pang of guilt for not thinking of rescuing the wizards myself, after all the times I had had to come to the aid of my master. There was just something overwhelming about being in the midst of two score sneezing wizards, something – perhaps the noise level – that made it difficult to think at all. A chill ran through my frame. Could this be yet another facet of the Netherhells' plot?

'Doom,' Hendrek muttered as he began to drag bunches of wizards outside the hall. Norei and Snarks turned to aid those few sorcerers still able to walk.

'That's not what I think it is,' Snarks whispered, his voice tinged with fear.

'Hi, there!' The Brownie waved from where he had been wandering among the prostrate mages. 'How are those shoes I made for you holding out? Talk about Brownie Power!'

Snarks groaned, his normal, sickly green face turned a sickly gray. 'No,' he moaned softly. 'What have I done to deserve this? I am banished from the Netherhells. This I accept. I am forced to wander through a strange world, and even battle my own kind whenever I should meet them. This, too, I accept. My human companions don't heed the helpful advice I give them that would so much improve their lives. Even this I accept. But the Brownie, again?' The demon drew a ragged breath, and fell to his knees. 'Is there no justice?'

'Why the sad face, friend demon?' Tap jumped merrily to Snarks' side. 'You have nothing to worry about. Now that I'm back, I've decided to take the time to show you the Brownie Way.'

'The Brownie –' Snarks began.

'Oh, there is no need to thank me,' Tap interjected before the demon could finish his sentence. 'I know it will take great patience, but making shoes teaches great patience. And if my efforts aren't enough to show you the light, fear not, there are a thousand of my fellows ready to take my place. You are in good hands with Browniedom. Soon you will know that there is justice – Brownie Justice!' The little man did an impromptu jig on the corner of Snarks' robe.

The demon stared back at the Brownie. Snarks opened his mouth repeatedly, and shut it as many times. No sound issued forth.

'Yes, it is all a bit overwhelming, isn't it?' Tap laughed infectiously. 'Come, what better time than now to begin our first lesson?'

The Brownie looked dreamily off into the middle distance. 'Lesson One: The Selection of Shoe Leather. All good things must begin somewhere. Shoes are no exception, and proper raw materials are essential. . . .'

Snarks rose unsteadily and staggered from the room. Tap paused at last and looked around, realizing that his audience had fled. 'Oh, how right you are!' he cried. 'How much better to conduct our lessons outside, in the warm summer air! I am coming, friend demon!'

Tap romped merrily from the room.

I stopped before a sneezing mass covered in royal blue.

'Master?'

Ebenezum looked up and nodded. 'Too much,' he managed. 'Outside –'

I helped the mighty wizard out onto the lawn that fronted the building. The grass was already crowded with prostrate mages. We had to walk some distance before we could find a place Ebenezum might sit undisturbed. He slid onto the grass with a groan. At least, I reflected, it wasn't a sneeze. In fact, the air out here on the lawn was remarkably sneeze-free.

'Thank you, 'prentice,' my master said after he had regained his breath. ' 'Twas an unhealthy situation in there. Too many magicians per square foot. The residual sorcery alone was enough to trigger the malady in all of us. And then, with the arrival of the Brownie, not to mention Snarks, and Hendrek's warclub . . .' Ebenezum shook his head. 'We will have to make plans' – the wizard stroked his beard contemplatively – 'but never again in such a large group.'

I did not say aloud what I thought; that the Netherhells had won a considerable victory if they could prevent the wizards of Vushta from ever using their collective magic against demonkind. The situation looked grimmer with every passing moment.

'Indeed,' Ebenezum replied to my glum expression. 'This proliferation of my malady is a serious setback. But we have faced other trials before, and triumphed.'

Snarks walked rapidly past us, a haunted look in his eyes. Tap was right on his heels. 'Now that we know all about the leather,' he called after the fleeing demon, 'just what do we do with it? This brings us to the second part of our lesson: Rudimentary Shoe Design!'

Ebenezum stroked his mustache as the Brownie also disappeared into the crowd of slowly recovering wizards. 'In fact,' he added, 'methinks I see the beginning of a plan.' He turned to me, an edge of excitement to his voice. 'Wunt!

Gather all our compatriots together and tell them to meet us at yon willow tree an hour hence.'

I glanced at the tree my master had indicated, a huge weeping willow at the far end of the courtyard from the Great Hall.

'All our compatriots?' I inquired.

The wizard nodded. 'Every single one. Meanwhile, I need to confer with one or two of my fellow wizards. By the time we meet, I will have put the final touches on our counterstrategy.'

I nodded and rushed away. We had made quite a few allies in our numerous adventures; I imagined them scattered all over Vushta by now. I somehow had to find all our compatriots in under an hour.

I found Snarks busily conversing with Hendrek directly around the corner of the building. The Brownie stood a few feet away, discoursing to no one in particular about the proper space one should put between eyelets. Here were three of these whom I sought. Perhaps this wouldn't be as difficult as I first had thought.

'Doom,' Hendrek remarked.

'Please!' Snarks pleaded. 'For the sake of all we've been through together! Only one tiny little blow from your warclub, and we'll never have to hear about eyelets again!'

'Doom!' Hendrek insisted. 'The Brownie has done nothing wrong!'

'Nothing wrong?' The demon groaned. 'The Brownie's very existence is an affront to demonkind! Just look at that little fellow, bopping up and down, talking about shoes as if they were the most important thing in the world. How can something that – that *cute* be allowed to live!'

Tap was indeed jumping up and down at this very moment, waving his hands and shouting at the top of his voice: 'You put one here, and you put one there! Shoe eyelets, shoe eyelets, everywhere!'

I had to admit that Snarks was at least partially right. Even lecturing about shoe eyelet placement, Tap the Brownie was adorable.

'Give me an S!' Tap continued. 'Give me an H! Give me an O! Give me –'

'Doom.' The large warrior shook his head. 'I couldn't do it. Violence is not always the answer, friend demon. Have you tried reasoning with the little fellow?' He turned to the Brownie, who was now leaping about in circles.

'What's that spell?' Tap cried. 'Shoe! What's that spell? Shoe! What's that spell? Shoe!'

'Doom,' Hendrek repeated. Snarks began to shiver.

'Hold, friends!' I called to the three of them. I had seen enough. If I was to accomplish my master's wishes, I would have to speak to them quickly and be on my way. 'Does there seem to be some problem?'

'No problem at all!' the Brownie piped up. 'We're talking about Brownie Power!'

'Whether we want to or not,' Snarks added quickly. He tugged nervously at my sleeve. 'You'll talk to him, won't you? My mother didn't raise me to be Brownie fodder.'

'Brownie fodder?' Tap replied. 'Brownie fodder? Sir, I want you to know that, to my knowledge, Brownies have never eaten demons for dinner. Or for lunch or breakfast either. Actually, we prefer to eat tiny cakes, baked to resemble boots, and even smaller sandal-shaped sugar cookies. Of course, when we are really hungry –'

'Doom,' Hendrek interjected. 'I believe the demon was speaking metaphorically.'

'Really?' Tap seemed taken aback. 'You'll have to excuse me. We in the shoe trade were never very good at metaphors. Similes are more our style! You know, like: "As industrious as a Brownie" or "As well made as a Brownie shoe." Now those are comparisons that mean something!'

The Brownie hesitated, doubt creeping into his enthusiasm. 'But metaphorical Brownie fodder? I had no idea you felt that way about the lessons. Perhaps His Brownieship is right. I do have a tendency to be too direct. Go for the gold, you know. That's a saying we wee folk have. I apologize if I have shocked you, friend demon.'

'Shocked?' Snarks replied, obviously startled by Tap's abrupt about-face. 'Someone who grew up in the Netherhells cannot be shocked. Being stunned by an excess of Brownie prattle, however, is another matter.' The demon took a deep breath, warming to his subject. 'And yet, you have apologized. Perhaps there is some hope for you little people after all. I could give you some advice on proper deportment. I'm sure if we worked on it long enough, we might find something for you to do that might even make a Brownie's life worthwhile!'

The Brownie nodded. 'It's obvious where I have gone wrong. I was too direct, too overwhelmed by Brownie Power! I must take a much more subtle approach, working by this deluded demon's side, showing him the truth in little ways every day, even though it may take weeks or months –'

'Months?' Snarks wailed, his rebuilt confidence evaporating at the very suggestion. 'Months?'

Tap nodded again. 'Perhaps even years. We Brownies have time. That's the joy of Brownie Power!'

'Joy?' Snarks' mouth began to work in a manner unnatural even for a demon. 'I'll give you joy!'

I restrained the demon's lunge with my stout oak staff and turned to Tap.

'Pardon me, but didn't you have a message to deliver?' I inquired.

The Brownie slapped his forehead. 'That's what happens when you start talking about shoes! I mean, the excitement just drives everything else out of your mind.' He hastily patted Snarks' footwear. 'Sorry, friend demon, but I have to go. Oh, what will His Brownieship think of me? I'll be demoted to buckles and laces!'

He waved hastily in my direction. 'I shall be back within the hour!'

'Meet us at the willow by the Great Hall –' I called after him.

A modest explosion, a small cloud of dust, and the Brownie disappeared.

'Gone?' Snarks asked, a slight quaver in his voice. 'Gone?'

'Doom,' Hendrek murmured, an immense, yet comforting hand on the demon's shoulder. 'Calm yourself. I have never seen you so undone before.'

'Yeah,' Snarks retorted. 'And I've never heard you use the word metaphor, either. Better watch out. High-flung language like that will get you kicked out of the Warriors Guild.'

'Doom,' Hendrek glowered. 'There is no such thing as a Warriors Guild. We mercenaries are all alone, forced to ply our trade without kith or kin. I am but a lone man, with a lone enchanted warclub. Is it any wonder that we take refuge in symbolism?'

The demon whistled. 'I didn't know anything was large enough for you to take refuge in.'

Hendrek raised his club.

'Now, now!' Snarks hastily took a few steps away. 'If you are not going to abide by some of those handy diet and exercise plans I have so helpfully given you, you have to expect comments like that! You should follow the apprentice's example here. Does he go on a rampage every time I show him how he might clear up his frightful complexion? I should say not! And I actually think my hints about his posture are having some positive effect!'

'Indeed!' I remarked neutrally. I had too much to do for my master to get into an argument now. I quickly explained how we needed both of them to meet the rest of our band by the great willow tree in under an hour.

'Doom,' Hendrek agreed.

'That means the Brownie will be there, too,' Snarks mused.

'He took me by surprise this last time, wouldn't let me gather my demonic wit. But that won't happen again.' A smile spread slowly over Snarks' bright green face. 'I'll be ready for him next time.' He turned to Hendrek. 'Are you sure I couldn't borrow your club for just a few minutes?'

'Doom!'

I decided to let the two of them continue their discussion without me. I still had to seek out the rest of our fellows. Most could be found close by the Wizards College, I knew, but there was a pair I would have to fetch from Vushta proper, where they were currently appearing under their professional names, 'Damsel and Dragon.' Perhaps it would be most economical to go after them first.

'Wuntvor!' a woman's voice called after me. 'Where are you running to?'

I turned to see Norei, my beloved, her hands upon her hips, her perfect mouth turned down to a perfect frown.

'I must fetch the rest of our compatriots to meet with Ebenezum!' I called to her. 'Pardon me, but is something wrong?'

'Well, it was awfully nice of you to tell me about it!' She sighed loudly and threw her arms open in a gesture of hopelessness. 'Wuntvor, one minute you are looking deep into my eyes, saying you will never leave my side. Then we go to help the sneezing wizards, and you vanish without a word of explanation! I swear, do you ever think about your actions at all?'

'Um, er . . .' I began. Everything she said was, unfortunately, true. When my master gave me this emergency task, I had quite forgotten that I was in the midst of a deep discussion with my beloved.

'Oh, I know you might tell me I'm being petty,' she continued. 'Here I am, thinking of my own concerns when we have another emergency at hand. But it seems like there's been nothing but one emergency after another since I've met you!'

'Um, er . . .' I tried to explain.

'Maybe it's because I've done nothing but rescue you from one bad situation after another. You seem properly grateful for a moment or two, and then – zip! – off you go again on some new adventure!'

'Um, er . . .' I said somewhat more forcefully. What did she mean, 'doing nothing but rescuing me'? Hadn't I rescued her in there somewhere?

'I should have known!' she went on. 'My grandmother warned me about wizards! I should have realized her dire predictions would hold true for wizards' apprentices as well! You sit there and pledge eternal fealty, then the moment my back is turned, you gallivant off looking for adventure and other women!'

'I do not run off all the time to see other women!' I shouted. Now she had gone too far!

'Well, perhaps I am being hasty,' Norei replied, somewhat mollified.

I nodded. She was being much more reasonable now. I knew I should have spoken up sooner.

'So you're going to Vushta?' she asked more quietly.

I nodded. Perhaps she would understand after all.

'To the Vushta Art Theater?'

I nodded again. Somehow, Norei's voice seemed to be growing colder.

'To talk with whom, Wuntvor?'

'Why Hubert, of course, and, uh . . .'

'See?' she cried triumphantly. 'It's always dearest Norei this and sweetest Norei that, but the minute my back is turned, off to see another woman!' She shook both her fists at the heavens. 'Off to Alea!'

'Um, er . . .' I responded. I had already explained to her a dozen times that Alea meant nothing to me.

'My grandmother was right all along!' she repeated, 'I might as well go back to the Western Woods.'

'But Norei,' I managed at last, 'my master – the meeting . . .'

'And you absolutely have to go see Alea personally and tell her about it? I understand! It is your duty as an apprentice! Men!'

'Norei?' I repeated. What else could I say?

'I will meet with the rest of you in an hour beneath the willow,' she replied coolly. 'As to what I will do after that, well, we will see.'

She turned and walked quickly away.

I wanted to call to her again, but the words died in my throat. How could my beloved think such a thing of me? Would she really leave us and go back to her home in the Western Woods? I shook my head and headed back into Vushta. I didn't see how things could get any worse.

But, of course, that was before I turned the corner.

THREE

ON DEALING WITH WIZARDS
(a fable)

Once a wizard was on holiday, far from his native land. He had journeyed to a distant kingdom to see the wondrous sights, as well as witness local custom. And, on this particular day, he was on his way to see the most wondrous sight of all in this part of the world, the Grand Palace high atop Emperor's Crag. He walked down a broad highway, curiously devoid of traffic, with tall woods to either side, and as he turned a bend in the road, caught his first distant glimpse of the palace's golden towers.

'Go no farther!' a gruff voice cried.

The wizard, in a strange land full of strange customs, halted immediately. A tall man dressed in crimson walked briskly towards him from the woods.

'This is an official road, you know,' the crimson-clothed man remarked as he approached. 'And as you are walking upon it, you are subject to a toll. A piece of gold, please.'

'A piece of gold?' the wizard repeated. It seemed to him a very hefty toll to pay when one was merely strolling toward a wondrous sight.

'Yes, yes,' the other man responded impatiently. 'I can see from your clothes you are a wizard, a man of learning. But I must have the toll. Unless, of course,

you want to conjure up a broom and fly away from this road entirely.' The toll collector allowed himself a little smile.

The wizard sighed. Still, he was in a strange land, full of strange customs, and one had to expect to put up with a little inconvenience now and then. He pulled his large and heavy money sack from his belt and handed a piece of gold to the other man.

'A wise man,' the toll collector remarked, 'for if you had not paid, I would have ordered the army to come out of the woods and kill you.'

So that was the way of it, the wizard thought. Of course, he couldn't see an army. But the trees were so tall and close together that they could have hidden anything. The wizard loosened his belt so that he might once again tuck away the money pouch.

'Not so fast!' the other man demanded. 'You have paid the toll, but you have completely forgotten the occupation tax!'

'Occupation tax?' the wizard replied.

'Another piece of gold,' the toll collector said, smirking. 'Unless, of course, you would like to call up a great storm to wash the road away.'

'I see.' The wizard recalled sadly how much he had wished to witness local custom. He reached back into his large and heavy purse.

'Ah, you have once again saved yourself from the army,' the crimson-clad official drawled. 'Oh, but I didn't mention, did I? That will be two pieces of gold. The occupation tax is double for wizards.'

'The occupation tax is double for wizards?' the magician repeated in disbelief. He had to admit, by now he was getting a bit too much of a taste of local

custom. Still, he did want to see the wondrous sight up
ahead. He reached once again into his purse.

'What'll you do?' The other man sneered. 'Turn
me into a frog? But then there's the army, isn't there?'
He jabbed the magician in the ribs. 'Of course, that
means you'll have to turn all of us into frogs, doesn't
it? Oh, I forgot. While you have the purse open,
there's one more tax you'll have to –'

There was a pause in the man's conversation.

'Ribbit, ribbit,' the toll collector remarked at last.

And the wizard was on his way, and was soon mar-
veling at great length at the wondrous sight, proud
now of all he'd learned about local custom, and revel-
ing in the newfound silence, which was only broken at
nightfalls from the direction of the lily pads.

– THE HOUSE AT WIZARD'S CORNER
(fourth edition)
by Ebenezum,
Greatest Wizard in the Western Kingdom

I turned the corner, onto the narrow street that led into the
heart of Vushta.

But my way was blocked by three young men, all close to
my own age and all dressed in brown. Two of them were
very large, perhaps taller than even Hendrek or the Dealer
of Death. One of the tall ones smiled in my direction, his
grin missing a couple of teeth. The other big fellow seemed
to hardly notice me at all. He appeared instead to focus all
his attention on a long, slightly curved knife which he
twirled absently between his palms.

The smallest of the three stepped forward. I was shocked

to realize that he was only an inch or two shorter than I was. Exactly how tall were his companions?

'Excuse us, fella,' the shorter one said. 'You wouldn't know where we might be able to find some guy named Wuntvor, would you?'

'Yeah.' One of the big ones laughed. 'Wuntvor.'

'Why, yes,' I began somewhat hesitantly. My battle senses were instantly alert. My palm sweated where I gripped my stout oak staff. I searched hard to explain this sudden feeling. For some odd reason these three newcomers seemed slightly threatening. Still, it must be my imagination, the result of spending far too long fighting in the Netherhells, where you might find danger lurking behind every stalactite. I must remember, I told myself: In our recent battle to defeat demonkind, all of Vushta had banded together to fight creatures of every description. After that, what need did humans have to fight each other?

I looked into the newcomers' faces, one after another. After a moment's hesitation I answered, 'I am Wuntvor.'

'Really?' the shorter fellow said. Somehow, he didn't look at all surprised. 'Not the same Wuntvor who is apprenticed to Ebenezum, a certain magician from the Western Kingdoms?'

'Ebenezum is the greatest mage in all the Western Kingdoms!' I replied far more quickly. I didn't like their tone. What were they implying about my master?

'Oh, no doubt, no doubt.' The fellow doffed his cap. 'I merely wanted to introduce myself and my companions here to the right person. You see, Wuntvor, we are apprentices, too. That's right. Just like you. Here, I want you to meet Slag . . .'

'Yeah.' The big guy to his left laughed. 'Slag.'

'. . . and over here is Vermin.'

Vermin doffed his hat with his knife.

'They call me Grott,' the shorter fellow continued as he placed his hat back on his head. 'We're all very pleased to meet you.'

'Yeah.' Slag snickered. 'Pleased.'

Vermin played with his knife.

'Now,' Grott said, 'you may be wondering what three busy apprentices like us are doing, hanging around on street corners?' He smiled ingratiatingly. 'Well, actually, we've been waiting here for you. You see, we have a little business.'

'Yeah.' Slag giggled. 'Business.'

Vermin used his knife to idly chip away large chunks of plaster from the building he leaned against.

'You see,' Grott continued, 'we represent a local organization, the Vushta Apprentice Guild.'

'Really?' I replied. I had obviously misjudged these three completely. They were naught but a welcoming committee. How much luckier was I than Hendrek! I had a guild of my very own. I asked the three if they wanted me to join.

'Well,' Grott went on, the smile still large on his face, 'I don't think you quite understand. If you're an apprentice, you're in the guild. Here in Vushta, there's no way around it. And since you're a member, we've got a little proposition for you.'

'Yeah.' Slag guffawed. 'Propo, uh . . . proposition.'

Vermin moved casually to the corner of the building nearest to me. He began to pry bricks out of the wall.

'It seems your master and our masters have been doing a little business together, too,' Grott said as Slag ambled across the road to a spot opposite Vermin. 'And that business has led to an unfortunate situation. Now, because of your master, "the greatest wizard in the

Western Kingdoms,'' all our masters are sneezing.'

'Yeah.' Slag smirked. 'Sneezing.'

Grott took a step in my direction. 'You probably don't realize how upset this situation makes us. Let me therefore give you a couple of examples.'

Slag and Vermin ambled toward me.

'Say you're a merchant in Vushta, used to paying a few pieces of gold each month as protection against evil sorcery. Now tell me, can a wizard who's allergic to magic protect anything?'

Grott didn't wait for my reply, but instead added: 'Let me give you another example. Say you're an apprentice, used to an occasional forbidden delight. What do you say when that delight's manager refuses to let you get near it, just because your master's malady might be contagious?'

Vermin walked away from his wall, sidestepping the stack of bricks he'd piled on the pavement. He used his knife to pick his teeth as he sauntered in my direction.

'Only one more example, Wuntvor,' Grott added ingratiatingly. 'Say, once again, that you are a magician's apprentice. This could give you a special standing with certain young women. Your job prospects are good. Full-fledged magicians have lots of power. And the ones that don't sneeze can make lots of gold as well, especially in Vushta. Now, it seems to me that the wise apprentice would find time to spend with all these young women, and show each one of them personally the advantages of a sorcerous career. But an apprentice won't be able to do anything of the kind if he has to spend all his time taking care of a sneezing wizard!'

I suddenly found Vermin's knife at my throat.

'It's very simple,' Grott continued, the smile gone from his face. 'All this sneezing around here is making our lives a little difficult. But we have a simple solution. Your master got us into this. And you're going to get us out of it.'

I opened my mouth to speak, but felt the knife point prick at my Adam's apple.

'We heard your master's hot stuff,' Grott went on, 'sneezing or no sneezing. We even heard you're pretty hot stuff, too, what with that jaunt down to the Netherhells and all. So we figure you can get everything back to normal by sometime in the very near future.' He reached forward to gently stroke the knife blade at my throat. 'Or else.'

'Yeah.' Slag towered over me. 'Else.'

'Are you threatening me?' I couldn't believe this. Fellow apprentices, resorting to violence! Is this what life in Vushta made of you? Perhaps I was happy I hadn't sampled any of the forbidden delights after all!

'Oh, no such thing.' Grott pulled his hand away. His smile once again dominated his face. 'We wouldn't think of causing you any harm. In fact, Vermin here is very good at improving the appearance of people he works on. He specializes in those little cosmetic extras, like cutting your ears back a trifle, or giving you an extra nose. But we wouldn't think of doing anything really violent.' He winked at Vermin. 'At least not yet.'

'Yeah.' Slag chortled. 'Yet.'

Vermin moved the knife point back a fraction of an inch, so that it but rested lightly against my throat.

'Well?' Grott prompted.

'Exactly what do you want me to do?' I asked. My hand still gripped my stout oak staff. I wondered how many of them I might be able to disable before they overwhelmed me.

'Why, that's simplicity itself,' Grott answered. 'We just need results – say, a cure for all our sneezing masters, or, failing that, a large quantity of gold to be handed over to us to repay us for this inconvenience.' The apprentice stroked his pointed chin. 'I think one hundred pieces might suffice.'

'One hundred pieces!' I exclaimed in disbelief.

'Oh, you are quite right.' Grott smiled broadly at his two companions. 'That was far too low an estimate. I am so sorry if I offended you. We'll have you bring us two hundred gold pieces instead.'

This time I remained silent, glaring at my captors.

'There, there,' Grott continued, 'much more reasonable of you. And you will see we are reasonable as well. We do not expect a cure for our masters, or failing that, the gold, until moonrise tomorrow!'

'Moonrise!' I sputtered. Grott shook his head. 'Still talking back? Maybe we should leave you with something to remember us by. What do you think, Vermin?'

And Vermin finally said something: 'Urracht!' he choked.

A hand, attached to an arm clothed in deepest black, lifted the large knife-wielder and tossed him a dozen yards down the road.

'I think this is possibly more fun than strangling wild pigs,' a mild voice remarked. I twisted my head around. The Dealer of Death stood behind me.

I moved quickly, swinging my stout oak staff about so that its end caught Slag full in the stomach. He sat down abruptly with a groan. I retreated a step, wary of a further attack from Grott, before I realized he was already held in the Dealer's viselike grip.

'Should I strangle this one, too?' the Dealer asked eagerly.

'No, no,' I replied quickly. 'I think we need to talk with them.'

'Oh,' the Dealer answered in disappointment. With some reluctance, and without completely releasing his grip, he lowered Grott to a point where the apprentice's feet touched the ground.

'Much more reasonable,' Grott whispered hoarsely once he had caught his breath. He nodded in my direction. 'So I trust you will honor our request?'

'Request?' I could not believe my fellow apprentice's audacity. Slag was still groaning on the pavement, and Vermin, while he had picked himself up from his recent toss by the Dealer, had lost his knife and seemed to be wandering about in a bit of a daze.

'Perhaps,' I added, 'you don't quite understand the situation. You are facing more than one simple apprentice here. My companion is known only as the Dealer of Death, a member of a secret league of assassins. I can assure you that he knows a greater variety of ways to kill people than there are apprentices in Vushta.'

The Dealer nodded eagerly. 'I have been getting a bit rusty on the finer points, though. Can I try something really elaborate on one of them, say a little number called ''The Princess and the Spikes of Death''? That one always was a crowd pleaser!'

'No,' I insisted, 'I think it's better if we talk to them. They are, after all, in the same trade as myself, only slightly jaded, I am sure, by a lifetime spent in Vushta.'

'Oh,' the Dealer replied, trying hard not to show his disappointment. 'Well, maybe I was being a bit too elaborate with the ''Spikes'' idea. It's just so seldom one gets a chance to do anything really major in polite society. How about something a bit simpler, say ''The Shepherd Girl and the Hundred Screaming Points of Doom''? It doesn't have quite the showmanship of the other piece, but it is still quietly effective in its way.'

'Please forgive the enthusiasm of my colleague,' I told the other apprentices, looking specifically at Grott, who was slowly turning blue from the Dealer's somewhat looser hold on his neck. 'If we can work together, none of this should be necessary. There is no need for threats, or for violence. I have fought demons and magical creatures from the Western Woods to Vushta, and then again down to the Netherhells and back, all for the sake of my master. I realize that you, too, fellow apprentices, are worried about the fates of your masters. But if we all work together, we shall persevere, and defeat whatever has overtaken the wizards, while we are ready for any other dastardly plan the Netherhells sends our way!' I threw my hands aloft, beckoning the others forward. 'Join with me, fellow apprentices! Together, we can rescue Vushta! Together, we can save the world!'

'Does that mean I have to let this troublemaker go?' the Dealer asked with a frown. 'I realize that even the "Screaming Points of Doom" might be a bit much for the middle of the day. But I was still hoping to perform at least "The Milkmaid and the Moment of Grinding Terror." That's one of the most sedate deaths I know that retains any bit of style at all!'

'Let him go,' I instructed the assassin.

Even though he didn't like it, the Dealer did what he was told.

'Much better,' Grott said as he rubbed his neck. He stepped back three paces to join his fellows, who stood on either side of the street, each leaning against a building.

'So,' Grott continued, 'we expect either the cure or the money by moonrise tomorrow.'

'What?' I replied in astonishment. 'Haven't you listened to anything I said?'

'I would have preferred not to. As it was, I was too busy choking in a death grip to pay it much attention.' The smile was back on Grott's face. 'We have our orders, Wuntvor. Moonrise tomorrow, or else.'

'Does this mean I get to perform the "Moment of Grinding Terror" after all?' the Dealer cried joyously.

But the three apprentices were already some distance down the street, traveling at an amazing speed, considering their injuries.

'Remember!' Grott called before he disappeared around a distant corner. 'There's more where we came from. We of the Vushta Apprentice Guild will not be stopped! Moonrise tomorrow!'

'Is it worth it to pursue them?' the Dealer inquired. ' "The Milkmaid and the Moment of Grinding Terror" is just as effective when performed in motion.'

I told the assassin not to bother. We would deal with the Apprentice Guild later, if we had to. I must admit that at the time, I still held the vain hope that, in a cooler moment, the Guild might agree to work together with us after all. In the meantime, though, there was the meeting with my master to consider. I asked the Dealer of Death to join us beneath the willow.

'Ah,' the Dealer replied with a smile, 'time for action again. I shall meet you there.' He flexed his large and powerful hands. 'In the meantime, though, this recent encounter has left me vaguely dissatisfied. It is time I strangled a wild pig.'

With that, the Dealer was gone as silently as he arrived. I turned and once again headed for the Vushta Art Theater.

A magnificently mellow voice spoke from the shadows before I had gone three paces.

'I would have saved you, you know, if the other fellow hadn't shown up,' the voice crooned softly.

With that, the most wondrous beast I had ever seen stepped out into the light. Sparks flew where its shining hooves hit the cobblestones. It looked at me and tossed its head, the motion of its flowing mane taking my breath away.

It was the unicorn, a beast I had met once before in our journey across the Western Woods. Its incredibly white coat was doubly blinding here on the dark streets of Vushta, and I found it almost impossible to look at the sunlight reflecting off its golden horn.

'Forgive me,' the exquisite creature murmured. 'I just couldn't stay away.'

'What do you mean?' I said, temporarily taken aback.

The unicorn looked at me with its soulful brown eyes. 'I'm talking about you, you wonderful apprentice. It's not often that a beast of my sort finds someone really worthy, someone in whose lap I can lay my heavy head.' The beautiful beast took a tentative step toward me. 'It's worth taking a trip, even to a place like this, when you find a lap like that.'

'All the way to Vushta?' I took a step away. I had forgotten how uncomfortable this beast made me. 'Certainly there must be hundreds of laps in Vushta worthier than mine!'

'Vushta!' the beast snorted. It took another step in my direction. 'They call it the City of Forbidden Delights, you know. Not much chance of finding virgins here.' The unicorn sniffed haughtily. 'Well, that is,' the beast hastily added, 'with certain exceptions.' It nudged me gently with its golden horn.

'That's all very nice,' I replied, trying to think of some way to escape this overamorous beast, 'But I have errands –'

'Oh, yes, the meeting at the willow tree with the wizard. I overheard you from the alleyway.' The magnificent beast sighed. 'I've come this far, I can wait a little longer. I'll join you at the willow tree with the others. Then' – the beast paused significantly – 'we'll talk again.'

I hastily agreed, and ran down the street toward the Vushta Art Theater. Time was growing short, and I had to fetch two more of our company. I sped about the corner and caught my first glimpse of the towering edifice that housed the theater. The first time I had come here, I had been quite taken aback by the size of the place, until I thought for a moment and realized how large a stage they would need to have to accommodate a tap-dancing dragon.

I walked in through an entranceway marked Stage Door, waving my stout oak staff at the elderly man who shouted at me from the stool just inside. There was no time to tarry now, and no need to ask directions. I could hear the pair I sought rehearsing in the distance.

'Hit it, damsel!' the great, deep voice of Hubert the dragon exclaimed. He was answered in song by one of the sweetest sopranos I have ever heard.

'Listen all you Vushtans, you'll be glad you came!
We'll tell you of a young man, and his claim to fame.
He might not be too bright. But still he did all right.
We've got a hero, and Wuntvor is his name!'

The two then repeated the last line, singing together, followed by a spate of very loud tap dancing. I climbed a flight of stairs and crossed an area filled with large painted canvases depicting various scenes from both Vushta and the countryside. Some of them even seemed to suggest a forbidden delight or two.

The singing sounded much closer when they began again. Taking an extra moment to study a couple of the finer canvases, I neglected to watch where I was going and thus tripped over something that looked like rock but was nowhere near as heavy. The thing that wasn't a rock slipped away from me at alarming speed. I grabbed at a nearby canvas to steady myself. Unfortunately, the painted backdrop did not appear to be well secured either, and fell firmly over my head, covering my entire body and the floor on either side for some distance.

This was terrible! How could I fulfill my master's wishes if I was trapped in canvas? I could barely move beneath the weight. One misstep and I would stumble completely into the tangling cloth. Still, somehow I struggled toward the singers' voices:

'Now Wuntvor is so clumsy, it's a wonder he's not
　　lame!
When he carries something, beware despite his fame,
His marching down the street
For he has two left feet.
We've got a hero, and Wuntvor –'

The song was interrupted by a piercing scream. Alea's scream!

Something was wrong! Damsel and Dragon were in danger, and I was trapped in my painted prison, unable to come to their aid! I tried to call Alea's name, but my voice was muffled by the endless yards of canvas.

I stumbled against something hard.

'Have no fear, Alea!' Hubert's voice cried. 'I've got

this hideous creature now! Should I fry it where it stands?'

At that moment I finally discovered the end of the canvas, and rapidly pulled my head through the newly found opening. I looked straight up into a dragon snout.

'Then again,' Hubert remarked, 'perhaps I shouldn't.'

'Wuntie!' Alea called, her voice tinged with delight.

I greeted both of them in turn. Hubert complimented me on my entrance and asked if I had ever seriously considered a career in show business. I told him I didn't have time to think of it now, and briefly informed the two of them of the situation at the Wizards College and the upcoming meeting with Ebenezum.

Hubert shook his head. 'You shouldn't be too hasty in a decision of this sort. There's a place for you in our act! Besides, as you probably heard, we're working on a major new opus, "The Ballad of Wuntvor," for the big victory celebration this weekend. You could do a guest appearance! What a natural!' Hubert paused and snorted, producing two perfect smoke rings from his nostrils. 'Of course,' he added, 'the way things are going, we may have to postpone the victory celebration . . .'

I agreed, and added that we should hurry, for the meeting was sure to begin shortly. All I had to do was get out of this restricting canvas.

'Oh, Wuntie!' Alea exclaimed. 'Let me help you!' And with that, she rushed to my side.

What could I do? I knew that once Alea had her mind set on something, she had to have her way. She had called me Wuntie since we had known each other long ago in the Western Woods, and nothing I said to her now could stop it. We had meant something to each other in that long ago time, but it had been naught but a boyhood crush on my part, before I met Norei and discovered what true love really meant.

'Here.' Alea giggled as she grabbed the pieces of canvas around my neck. 'We haven't had a chance to be this close in weeks, Wuntie!' Her long blond hair fell in my face, tickling my nose. Her blue eyes were mere inches away from mine, as were her full, red lips.

It was getting awfully hot, trapped in this canvas. I began to sweat.

'I think I found where it starts,' Alea cooed. 'Wuntvor, I'm going to pull this way. If you pull opposite me, maybe we can unravel this.' She giggled again. 'I've always wanted to have a captive male.'

'This is perfect!' Hubert exclaimed above us. 'Are you sure you didn't want to go into show business? Talk about your escape acts! I tell you, it's a natural!'

Perhaps I overreacted then. Perhaps I was still far too worried about what Norei had said to me, and that if I didn't change my ways, she would leave me forever and return to the Western Woods. Perhaps I was worried what Norei might think if she found me in such close conversation with this other woman. Perhaps I thought about how far away the Western Woods really were.

Then again, perhaps I didn't want to be anybody's captive male.

Whatever made me do it, it happened thus: I pulled away from Alea, just as she had indicated. Unfortunately, I pulled away with far more force than she or even I was expecting. The canvas, amazingly resilient piece of fabric that it was, stayed firm, but the force of my movement instantly caused me to lose my balance. As I fell, I saw Alea swept off her feet, pulled by her own steel-fingered grip on the canvas. Once again she screamed.

'Then again,' Hubert suggested, 'you could perform a credible comedy act.'

How could the dragon joke at a time like this? I was completely lost within the folds of the huge canvas. And what's more, Alea was lost with me!

This was not at all what I had planned to do.

I had meant to tell Alea, once and for all, about my feelings towards Norei. I had meant to tell her that for the time being it might be better if we did not spend any time in close contact. Now we were wrapped together, overwhelmed by a mass of scenery!

But I realized then that I was needlessly panicking; I, the apprentice who had rescued Vushta from the Netherhells. This was all an accident. Both Alea and myself were innocent, completely without ulterior motive. There was no need for my beloved to be informed of this little incident, ever. If I just stayed calm, I could extricate myself in no time, with no harm done.

'Pardon me,' a woman's voice called outside my canvas prison, 'but is Wuntvor here?'

I knew that voice. It was Norei!

'May I help you?' Hubert called in his most ingratiating tone.

'Well, mayhaps,' Norei said hesitantly. I managed to peer again through a hole in the canvas. She looked up at the dragon, and did not see the point where Alea and I lay tangled upon the stage. 'If you can aid me in finding Wuntvor.' She blushed. How beautiful she was with those red cheeks! 'You see, we had an argument. Oh, it was all my fault!'

She had come to apologize! I redoubled my efforts to free myself of the neverending canvas, doing my best to remain silent at the same time. If I could only get out of this one, Norei and I could live happily ever after!

'We had a fight over –' she paused – 'well, over something stupid. I don't know what came over me. I think I wanted this whole trip to Vushta, with all the fighting, and all the nights not knowing whether I'd wake up in the morning or end up as some demon's dinner – I just wanted all that to be over. When I found that it wasn't, I took out my frustration on the person closest to me. And I'm afraid that person was Wuntvor.

'Oh, the argument was so foolish.' She laughed as she looked about the room. 'I have to tell him, to make him understand. Is Wuntvor here?'

At that moment I finally rolled free of the canvas.

'Wuntvor!' My beloved cried. 'You heard me talking to the dragon, then? What can I say –' But her smile turned almost instantly to a frown.

'Norei –' I began.

Alea rolled out of the canvas and bumped into my posterior.

FOUR

'The truly professional wizard must consider the needs of not only humans, but every manner of creature he might come in contact with in the course of his sorcery. He is required to know, for example, precisely what sphinxes like to eat for a midnight snack; that trolls, as a rule, do not know the meaning of the word erudition, or that most fairies are violently allergic to horse-radish. However, all these facts pale before the most important part of a wizard's knowledge, which is just exactly what each and every creature can afford to pay for your services.'

— THE TEACHING OF EBENEZUM,
Volume XI

'What can I say?' my beloved repeated, although the tone of her voice had changed. 'I know just what I can say, but I'm too civilized to repeat it in front of others!'

Norei turned and stomped from the stage, her footsteps somehow even louder than the noise the tap-dancing dragon had made earlier.

'I'm glad she's gone,' Alea breathed on the back of my neck. 'Now we'll have time to get reacquainted.'

I didn't answer her. I was far too upset. Was Norei leaving me for the Western Woods? How would I ever see her again?

'Alea,' Hubert reminded her softly, 'we have to rehearse.'

'Oh, Hubert! Honestly!' Alea pushed herself to her feet, somehow managing to lightly kiss my ear in the middle of the process. 'Sometimes, working with a dragon . . .' She left the rest of the sentence unfinished as Hubert puffed impatiently.

'You'll forgive me, Wuntvor,' she murmured, 'but I have to get back to work. While you're very nice to dally with, the stage is my life.'

I somehow managed to get to my feet as well. I might not be able to dally with Norei ever again. I felt as though my life were over.

But I had to get back to my master! While Norei was gone, I still had a purpose – to save Ebenezum, Vushta, and the Western Kingdoms from whatever machinations the Netherhells had devised this time. I would go boldly into battle, heedless of life or limb, with no one to mourn for me after I was gone.

I marched from the stage, heading resolutely for the street.

'Hit it, damsel!' the dragon yelled behind me.

Alea's voice followed me as I made my way back through the storeroom to the stage door:

'Wuntvor's not that handsome, he's a hero all the
    same!
It's not just that he's awkward, it's his face that
    takes the blame!
For you can't see his dimples,
Beneath those mounds of pimples.
We've got a hero, and Wuntvor –'

Their voices cut off abruptly as I walked from the theater into the street. It didn't matter. I wasn't really listening to the words. I was hoping to hear another sound, like the light, rapid footsteps of a young woman, returning to seek me out again, or mayhaps that same young woman's voice, saying she forgave me.

There was a noise ahead of me, a cart being pulled across the cobblestones, a man's voice crying cheerfully through the afternoon air. I looked ahead, full of the faint, foolish hope that where there was activity, there might also wait my beloved. Alas, it was naught but a costermonger going about his business. He tried to draw my attention to his wares, but I had no heart for it. He could go on mongering his costers around me for the rest of time, it made no difference. My thoughts would forever be elsewhere.

'Norei,' I whispered to the empty street.

But enough was enough. I drew a ragged breath and reestablished a firm grip upon my stout oak staff. This mooning over lost love would do nothing to save us all from the clutches of the Netherhells. I had to return to the willow outside the Wizards College in time for the meeting. I had managed to gather all our allies – well, almost all.

I moved quickly to perform my final errand. It was on my way, at the corner of the field that the college used for their sorcerous athletic activities.

Dozens of furry faces seemed to light up as I approached their pen.

'Eep!'

'Eep eep!'

'Eep eep eep!'

I opened the door and was immediately surrounded by adoring ferrets. I worried sometimes, what with the way I had produced them – quite by accident, out of this old magic hat – that they all thought I was their mother. Their affection, especially right after I opened their pen, could sometimes be quite overwhelming. Still, I had grown rather attached to them on our travels to rescue Vushta from the Netherhells, and I admit that there had been one or two occasions when the hustle and bustle of Vushta had grown too much for me, and I had come to tend these cages, seeking solace.

'Come on now,' I called softly, although I doubted that they really understood me. 'It's time for us to go to a meeting.'

'Eep!' they cried. 'Eep eep! Eep eep eep!'

I laughed despite myself. They milled about me as I turned to lead them to the willow. What use had I for love? What need had I for human companionship? I had my ferrets to keep me warm!

Still, I didn't recall producing quite this many of them. They rubbed against my ankles and rose upon their hind legs to nuzzle my knees. A few of them, even merrier than their brothers and sisters, leapt joyfully for my head and shoulders so that they might rub their cold noses against my forehead and ears. There was a good score of them before me on the path, and two score of them to either side, while even more were emerging from their pen at a rapid rate.

Exactly how many were there? A momentary thought chilled me: Could magically produced ferrets reproduce magically as well?

'Come,' I repeated, 'there is no time to lose.' I brushed the overenergetic creatures off my person and strode in the direction of the willows, being especially careful not to tread on any ferret parts as we made our way to the meeting. We skirted the large building that contained the Great Hall, and stepped into the college's main courtyard.

'Doom!' Hendrek hailed me, waving his warclub so that I might better see him beneath the willow. The ferrets all about me eeped merrily in reply.

A short, green blur paced rapidly back and forth behind the large warrior's bulk. It was Snarks, hopping, then walking, even running a pace or two, his fists occasionally darting out to hit something that wasn't there. Even allowing for his demonic demeanor, he seemed agitated.

'Oh,' Snarks remarked distractedly as we approached. 'I didn't know you'd be accompanied by a sea of rodents.'

'Indeed?' I replied. 'Rodents?' Just what did Snarks mean about my little charges? Perhaps I was being a tad oversensitive on the issue, but I thought the demon should show due respect for my ferrets. 'Please, friend Snarks. These are anything but a sea of rodents!'

'What else could you call them, a living rug?' Snarks shrugged, as if it no longer mattered quite what they were. 'Oh, well, I suppose they might make somebody a good coat someday.'

'Coat?' I demanded. This was really too much. The ferrets nearest my feet, catching my mood, bared their teeth as they crept in Snarks' general direction.

The demon, seeing the change in my little charges, threw his hands up into the air. 'Wait!' he called. 'I am forced to agree with you. Ferrets are wonderful creatures, and a boon to our cause!'

I realized then that this was the second time today I had heard Snarks apologize. This went beyond mere agitation. Snarks was being pleasant and polite. There must be something seriously wrong.

I quieted my ferrets with a glance, and asked the demon what troubled him so.

' 'Tis a small matter,' Snarks murmured, still intent, it seemed, on making light of the situation. But his anger broke through when he spoke again: 'And it makes shoes!'

I had never seen the demon so undone before. 'The Brownie?' I replied.

'The Brownie!' Snarks shrieked. 'Always the Brownie!' He fell to his knees, his small, green fists flailing at the gnarled roots of the willow.

'Doom,' Hendrek remarked.

I merely nodded, and gave myself a moment to collect my thoughts. For the first time since I had met him, Snarks seemed completely undone. What was even worse, his anguish concerned not an enemy, but another one of our allies, a magical creature who had helped us in the past and might be of use to us again.

I could see a potential for this situation to get out of hand. I wished then that I could have called my master over and allowed him to directly settle the dispute between demon and Brownie. But Ebenezum's malady would not abide such close contact with these two magical creatures. Therefore, unless I wanted to see my master once again turned into a sneezing wreck, I would have to handle at least the up-close, personal end of this dispute. I looked at the demon and tried to think like a wizard. How would my master handle this?

'Indeed,' I replied. 'And yet you have dealt with the Brownie before for much of our adventures. Why, then, this sudden consternation?'

Snarks paused mid-tantrum. 'Funny. I never thought of it that way. Yes, now that you mention it, I have stood up to the Brownie many times. I've even stood up to groups of Brownies!' I could hear the confidence creeping back into his voice. 'After all, even in groups, they are still very short.'

'Doom.' Hendrek nodded encouragingly. 'So you do not fear the Brownies?'

'No, not at all.' Snarks allowed a demonic smile to settle upon his countenance. 'Fear, no. Dislike, however, is another matter entirely. Yet that would not be enough to explain my actions.' Snarks' smile faded as dark green furrows appeared on his forehead. 'For I admit, I have been acting strangely. My behavior has been totally undemonic. What would my mother think?'

'Doom,' Hendrek agreed. 'Then you must fear something besides the Brownies.'

Snarks stared at the large warrior. 'You never cease to amaze me. First symbolism, and now this. And I used to believe your warclub did all your thinking for you!'

'Indeed,' I interjected before Hendrek could become further embroiled in the discussion. 'But has Hendrek hit upon the truth?'

'Is it fear?' The demon paused, and looked away from us to stare out into the middle distance. 'In a way, yes. I fear it is this constant battle with my homeland. Even though I am a demon in exile, still I am a demon. When, at first, it seemed as though we had one great battle to win – to rescue Vushta from the Netherhells and defeat Guxx Unfufadoo, who I never much liked in the first place – well, that was a fight I could believe in. But now . . .' Snarks sighed.

'I was fine until I went back there,' he continued. 'I could have visited my mother, you know, when we returned to the Netherhells. But I chose to slink around like an outsider, as if my time with humans had tainted me.' The demon looked from Hendrek to me and back again. 'Which, of course, is a distinct possibility.'

'Doom,' Hendrek interjected, refusing to be lured away from the real topic. 'Then you fear your mother?'

'Well, of course!' Snarks replied. 'If your mother was a demon, you'd be scared of her, too! But that, I think, is beside the point. Returning to the Netherhells has dredged up old memories, and old emotions. Now, we find our battle might not be over. My real fear is that, the longer the battle lasts, the more these emotions will overwhelm me!'

'Doom!' Hendrek stated with grim finality.

'Indeed,' I added, to show that I realized the weight of Snark's problem as well. But I was afraid to share the rest of my thoughts.

I was chilled by how his complaints seemed so similar to those of my beloved. Both were tired of battle, and both seemed to be no longer quite themselves. I could think of no two creatures among my close acquaintance so dissimilar as Snarks and my young witch. Odd, then, that the demon's feelings should so echo those of Norei.

'Hello.'

The mild voice was so close behind my shoulder that it made me jump. The black-garbed Dealer of Death strolled into our midst.

'I hear you are discussing problems. I, too, have a problem.' The Dealer absently flexed his powerful hands. 'One more profound than the recent shortage of wild pigs in the vicinity.' He paused and looked at me, his usual smile gone from his face.

'You know, of course,' he said slowly and precisely, being careful to flex his jaw and cheek muscles, 'that I still hold a contract to assassinate at least three of you.'

'Doom.' Hendrek's hand moved quickly to the hilt of his warclub. Perhaps the warrior had hoped, as I had, that our time fighting side by side with the Dealer of Death had somehow negated the death contracts the assassin had on Hendrek, the wizard, and myself.

'There is no need to be hasty, good warrior,' the Dealer remarked as he idly flexed his legs, 'although the exercise certainly would be pleasant. Let me first tell you my thoughts on said problem.'

Faster than the eye could see, the assassin snatched a buzzing gnat from the air and captured it within his closed fists. ''Tis a funny thing about contracts. You might recall that there is no termination date on this particular piece of parchment. You might also recall that, through the wiles of the contractee, King Urfoo the Stingy, I end up paying to kill you rather than getting paid for my services.'

The Dealer paused to clear his throat. Talking about this particular clause of the contract, especially since he was personally responsible for its negotiation, seemed to affect him emotionally. But at last the Dealer smiled, and as he began to speak again, he lifted aloft the hand that held the gnat.

'Because of these complications, I had thought about delaying said contract's completion. I was wondering if we might agree upon some future occasion, say perhaps when we meet in some future lifetime.' The Dealer opened his fist, and the gnat flew away.

'Doom,' Hendrek murmured, his voice tinged with relief.

'However,' the Dealer continued, 'life is seldom as simple as that. I also have my superiors in the Urracht sect to consider. It might be fine now to make a decision to delay your deaths, but what happens when my actions come up for their quarterly review?'

'Quarterly review?' Hendrek repeated, his hand once again reaching for the warclub. 'Doom.'

The Dealer nodded soberly. 'The good assassin is accountable for every death. It's right there in our bylaws. The Urracht is a strict sect, but fair.'

The Dealer stretched, languorously extending his huge shoulder muscles. 'Before, as the battle was being joined, there was no time to think of contracts. Now, although I welcome the fact that the battle might soon be joined again, I worry more about just when such contracts should be fulfilled.' He shook his head, a sad smile on his face. 'I really should have killed some of you by now.'

'Indeed,' I interjected nervously, 'but there have been extenuating circumstances. After all, the fate of the world may be at stake!'

'But will that be enough of a reason when my review comes up?' The black-clad assassin flexed his knees, obviously troubled. 'Well, the fate of the world . . . It does have possibilities. I think my Urracht superiors may give me an extension.' He hesitated again. 'Still, a contract is a contract.'

A deep voice shouted across the courtyard, causing even the brooding Dealer to take notice.

'Hey gang! It's showtime!'

Hubert the dragon circled overhead, angling to land in the grassy area at the courtyard's center. Alea waved to me from her perch at the base of the dragon's neck.

'Hit it, damsel!' Hubert cried as he executed a perfect four-point landing.

Alea began to sing:

'What's the show with so much class,
It stars a dragon and a pretty lass!
Yes we're the pair of Vushtan fame,
Who send the audience up in flame!
So if your theater's receipts are flaggin'
You know who to send for – Damsel and Dragon!'

'Just a little publicity,' Hubert remarked as Alea handed him his top hat. 'I thought it was time we classed up our act.'

'I agree entirely,' Snarks commented. 'Let me know when you've come up with some way to do it.'

'We've come for the meeting,' Hubert continued,

choosing to ignore the demon. 'Are we on time?'

I told the dragon that they were perhaps a moment early and that we still awaited the arrival of my master.

'Early!' Hubert grinned. 'What an opportunity! Damsel and I have been working up a new routine, including some brand-new snappy patter. We could not ask for a better audience than our friends here. Quick: Why did the dragon cross the road?'

'Wait a moment,' Alea interrupted. 'Shouldn't we be working on our song lyrics?'

Hubert harrumphed, sending a column of smoke into the air. 'Alea, please.' He turned to the rest of us. 'It appears that the Damsel and I have some small artistic disagreement over song content.'

Alea crossed her arms and glared at her partner. 'We may have a disagreement, but I don't think there's anything artistic about it.'

'Alea, please!' When the dragon snorted this time, flame shot from his nostrils. 'Must we air our dirty laundry in front of our fans?'

'Exactly.' Alea looked at the rest of us with a knowing smile. 'And let me tell you, you've never dealt with dirty laundry until you've cleaned up after a dragon!'

She walked quickly over to where I stood. Somehow, I found her arm intertwined with mine. I remembered then that I had meant to tell this woman that our days of easy familiarity were over. But what with one thing and another, I hadn't quite gotten around to it.

'This all has to do with you, Wuntie.' Her face was all too close to mine. Why did it always get warmer when Alea was around? 'It's about your song: "The Ballad of Wuntvor".'

'The Ballad of Wuntvor?' Snarks repeated.

'A deep and meaningful ballad!' Hubert boomed. 'Perfect the way it is!'

'How could anything called "The Ballad of Wuntvor" be perfect?' Snarks interjected.

'I feel we have gone slightly astray,' Alea admitted. 'We thought that by showing your fallibility, it would make your deeds that much grander. We wanted to show the human behind the hero. I'm afraid, Wuntie, that we made you a bit too human.'

I realized then that I had heard bits of 'The Ballad of Wuntvor' when I had come to fetch Damsel and Dragon earlier that day. I reconsidered the verses I had overheard in the theater. Now that I thought of it, that verse about my complexion had been a bit much. I told Alea I agreed with her, for that very reason.

'Complexion?' she replied a bit uncertainly. 'Oh, yes, we *did* have a verse about that, didn't we? No, I'm afraid it was another verse entirely that made me realize we'd gone too far. The one about the stomach noises.'

'Stomach noises!' Hubert retorted. 'That verse? I'll have you know that I thought that particular verse was among the best . . .' The dragon hesitated. 'Oh, dear. That was the one with the growl/howl rhyme scheme, wasn't it?' Gray wisps wafted upwards as Hubert cleared his throat. 'Damsel, you may have a point.'

'Complexion?' Snarks considered. 'Stomach noises? Maybe "The Ballad of Wuntvor" *is* perfect after all. Do you have a verse about posture?'

'No, we don't,' Alea said thoughtfully. 'Perhaps that would make a good substitution.'

'Yes, of course!' the dragon replied. 'We don't have to explore every nuance of Wuntvor's character. I think the twenty-eight verses we've already written cover most of his faults, anyway.'

'Twenty-eight?' Alea asked, slightly surprised. 'Oh, did you finally come up with a good rhyme for "dandruff"?'

'No, I had forgotten all about that. I'm afraid I'd gotten caught up in that verse about nose hair. Thank you for reminding me, damsel. Perhaps we should have twenty-nine.'

'Nose hair?' Alea clapped her hands in glee. 'Oh, that's right! And then we contrast Wuntie's nasal curls with the nose hair of Guxx Unfufadoo? What pathos! A master's touch!'

'What can I say?' Hubert blew gently on his foreclaws. 'I was born to write for the stage.'

'Hello, Wuntvor,' said a woman's voice so cold that I felt ice run up my spine. I knew, even before I turned to look, that it was Norei.

'I don't know why I keep giving you another chance,' she said in a voice barely above a whisper. 'I thought, after walking out on you at the theater, that perhaps I had been hasty, that I should have listened to what you had to say. There might have been a reasonable explanation for why I found you wrapped up in a canvas with that woman.' Her lower lip began to tremble. 'Still, I came here thinking for some reason I'd give you one more opportunity to make a choice between us. Well, I see that the choice has already been made!'

What was my beloved talking about? Was she upset because I hadn't noticed her arrival? 'Twas true that I had become quite engrossed in the discussion of what should or shouldn't be in that song named after me, but that was understandable, wasn't it? Well, then there was the way Alea was holding onto my arm. That, perhaps, was a bit more difficult to explain, but I was sure if my beloved would but take a minute to hear me out –

'Norei –' I began.

'Don't even start!' she replied.

'But . . .' I added. What could I say? This was terrible. Now she would go to the Western Woods for sure! What could possibly be worse than this?

There was a small explosion by Snarks' foot. I used the momentary diversion to disengage myself from the clutching damsel.

'Surprise! Did you miss me?'

'You're right,' Snarks replied. 'Next time I'll have to take better aim.'

It was Tap the Brownie.

'Good news!' he exclaimed in his tiny Brownie voice. 'His Brownieship has given me another chance!'

'Good news?' Snarks repeated. 'If that's good news, I'd hate to think what's bad news!'

'Oh, yes!' Tap added. 'And in a few minutes we'll be visited by His Brownieship in person!'

'Yes, you're right,' Snarks responded. 'That's bad news.' A shudder ran through the demon's sickly green frame. 'His Brownieship?' Snarks wandered away to collect his thoughts.

Something poked me in the back. Could it be? Maybe she would give me a chance to talk to her in private! I turned quickly.

'Norei . . .' Her name died on my tongue. It was the unicorn.

'I said I'd come.' The magnificent beast tossed back its flowing mane. 'Unfortunately, it's much too crowded around here for us to *really* talk.'

I told the unicorn that that was really too bad, but we had to wait for Ebenezum.

'I realized,' the beast continued, its voice tinged with a

magnificent melancholy, 'when I followed you all the way from the Western Woods, that I would have to make sacrifices.' The unicorn lifted its golden horn to the sky, its dark eyes staring into the distance. 'If only my head were not so heavy. If only there were a lap somewhere where I might rest.'

'Wuntie!' Alea called to me from a few feet away. 'You weren't going to wander off and leave me all alone, were you?'

'Um, er . . .' I began. 'I've been meaning to talk to you –'

'Wuntie!' Alea stopped and stared at the unicorn. 'I remember this magnificent creature.'

'Um, yes . . .' I began.

She walked rapidly toward us. 'Well, don't you think it's time to introduce me?'

'Um . . .' I began. 'Surely.' Perhaps here was the chance I was looking for. While Alea and the unicorn were temporarily involved, I might at last seek out Norei and explain. I turned to the unicorn. 'Do you recall this young lady –'

'I would rather not,' the beast interjected. 'Isn't there someplace we could go' – the creature allowed the slightest mournful sigh to escape from between its perfect teeth – 'only the two of us?'

'My name is Alea.' She smiled enough for her dimples to show. 'I believe we met before. In the Western Woods.'

The creature shrugged its silken shoulders and pointed its golden horn in my direction. 'I was speaking with Wuntvor. Isn't there someplace quiet we can go? This sort of thing always happens when unicorns get stuck in crowds.' The beast snorted its magnificent defiance of the ways of the world. 'If only I hadn't wanted to see you so badly! If only I could find a place to lay my weary head!'

'I have a very nice lap,' Alea suggested.

'This is what happens when unicorns get stuck in crowds in Vushta!' The beast nudged my shoulder gently with its horn. 'It seems I am offered a never-ending succession of laps! But never' – it paused to nudge me again – 'the right one.'

'Wuntvor!'

'Norei!' I replied, for it was she, the woman with a voice only slightly more frigid than the coldest of winter days.

'We have been waiting here for quite some time. Isn't Ebenezum ever coming?'

Now my beloved was becoming impatient. It seemed very unlike her, as if, when she lost her faith in me, she had lost her faith in my master and all of Vushta as well.

I swallowed hard, knowing that whatever had happened to her, it was all my fault.

'Norei,' I began. 'We have to talk. No matter what you may think of me –'

'Weren't *we* talking?' the unicorn reminded me.

'Later,' I said, ignoring the beast's insistent golden horn. 'Norei, we've been through a great deal together –'

'Oh, for a lap to rest my weary head!' the magnificent beast interrupted.

'But I've already offered you mine!' Alea interjected. She glanced at me as she sidled toward the unicorn. 'If Wuntie wants to waste his time elsewhere, let him. After all, I'm available!'

Alea ran around the beast so that she might sit directly in front of it. The unicorn's well-polished hooves took a pair of steps in the opposite direction.

'Oh!' the beautiful beast moaned. 'To be in want of a lap in Vushta!'

I looked up to see Norei standing directly before me. Her lips trembled as she tried to speak. Finally she managed:

'Wuntvor? You started to tell me something. What –'

'It's after me again!' Snarks ran between us, his lips curled back in a grimace of fear that showed his every fang. 'The Brownie is after me!'

But I turned my attention back to my beloved. I could not let the crisis of the moment dissuade me from my task. What Norei and I meant to each other was too important for that.

Snarks ran on. The Brownie followed.

'Norei,' I tried again. 'In our brief time together, we have become very –'

'I just want to help you with some Brownie etiquette!' Tap yelled at the retreating demon. 'Like those times when you should refer to His Brownieship as his Master of Buckles, or mayhaps the King of Sole –'

'Wuntvor,' Norei said, taking my head in her hands. 'Are you trying to say –'

The unicorn's majestic horn came between us, pulling us apart.

'Why not rest awhile?' Alea insisted as she pursued the grandly trotting beast.

'Ahem. There are laps, and then there are laps,' the unicorn replied haughtily.

'Norei –' I began, as Snarks ran screaming between us once again.

'And you need instruction in some of our sacred ceremonies!' insisted the Brownie, close upon the demon's heels. 'You know, like the ritual tying of laces –'

'Wuntvor!' Norei complained. 'It's impossible to talk to you!'

'Yes, it is, isn't it?' the unicorn agreed sadly. 'Oh, what a heavy head!'

'Wuntvor!' another voice called out from across the clearing. It was the voice of my master, Ebenezum.

'Norei –' I turned to excuse myself, but my beloved was already marching away to the opposite side of the willow, with no sign that she had even heard me call her name.

But I had no time to worry about what would happen now. Ebenezum needed me. I jogged across the grass to my master.

'Wuntvor,' the wizard addressed me as he pulled upon his long, white beard. 'I am sorry to have kept you, but it has taken me somewhat longer to confer with my colleagues than I had at first anticipated.' He nodded to both sides. I followed his gaze, and saw a pair of wizards, one left, one right, each a good twenty paces distant, and twenty paces beyond each of them, another pair of magicians, and so on. I realized then that wizards circled the entire courtyard.

'Indeed,' Ebenezum replied to my questioning glance. ''Tis but a precaution against further mischief on the part of the Netherhells. We wizards are close enough to form an effective magical unit, but not so close as to affect our immediate maladies.'

My master scratched at the shock of white hair that protruded from beneath his handsome wizard's cap. 'But we must discuss our plan, for even with precautions such as these, who knows when another . . .'

Ebenezum paused as we both heard a low rumble which seemed to come from deep beneath the earth. The ground where we stood began to shake.

I knew this kind of quake. This was no little Brownie explosion. This was an attack, by the demons of the Netherhells!

'And so it begins,' my master remarked grimly.

FIVE

'The successful wizard must plan to spend a fair amount of time away from home, whether in the company of other mages or working for the common man.

'I have known the occasional wizard who had attempted to buck this trend and work completely and forever alone, but there is danger here as well. A close personal acquaintance of mine locked himself inside his lair for sixteen years, until at last he discovered a spell for turning dirt into gold, and spent the last few months of his exile amassing a great pile of his magical wealth.

'What could be wrong? you might ask. Ah, but sixteen years away from human contact had taken its emotional toll. This wizard had become afraid to even walk outside his home, and confessed to me, through his closed and bolted door, that he was even more afraid to leave his horde of gold, and cursed his riches for a burden!

'The solution, of course, was simple. Whenever such a tragedy occurs to a fellow sorcerer, the wise wizard should always be prepared to take the burden from their hands.'

– WHEN BAD SPELLS HAPPEN TO GOOD WIZARDS
(fourth edition), by Ebenezum,
greatest wizard in the Western Kingdoms

Ebenezum nodded to the wizard on either side of him, and they, in turn, nodded to the wizards on either side of them. Everyone seemed to be nodding, although it might have been the earth shaking at our feet that caused heads to bob up and down so. My master raised both his arms, and the other wizards in the circle mimicked his action, so that all arms pointed to the sky. Then the whole circle of magicians called out a string of syllables as one, their voices close to drowned out by the crashing rumble of the ground, and slowly lowered their arms so they pointed at right angles to their wizardly frames.

'Now!' Ebenezum shouted above the earthquake.

The circle of mages all turned their outstretched palms to the ground and pushed.

The quake noise seemed not quite so loud as before.

The wizards pushed downward, seemingly against the air, although their arms shook as if they were struggling with a great weight.

The ground beneath my feet was not lurching about so violently as it had before.

The wizards' palms were now parallel with their waists as they continued to struggle against the invisible force. I looked back to my master. Sweat matted his white hair to his forehead.

But the noise of the quake was quieting. It was now no louder than distant thunder. And the earth beneath my feet was hardly moving at all.

The magicians pushed their hands as far as they could reach down their sides.

The earthquake stopped. For an instant the world around us was completely silent. And then the birds began to sing.

'Master!' I called, almost overcome with joy. 'You

have defeated the attack of the Netherhells! How . . .'

I paused in my exclamation when I realized that Ebenezum, along with every other mage in the circle, was now lost in a sneezing fit.

My master was the first to recover. He blew his nose quickly on a silver threaded sleeve, then beckoned me to come closer.

'Indeed,' he began, 'we have won. But you have seen the cost.' He swept out his arm to include the circle of wizards, all the rest of whom were sneezing still. 'And what has worked once may not work again. The Netherhells will be more prepared next time. We will have to develop new counterstrategies.'

My master stood and regarded me for a silent instant as he tugged absently at his beard. 'Wuntvor, it is time we had another talk. What we wizards of Vushta can do against the Netherhells will result in nothing more than a stalemate. I'm afraid we have need once again for someone not afflicted by my malady to make another quest.'

I swallowed hard. Whatever my master wished of me, I knew I would obey.

'Must I go to the Netherhells again?' I asked, and this time my voice barely qualified as a whisper.

My master shook his head. 'Indeed, no. Our salvation, if we are to find it, lies elsewhere, although I fear your new destination is not much preferable to traveling in the land of demons. Wuntvor, little as I like to do it, I must send you to the Eastern Kingdoms to enlist the aid of their leader.'

'Eastern Kingdoms?' It was the first I had ever heard of them.

'Indeed,' my master agreed with my confusion. 'We in

the magical trade do not discuss the Eastern Kingdoms overmuch. I suppose we are embarrassed by any associations with them. You see, Wunt, things are' – Ebenezum cleared his throat – 'different there.'

'Different?' I inquired.

My master nodded his head. 'They have strange customs thereabouts.' He paused, considering his words. 'They have a different way of looking at the world.' He paused again, and when he spoke for a third time, it was in a whisper. 'But mostly, they have Mother Duck.'

'Mother Duck!' I exclaimed.

'Indeed,' Ebenezum continued in a whisper. He stroked his mustache agitatedly. 'Not so loud, Wuntvor, if you please.'

He stared at the ground and surreptitiously motioned me to walk with him a little farther from the crowded clearing. Rarely had I seen my master so uneasy. I glanced briefly around the courtyard in which we stood. Those wizards who had recovered from their sneezing fits all seemed to be glaring in our direction.

'Mother Duck?' I repeated, this time matching my master's quieter tone. 'Who is Mother Duck?'

'Who indeed?' my master replied. 'She is the ruler of the Eastern Kingdoms. She is also the reason that none of the wizards here want to visit her domain.'

'Doom!'

I had become so engrossed in my master's conversation that I hadn't heard the approach of Hendrek and Snarks.

'Forgive us for eavesdropping,' the large warrior began, 'but you wizards have only narrowly averted a skirmish with the Netherhells. We were wondering if we might be able to offer you any aid.'

'It also gave us an opportunity to get rid of the

Brownie.' Snarks, who stood somewhat farther away to avoid affecting my master's malady, nodded his head happily.

My master pondered briefly. 'Perhaps you heard that Wuntvor will have to go on another quest? He will once again need companions to aid him and protect him against dangers along the way. Still, I do not think we can utilize all the magical and heroic allies who have gathered here. I believe a small fast-moving group would be best for our purposes. Once all the wizards have recovered, we will discuss strategy and determine the party that will best serve our needs.'

'Doom.' Hendrek nodded his head, acknowledging the wisdom of my master's counsel.

'So we have a chance to leave Vushta?' Snarks added. 'Not that Vushta isn't a wonderful place' – he glanced nervously at the area around his shoes – 'but some of the creatures that tend to congregate in the area . . .'

'Doom,' Hendrek agreed. 'It will do my warclub good to once again taste battle.'

'What's this about tasting battle?' I started at the nearness of this new voice. The Dealer of Death had once again snuck into our midst.

'My master has suggested another quest,' I explained.

'Yeah!' Snarks rejoined. 'One without any Brownies!'

There was a miniature explosion at the demon's feet.

'Did somebody call?' a small voice demanded. 'Come on now, I'm sure I heard my name.'

'Why would anyone mention you?' Snarks asked defensively. 'You've heard of the phrase "beneath notice"? I think that that perfectly fits anyone who doesn't come up even to my knees!'

The Brownie shook his head sadly. 'It's tragic to meet a

being who can't see the beauty of Brownie Power. I'm afraid I tried to show our friend here the glories of Browniedom too quickly. Listen to me, friend Snarks!'

'Sorry,' the demon murmured, trying hard to maintain his composure. 'Not interested.'

Tap tugged at the demon's robes. 'I will start where I should have all along: In the beginning, long ago, before there were Brownies . . .'

'Maybe I'm interested after all!' Snarks brightened momentarily.

'. . . or before there were demons,' the Brownie continued, refusing to be sidetracked. The little fellow looked at the rest of us. 'Or before there were wizards, or warriors, or apprentices, or trained assassins. Before all these things, there was the Great Shoe!'

'Now I'm really not interested!' Snarks exclaimed as he began to sidle away from the little person.

'I'm not very interested, either,' another voice said behind me. 'At least, I'm only interested in certain very special individuals.'

It was the unicorn.

'But what I wouldn't do for those individuals!' the magnificent beast continued. 'Oh, if only I could find a place to lay –'

'If you'll excuse me.' My beloved stepped between me and the unicorn's horn. 'I thought that I might like to be included in the discussion. Who knows? Perhaps I can be of some help' – she looked pointedly in my direction – 'at least for that short time that I am still available.'

'Hey, what's going on here!' A deep voice cut off the unicorn's complaint. 'It looks like a victory celebration, damsel! But what sort of celebration would it be without entertainment!'

The Brownie continued his speech, eyes closed, in a clear, high voice, as if everyone else was not shouting simultaneously. '. . . and the Great One looked out upon the void, and saw nothingness. So the Great One reached out its laces to the Void, and said "Let there be shoes!" '

'What we need here,' the dragon continued, 'is a funny story from our new act. How about this one? Seems there was this thirsty dragon decided he needed to have a drink. So he goes into this local tavern, see –'

'Ahem,' my master intoned, holding his nose against the ever-increasing scents of magical creatures in the immediate vicinity. 'I think, Wuntvor, that the time has come for us to consult briefly in the college library. Alone.' He turned and called to the others. 'Wuntvor and I will return anon. Please wait for us. We beg your –'

My master sneezed once. He turned upon his heel and rapidly strode across the courtyard. I did my best to keep up.

'And there were shoes!' the Brownie continued behind us, his voice filled with wonder. 'And boots, and sandals, and slippers with pointy toes –'

'So, anyway' – Hubert's booming voice drowned out the little person's – 'the tavern keeper brings the dragon a tankard of mead and says, "That will be five hundred golden crowns." Then the barkeep adds, "You know, we don't get many dragons –" '

Ebenezum slammed the door of the library after I had followed him inside.

'I fear,' my master remarked, 'that this situation may be getting out of hand.'

I agreed with the mage.

Ebenezum pulled absently at his beard. ' 'Tis always the way when great magic is involved. One way or another, magic creatures appear in great numbers and stand around being magical. Unfortunately, it can be very disruptive' – he paused to blow his nose – 'especially considering our present circumstance. Like all things sorcerous, magical creatures must be kept under strict control. They need a firm hand. They need a leader.'

'Master?' I asked, not quite seeing his point.

'Indeed.' The wizard fixed me with his steely gaze. 'They need you, Wuntvor.'

'Master?' I repeated, a bit of panic in my voice.

'Yes,' Ebenezum continued. 'There's no use denying it, Wuntvor. This situation needs a leader, a focus to direct all those magical actions we will require to defeat the Netherhells. Unfortunately, my malady prevents me from being that focus. And now all the wizards in Vushta seem to have caught that same malady. It is therefore up to you, Wuntvor, to become the magician who will lead our forces to success.'

I did not know what to say. Me, Wuntvor, a mere unschooled apprentice, the leader of all our forces? I was quite overwhelmed by the amount of faith my master held in me. I looked at the wizard, resplendent in his new robes of deepest blue, and he nodded solemnly.

I swallowed and took a deep breath, careful to stand at my full height. Perhaps my master was right after all. I had shown that I could perform magic in a pinch, both in our trip to Vushta and in my quest to the Netherhells. Now that I thought of it, I _had_ conjured dead fish and turned myself into a grackle.

Very well. I folded my arms and nodded, ready to fulfill my destiny.

'Indeed,' my master continued when it became apparent that I had no objections. 'Now we must prepare for your quest. And Wuntvor, the best preparation a wizard can have is that of a ready mind and positive attitude towards what is to come.'

'Indeed,' I replied, ready to shoulder a wizard's responsibility.

'Therefore,' Ebenezum resumed, 'you must keep a cool head, no matter what should occur or what people should tell you. There are many rumors about the Eastern Kingdoms, and while most of them are completely unfounded, there are many in Vushta who enjoy spreading these rumors about.' He paused to stroke his mustache thoughtfully. 'You should know, then, to pay no heed to the stories of Mother Duck's kingdom, especially those about her cooking magicians and heroes in those ovens she keeps for her giants. And, of course, give not a thought to those unfounded tales about how she can twist the very fabric of reality and turn men into beasts and shrubs.' Ebenezum's great white eyebrows rose as he made his final point. 'Remember, no matter what happens, your magic will be able to save you!'

Beasts and shrubs? Then again, it occurred to me that there might be some situations that required spells other than grackles and dead fish. I cleared my throat. Perhaps I had objections after all. But how would I best be able to express them to the mage?

'But master,' I began hesitantly, 'will I be able to learn the spells required? I mean, my magical background –'

' 'Tis true, Wuntvor.' Ebenezum nodded sagely. 'I have been slightly remiss in your education. During your first two years of apprenticeship I had meant to begin your course of magical lessons. Still, you know how things go – one thing leads to another, and the time is gone before you know it. Well, it is no use crying over broken spells. We will have to remedy your lack of education, beginning now.'

Ebenezum turned to the rows of books that stood behind us. 'Indeed, Wuntvor. I brought you to the library for more reasons than to free ourselves of the crowd. There is a certain tome here that I feel might be of assistance to you.' Holding his nose, he scanned the shelves.

'There!' he said at last, pointing to an aged volume on the uppermost shelf. 'Could you reach it for me?'

I pulled down the book, which was bound in dark blue vellum. At first glance it was a quite impressive-looking tome, although the parchment within appeared a touch dog-eared, as if it had seen frequent use. The cover bore a title, in highly illuminated script of pure gold leaf: *Magic for the Millions – A Home Study Course*.

'A home study course?' I replied.

'Even more than this,' my master intoned. 'It is the finest home study course ever invented.'

'Pardon, master,' I asked with some trepidation, 'but what is a home study course?'

'Indeed.' The mage pulled at his beard. ' 'Tis a series of lessons that are self-contained, so that you might gain the advantages of a schooling in magic without actually attending the school. There are a great many advantages to learning magic in this method. Think, Wuntvor. For one thing, you don't have to sit through the study halls, and you'll never catch yourself glancing at the classroom hourglass while your teacher goes on and on about something you could care less about.' The wizard sighed. 'Of course, you also aren't able to try out for the sports teams, sorcerous soccer, and the like, and I would imagine that the senior play might have to be a monologue – but I digress.' Ebenezum paused to clear his throat and straighten his robes.

Study halls? Sorcerous soccer? I had no idea what my master was talking about. I hoped there was enough in this book so that I might make some sense out of it. I hastily opened the cover and read aloud the words imprinted on the first page:

'Compiled by Ebenezum, Greatest Wizard in the Western Kingdoms. Fourth Printing.'

'Indeed,' my master remarked. ' 'Twas part of my association with the Famous Wizards school. Made me quite a bit of – but that is beside the point. We must address our present task!' He waved with a flourish at the book I held in my hands. 'You have before you everything you need to become a full-fledged wizard, competent in all the basic sorcerous arts – alchemy, healing with herbs, love potions, how to predict the arrival of tax collectors. And that is but the mere beginning!'

Love potions? All thoughts of quests and battles with the Netherhells fell away from that one glowing thought. My master had said love potions, hadn't he? I tried to contain my excitement. Perhaps there was some way Norei and I could be reunited after all! I could barely wait to begin this 'home study course.' Love potions, indeed!

'No matter what danger you might face,' the wizard resumed, 'within this book there is a magical solution. If you would turn to the back, you'll find an index.'

I struggled to put thoughts of a happy reunion out of my mind, and did as Ebenezum bade, opening to a page titled 'Easy Wizard's Index.' I scanned quickly down the righthand column:

'As you can see,' my master continued, 'quick reference to this index can prepare you for virtually any eventuality. In all, I think this home study course will go some distance toward remedying your lack of education. Of course, while you are on the quest you might have difficulty in mailing your lessons, but we'll devise some method to overcome that.'

I closed the tome and looked to my master. The index certainly did seem thorough. I was happy that he was so sure of my success. There was a damp spot on the vellum where my sweaty palm grasped the book. Suddenly my brain was no longer filled with thoughts of my beloved. Instead, the words I had read in the index were sinking into my overworked consciousness: 'Demons, who have already begun to eat you . . .'

I had been thinking too much of Norei and not enough about the quest. I would have to study this book in some detail before I began my journey. Then, when there was time, I would study the love potions.

'Indeed,' my master remarked. 'I have also spoken with Snorphosio, and he shall supply you with a map of the region.' He pulled at his beard. 'Or at least what we know of that region. But what say, Wunt, that we go over the introductory lesson together? I may have to hold my nose a bit, but I think I can make it through. If we work on it now, in the library, we should be able to speed through it without interruption.

I had barely reopened the book when the earth began to shake again.

'Then again,' the wizard muttered, 'we may never again be able to do anything without interruption.'

I hurriedly followed my master back into the courtyard, ready for our next confrontation with the Netherhells.

Or so I thought.

SIX

'Demons do not generally make the best of friends, unless, of course, you like to center all your social activities around eating, and furthermore, enjoy serving yourself as the main course.'

– THE TEACHINGS OF EBENEZUM, Volume XLI

'To the circle!' my master cried as he ran from the library. The other wizards, alerted by Ebenezum's warning, hastily moved to their preassigned positions.

The circle of wizards raised their arms as one. Then in unison each magician began to sneeze.

The quake intensified. The ground heaved, shaking me from my feet. By the time I regained my balance, I saw that a great rift had appeared in the earth at the center of the courtyard. I watched, horrified, as a demonic apparition rose from the bowels of the Netherhells to fill that rift.

The quake ceased as suddenly as it had begun. I gripped my stout oak staff as the dust settled, and I could clearly see what the foul fiends of the Netherhells had brought into our midst.

It appeared to be a stout oak table, behind which sat five of the largest and ugliest demons I had ever seen. The one in the center pounded on the table with a huge gavel.

'I now bring this attack to order!' the thing announced in a voice far too coarse to be called gravelly.

What sinister trick of the Netherhells was this? I turned to my master, but he was lost, sneezing deep within his robes. It was up to the warriors, then. I nodded to my fellows still standing amidst the sneezing mages.

'Doom,' Hendrek agreed.

We all took a cautious step forward.

'Wait a moment!' the slightly smaller, purplish demon cried from the end of the table. 'Who gives you the authority to begin the attack? We have to have a consensus here!'

'My dear Blecch,' the demon with the gavel calmly replied. 'I beg to differ. We don't need a consensus. In cases like this, a simple majority is fine.'

'Majority?' Blecch laughed derisively. 'My fellow demon is completely out of order!' It pounded its demonic fist on a large and ugly tome that it had just opened. 'It states clearly here, in the *New Netherhells Bylaws* –'

The demonic group seemed a bit disorganized. If we were going to win, we should attack now.

I lifted my stout oak staff above my head, and with the mightiest cry I could muster, ran towards the demons. Luckily, my fellows followed my lead. As I ran to face our enemy, I glimpsed Hubert galloping, Hendrek trundling, and the unicorn prancing magnificently forward to attack.

The Dealer of Death got there before all of us.

'Point of order!' one of the demons cried. 'We seem to be under attack!'

'I vote for retaliatory action!' Blecch added 'All in favor say' – he paused as the Dealer grasped him by the throat – 'Urracht!'

'No, no,' the gavel demon insisted. 'A show of hands is more appropriate. All in favor?'

The four demons not currently being strangled raised

their hands. Blecch, with some considerable effort, managed to follow suit.

'It's unanimous, then!' the gavel demon announced. 'Time for the boiling blood!'

All five demons turned to regard the Dealer.

The man in black gasped. His face turned bright red and steam shot from his ears. Blecch gave him a gentle push. The Dealer collapsed on the ground.

'Now we can get on with our own attack,' the gavel demon remarked.

'I think not!' Blecch countered as it massaged its throat.

'We still have not resolved this important procedural issue. To recklessly continue without putting this matter to rest would be a breach of authority one might expect of Guxx Unfufadoo!'

'What?' the gavel demon blustered. 'You dare compare me with the ex-Grand Hoohah? Just for that, Blecch, I'll –'

We never found out what the demon would do, for that was the moment my fellows and I attacked.

'Point of urk!' Blecch yelled as the dread warclub Headbasher came squarely down upon his purple head.

I swung my stout oak staff at the demon on the table's far end. 'Point of order!' it cried as it deftly ducked the blow. The staff bounced harmlessly off the table, forcing me to stagger back a pace.

'I think we should vote on retreat!' the ducking demon continued.

The demon at table's center lifted its gavel to pound for order, but found the wooden mallet burnt from its fingers by Hubert's dragon fire. 'Show of hands!' the demon yelped. It didn't wait for any response from its fellows, who were busy fending off Snarks, myself, and the unicorn. 'Majority rules! the ex-gavel demon shrieked.

The table and its occupants disappeared in a puff of smoke.

'Doom,' Hendrek muttered as his enchanted club swept the air where a demon had sat scant seconds before.

'What an exit!' Snarks whistled in admiration. 'Unfortunate, wasn't it, that it was the only successful part of their attack?'

I turned to Norei, who knelt over the prostrate Dealer of Death. He lay so still. A chill slithered down my spine.

'Is he –' I began in trepidation.

'I feared the same,' Norei replied quickly. 'But there is still a spark left deep within him. The demons' attack appears to have put him in a deathlike trance. And who knows how long that life spark will last?'

'Doom,' Hendrek intoned, echoing the sympathies of all those assembled.

The chill I had felt when I had seen the stillness of the Dealer had stayed with me. We seemed to be facing a new and very different strategy from the Netherhells. As ineffectual as their first attack had been, the threat somehow seemed much more sinister.

I heard a nose blow behind my right shoulder. My master stepped forward.

'Indeed.' He spoke as if he had read my thoughts. 'An attack of this nature can be truly serious. I have never before seen this particular Netherhells strategy, but I have read about its devastating effect in my ancient wizardly lore.' He paused to blow his nose a final time. He wiped his mustache clean and redeposited the kerchief in one of his voluminous sleeves.

'From observation,' the wizard resumed, 'it appears that this particular plan of attack has fallen out of use among the demons as well, for the proficiency of the strikes against us has so far been somewhat lacking. However, we should not let this temporary incompetence lull us into complacency.' He extended his foot to gently nudge the still form of the black-clad assassin. 'We have seen from the current condition of the Dealer of Death that this new strategy can be devastating. The forces of the Netherhells are stubborn. They will come against us again and again, until they get their attack right. When that happens, I fear we are all doomed, for there is no Netherhells strategy deadlier than the one we saw today: Conquest by Committee!'

'Doom!' Snarks exclaimed in agreement. ' 'Tis the only thing worse than the Grand Hoohah.'

'What –' I began.

'You don't want to know!' Snarks interjected rapidly.

'Indeed,' my master continued. 'This situation makes it that much more imperative that we begin the quest for aid at once.' He motioned to the other mages, most of whom seemed to have recovered from their sneezing bouts. 'We must confer for but a minute, and then the selection shall be made.' He turned to Norei. 'I am sorry, young witch, that we will have to exclude you, but I feel such a move is for the best. You see, I have discovered that when magic arises, my malady becomes contagious.'

My master turned and walked back in the direction of the library, the other wizards at his heels. I paced in the opposite direction, eager to pick up the Home Study Course where I had dropped it in the heat of battle. On my way there, I chanced to pass close to my beloved, who shook her head in disbelief.

'Can you believe it?' she asked.

Well, I could believe anything that came from those beautiful lips. Still, of late, whenever I had tried to express my devotion to Norei, it seemed to come out incorrectly. I decided, therefore, to take the safer path.

'Believe what?' I asked.

'Your master kept me from casting a spell in the recent battle. I did not know that was his intention at the time, of course. He kept leaping in front of me, his head covered by his great robes, so that all I could hear were his muffled sneezes.' Norei chuckled. 'I thought the great wizard had taken leave of his senses.'

I nodded solemnly at Norei's explanation. With hardly any thought of his own malady, Ebenezum had prevented this young witch from suffering a similar fate. He was, truly, a great wizard. How many times had he saved me from similar misadventures? But with that thought came another: How would I survive my coming quest without him by my side?

I turned to Norei, intent on confiding my doubts. But my beloved was nowhere to be seen in the milling aftermath of battle. Was this what it had come to, then? Had I lost Norei's confidence completely? Would I be forever alone, without another soul to speak with?

There was a small explosion by my feet.

'A happy Brownie hello!' an equally small voice exhorted. 'You haven't perchance seen my student hereabouts?'

'Your student?' It only occurred to me once I had spoken that he must mean Snarks.

'Yes, the green fellow,' the Brownie replied, confirming my suspicions. 'That rapscallion led me to the official college bootery. Well, let me tell you, time can really fly when you get a chance to examine quality footwear. And how much more fascinating is it when that footwear is magical!' The Brownie whistled softly. 'There was one pair of ruby slippers that really caught my . . .'

Something pricked at my throat. I found it was a knife. It

was attached to an arm, which was attached in turn to Vermin, that large, unspeaking member of the Vushta Apprentice Guild.

'What a surprise!' said Grott, whom I was sure could do enough talking for the both of them. He doffed his cap and bowed in what I thought was a rather exaggerated manner. 'To find you here at the Wizards College just after a battle. But how fortuitous. It seems we have a little unfinished discourse.'

A huge shadow blocked the sun. I looked up to see Slag grinning at me.

'Yeah,' the huge man said. 'Disco – uh, disc –.' He swallowed. 'Yeah,' he began again. 'Seems.'

'It also seems,' Grott continued all too jovially, 'that a certain party of our mutual acquaintance has just had his blood boiled and can no longer come to your rescue!'

'Yeah,' Slag smirked. 'Seems.'

'So we simply waited until the courtyard here was a little less populated,' Grott continued. I glanced about me as much as the knife at my throat allowed. It was true. My surroundings were quite deserted. 'When that happened, we knew it was time to become reacquainted and remind remind you of our simple demands: A total cure for our masters, or four hundred pieces of gold for –'.

'Hey!' a small voice piped from near my foot. 'Are these fellows bothering you?'

'Eh?' Grott said. 'What's this?' Obviously, in their haste to threaten me again, my three fellow apprentices had completely missed my tiny companion. Grott glared down at the Brownie. 'Oh, an insect of some kind.'

'Only if insects are equipped with Brownie Power!' Tap exclaimed.

Grott laughed at that. 'No matter what defenses an insect has, it can easily be squashed.'

'Yeah.' Slag chuckled as he raised his foot. 'Squashed!'

The Brownie danced, a frown of concentration on his tiny face. The laces on Slag's rapidly descending shoe suddenly snaked out and tied themselves around the man's arms, causing the large apprentice to totally lose his balance. Slag fell beyond the Brownie with a considerable crash.

'What happened?' Grott demanded.

'Yeah.' Slag struggled to put words in a sentence. 'What . . . uh, shoe . . . uh, tie. No. Untie!' The large fellow pointed gleefully to his unlaced boot, happy that he had found the right word.

'What?' Grott repeated incredulously. 'Oh, never mind. We'll figure it out later, after Vermin takes a little prize from our apprentice friend here. Something to remember you by, Wuntvor, a little keepsake – say, a piece of your ear.'

Vermin's knife pressed even harder against my throat.

'Don't worry,' Grott added. 'We'll give it back to you when you deliver the four hundred pieces of gold.' He cleared his throat and smiled. 'Did I say four? So sorry. A slip of the tongue. I meant, of course, five hundred pieces. Vermin, if you would?'

'Not while there's Brownie Power around!' Tap cried triumphantly.

'What?' Grott's voice held a note of panic. 'What's happening to my shoes?'

'Yeah!' Slag replied hoarsely. 'Untie!'

And that was what Grott's soft leather boots were doing: the laces seemingly untying of their own accord. The knife was no longer at my throat, so I was free to turn my head

and see the same thing happening to the footwear of both
Vermin and Slag. Six sets of laces untied, then stretched to
perhaps three times their natural length, swatting away the
apprentices' hands when the guild members tried to control
them. Then just as rapidly the individual laces found each
other and tied new knots, so that Grott, Slag, and Vermin
were joined together by their footwear.

'I'm warning you!' Grott screamed as his feet were pulled
from under him. 'A cure for our masters or six hundred
pieces of gold!'

The six shoes, with the apprentices' feet still inside, began
to bounce up and down.

'Did I say six hundred? I meant seven hundred!'

The bouncing grew more pronounced.

'Eight hundred!' Grott, Slag, and Vermin caught each
other's arms to keep from falling. The shoes bounced away
from me and the Brownie. 'No! A thousand!' Their bouncing took on height and speed as the three took great six-foot
leaps across the courtyard. 'And by moonrise tomorrow, or
you'll be really sorry!'

Their leaps grew higher still, so that by the time they
reached the far end of the courtyard, their final jump sent
them clear over the Great Hall.

'A thousand?' Grott shrieked with all his might. 'That is
not enough! Twelve hun –'

His voice was cut off by the intervening building.

'What will happen to them?' I asked the Brownie.

'Eventually they will reach the Great Vushta Canal,' Tap
replied. 'There, they will sink.' He grinned broadly. 'Is that
Brownie Power or what?'

I had to agree with the little fellow. He certainly did have
a way with shoes.

'Wuntvor!'

My master's voice called to me from directly outside the library. He approached, trailed by his fellow wizards. The crowd of heroes and magical creatures was also filtering back into the courtyard, although Snarks, on spotting the Brownie, seemed content to lurk about in the extreme edges of the greenery, generally behind some concealing bush or boulder.

My master stopped a few paces before me. 'It is time for our decision,' he intoned.

'Indeed?' I replied.

'Indeed,' my master rejoined. 'Heed well, 'prentice, what transpires in these next few moments. Your life, very probably, will depend upon it.'

SEVEN

'The working magician will sometimes find himself in less than ideal circumstances. For example, say you are employed to fight some dire enemy, and having begun the fight, find the enemy has hired a wizard as well. The professional magician, ready for any eventually, will thereupon redouble his efforts while constructing mystical barriers against the other mage.

'But the enemy has also hired assassins, equipped with enchanted weapons, to kill our hypothetical magician. In such cases the fully prepared wizard will reach deep inside himself for those special inner resources, gained through years practicing the magical arts, that will help him to survive.

'But then it grows even worse, as our mage discovers the enemy has enlisted the services of a demon horde who are headed straight for our magician's redoubt to tear him into little pieces and then serve those pieces, impaled with toothpicks, as a part of their victory celebration. What, then, is the working wizard to do?

'The first thing to tell yourself is not to panic. Remember, rather, to keep a calm head, and to heed these words that have helped other wizards, in similar situations to your own, throughout the ages:

'When in doubt, run.'

— THE TEACHINGS OF EBENEZUM,
Volume LXXXII
(annual supplement)

So the moment of decision had come at last. I was relieved, in a way. Now, at last, I could put all the petty little things that had been happening of late behind me and concentrate on the quest.

'Get away from me!' Snarks shrieked.

'You are only delaying the inevitable,' the Brownie replied calmly as he chased the frightened demon across the courtyard. 'We must prepare you for the arrival of his Brownieship. Soon you will know the truth about shoes.'

'Indeed,' my master interrupted, primarily, I suspect, to regain my attention. 'As the rest of our group assembles, let me give you a final reassurance. As you know, my malady prevents me from joining you personally on your quest into the realm of Mother Duck. However, you will not be without my guidance. I have made arrangements so that we will stay in constant contact –'

My master sneezed.

'Must you?' the unicorn chided as it stepped between us. 'You'll tarnish my wondrous golden horn.' The beast shook said horn dry, the golden sheen flashing magnificently with reflected sunlight. It turned its amazingly soulful eyes in my direction. 'I only wanted a few' – it paused – 'private words with our' – it paused again, blinking at me – 'young hero.'

My master sneezed in disbelief.

'Indeed,' I said quickly, doing my best to substitute for the temporarily ailing wizard. 'Do you think it might be possible to give the two of us a moment's privacy?'

The unicorn looked at me in shock, as if I had wounded it by the very suggestion we might not want it around. 'So that's the way it is, then,' it murmured, its voice soft and mournful. 'I, the most magnificent of beasts, am to be turned away. Who would have thought it would come to this?' The creature glanced at me a final time, its eyes filled with wondrous despair. 'If only my head were not so heavy!'

'There, there,' I said, momentarily taken aback by the unicorn's show of anguish. 'Nobody's disputing your magnificence.' The unicorn stopped moaning softly to itself and looked at me. 'In fact, it is that very magnificence that would stop us from fully concentrating on an important decision. That is why you must leave. After all, how can we defend ourselves when we are blinded by your beauty?'

'Yes, being as wonderful as me can be a tremendous burden,' the beast agreed as it tossed its shaggy mane from its eyes, a gesture that took my breath away. 'It's good to know that others can realize that.' The creature once again looked deep into my eyes. 'And it's also nice to know' – the unicorn paused meaningfully, – 'that you care.'

'Indeed,' I replied after a moment's pause.

The unicorn nodded a final time and strutted away, the royalty of magic creatures.

My master blew his nose. 'Indeed,' he remarked once he had regained his breath. 'With such diplomacy, Wunt, you may become a first-class wizard after all. I had feared that my malady might stunt your growth in the wizardly arts. But now I see that you have used the adversity of the past few weeks to your advantage.' The wizard beamed at me. 'After dealing with Brownies and unicorns, Wuntvor, you should be able to handle regular clients with both hands tied behind your back while you are concurrently balancing a ball upon your nose and midway through a short, refreshing afternoon nap.'

I was quite taken aback. Rarely had my master heaped any praise at all upon me, and never, I thought, had he complimented me quite so directly. For the first time I began to feel just a bit like a hero.

'But there are things we must discuss,' the wizard added quickly. He pulled for a moment at his long white beard. 'Now, let us see. You have been given the home study course, and I mentioned that we would stay in contact, although I have not yet explained the means –'

The earth shook, ever so briefly. I feared another Netherhells attack until I saw that Hubert had landed in front of us, accompanied by his beautiful partner, Alea, who sat upon the dragon's back.

The two began to sing:

'The young man, he came from the West,
Bound on a Mother Duck quest!
From his grim task he would not sway,
Though certain death stood in his way!
But Wuntvor was bound to endure,
Though he would get eaten for sure
By dire creatures out for his blood,
Who would then stomp his bones in the mud,
And break them in two for a wish!
They'd hollow his skull for a dish,
And make a soup using his eyes.
From the rest, they'd make Wuntvor Surprise!
Although they might spit out an ear,
While they noisily chomped on his –'

'Indeed!' my master interjected very loudly, at the same time holding his nose so that the dragon's scent would not bring about another sneezing fit. 'I am sure this is all very, musical, but what does it have to do with our present situation?'

'Good wizard,' the dragon replied, bowing so low that

his snout touched the ground. ' 'Tis but a small token of our appreciation for being included in this adventure. You know that we feel it is our duty to lighten the grim load of responsibility with an occasional entertainment. And what better time than right now, with a new quest about to begin!' The dragon tossed his head aloft, shooting forth a banner of flame.

'Yes,' my master began. 'But –'

'So glad you agree,' Hubert replied quickly. 'Let me tell you, it was a dilemma. This is such an important moment, we wanted to choose something appropriate. After much discussion, we decided that a touching farewell song would be best, and so put together a haunting melody tinged with sadness as we send our hero off to certain doom. You know, the sort of thing that tugs at the strings of your heart. We humbly think that if you are here to provide the wisdom, we are here to provide the art.'

Tug at the strings of my heart? I had felt more of a reaction to the song in my stomach.

'Indeed,' I attempted to interject. 'But –'

'Thus,' Hubert continued, 'we thought it appropriate to give you a small sample of our strengths now, when you are about to choose those who are to go on this most important mission. Yes, that is correct: Damsel and Dragon would like to volunteer! The expedition surely needs a couple of cheerful minstrels to keep spirits high in times of trial! We laugh at demons! We sneer at sorcery! We scoff at danger!'

The dragon chortled, producing a pair of smoke rings from his nostrils. 'Plus, should we succeed, think of the publicity! "Damsel and Dragon Help Save the World from Demonkind!" ' Hubert sighed happily. 'We will be booked forever!'

Hubert's dragon jaws closed with a snap. Apparently his oration was over.

'Indeed,' my master replied after a moment's hesitation.

'Thank you for your offer. I assure you it will receive careful consideration.'

Alea blew me a kiss as the two of them left to join the crowd. Ebenezum took a second to tend to his nose.

'Sometimes,' he remarked as he once again tucked his dark blue handkerchief, tastefully embroidered with silver moons and stars, within his voluminous sleeve, 'I long for the days when it was just the two of us, Wunt, struggling across the Western Kingdoms toward Vushta, with only nature and the forces of the Netherhells to contend with.' He shook his head. 'But this is no time for nostalgia. It is time for action. Now where were we? We have covered the home study course, and delved, however briefly, into the fact that I shall still be able to advise you. Now, I think it is time for a bit of wizardly advice. Heed my words carefully Wuntvor, for they may mean the difference between success and failure, life and death, a carefree existence for us all or an eternity of pain and torture at the hands of –'

'Doom.' Hendrek's voice resounded over my left shoulder. 'Forgive me for interrupting, but they have brought the weapons.'

'Indeed,' my master replied as he glanced over his shoulder. 'So they have. Now, if you would excuse us for but a moment –'

'Doom,' Hendrek interjected. 'You must forgive one further interruption, but as we speak of weapons, I feel I should remind you of my prowess with Headbasher. If you are about to go on a quest, how much better if you are to include a man inured to battle like myself, a warrior, steeped in blood. A berserker, ready to kill at the slightest provocation.'

'Indeed,' Ebenezum concurred. 'Still –'

'A lit fuse,' Hendrek glowered. 'A powder keg ready to explode. It is best that a trained mercenary like myself does not remain idle.' He fingered the sack that held Headbasher. 'Please consider me when you choose companions for the quest. Doom!'

And with that, the large warrior left us.

'Well,' Ebenezum remarked. 'And now quickly back to our discussion, before we can be interrupted –'

Someone cleared her throat behind me. It was the most musical throat-clearing I had ever heard. It had to be Norei.

'Excuse me,' she said, looking straight at my master. 'I know it's rude to interrupt, but I was wondering if you might be able to give Wuntvor a message from me.'

'Norei!' I began. Why wasn't she speaking to me? 'But –'

'I am well aware that you are about to choose those among us who are to accompany Wuntvor on a quest of some importance. I wanted to inform you now, so that there would be no misunderstanding, that I do not wish to be among those included.'

'Norei?' I gasped, astonished. What did this mean? 'But –'

'I want to be very firm about this,' my beloved continued. 'You see, Wuntvor and I once meant something to each other.' She sighed wistfully, as if recalling some far distant memory.

'Indeed?' my master remarked as he stroked his beard in thought. He glanced in my direction.

'Norei?' I asked forcefully. Whatever her problem with me, I would do my best to solve it now. 'But –'

'It is for this very reason,' my beloved continued as if she had not even heard me, 'that I do not wish to be included in any other adventures. The very nearness of that apprentice would remind me of better times, happier moments that Wuntvor apparently never wishes to repeat. Therefore, you should not even consider me for the quest. That is' – she paused, her eyes fluttering ever so slightly (dare I hope?) in my direction – 'unless you really need me.'

Ebenezum cleared his throat rather noisily. 'Well, I will be certain to tell Wuntvor of your wishes. And we will assuredly take your feelings into account when choosing our party.

'Norei?' I called a final time. She seemed to hesitate as she turned away. My heart quickened. Perhaps she would give me one last chance.

'Oh, Wuntie!' Alea called to me as she skipped across the courtyard. Her ash-blond curls shone blindingly as they bounced in the sunlight. 'Hubert wanted me to talk to you about that act we were going to do together!'

To my dread I saw my beloved Norei mouth Alea's last few words: 'Act we were going to do together?'

Norei looked at me for the first time. From the intensity of the emotions in her eyes, I wish she hadn't.

Alea interposed herself between Norei and me. 'You'll excuse us, won't you dear?' Alea called over her shoulder to my beloved. 'Wuntie and I have things to discuss.'

It was too much for the young witch. 'Act?' she yelled. 'Things to discuss? I'll give you –'

She stopped abruptly, caught short by the sudden appearance of a golden horn so wonderful it put even Alea's hair to shame. The unicorn pushed between me and the two others.

'Pardon me, but are these women bothering you?' the incredible beast inquired.

'Um . . .' I replied.

'Bothering you!' Both women cried in unison.

'Um . . .' I repeated. This was all going too fast for me. What should I say?

'I never bother Wuntie!' Alea insisted vociferously. 'Wuntie and I were having another of our sensitive conversations about –'

'You wouldn't know a sensitive conversation if one bit you in the –' Norei interrupted just as loudly.

'Obviously, then, my first reaction was quite correct,' the unicorn sniffed. 'A sensitive lad like you needs protection' – it paused meaningfully – 'and perhaps a little guidance.' The beast looked soulfully into my eyes. 'I thought if I took a more active interest, you might see the light. Who, after all, can resist a unicorn? Especially when the alternatives are such as these.'

All three of them turned to look at me. I swallowed loudly and turned to look at my master.

'Indeed,' the wizard said as he stroked his mustache. 'Wuntvor and I must confer privately about the choice of weapons.'

My master hastily pulled me aside.

'What do you mean,' I heard Alea shout behind me, 'I wouldn't understand a sensitive conversation?'

My master spoke to me quickly, in hushed tones. 'We have a situation here that would best be left alone for a time.'

'So you want sensitive?' Norei retorted. 'I'll make you sensitive!'

'Say the time it takes to complete a quest,' my master added.

'Of course,' a third voice remarked calmly, 'no one is as sensitive as a unicorn.'

'Oh, shut up!' Norei retorted. 'You're nothing but an overstuffed horse!'

'Or perhaps two quests,' the wizard amended. I could see the wisdom in my master's words. 'But we must confer quickly now, before we suffer further –'

'I never want to hear about shoes again!'

My master almost tripped over the rapidly traveling Snarks. I suppose it was only natural, then, that I should trip over the Brownie.

'You must face the inevitable – yelp!' Tap shrieked as he collided solidly with my left foot.

As I picked myself up, I was startled to see Snarks on his knees, clutching frantically at my master's robes.

'Oh, great wizard,' the demon pleaded. 'I have heard there's another quest in the offing, and I was wondering if I might be considered –' The demon drew back as he saw Tap stand and happily brush himself off. 'No, I'm not wondering at all!' Snarks added quickly. 'Take me on the quest! I don't care where it is! As long as there aren't any Brownies!'

I turned and began to apologize to the little fellow, but Tap waved me to silence.

'No harm done,' he remarked cheerfully. 'Brownies don't bruise easily. It's one of the advantages of being built short. You're much closer to the ground when you fall. Besides, I should have been looking where I was going. Once I get talking about shoes, though . . .'

The Brownie sauntered casually in the demon's direction. Snarks shrieked and ran. I looked after him with astonishment. Before today the demon had always had a ready answer for everything. Could one Brownie make that much of a change?

Ebenezum blew his nose and tapped me on the shoulder.

'Indeed,' my master whispered hoarsely. 'Quick –'

'Eep! Eep! Eep!' My ferrets,dispersed by the recent battle, seemed to be regathering around us. As happy as I was to see them, I had to admit that their joyful cries made it difficult to listen to anything else in the immediate area.

'Oh, never mind,' the wizard muttered: 'Let's look at the weapons.'

The aged wizard Snorphosio nodded as we approached. He was tastefully tucking his own recently used handkerchief within a bright red sleeve.

'We have here what weapons we could find in the college storeroom.' The scholarly mage sniffed. 'I am afraid there have been some problems.'

'Problems?' Ebenezum asked.

'Yes.' Snorphosio nodded his head sadly. 'Although who among us does not have problems? It is in the nature of existence, is it not, for wizards must exist like any others. And what is the true nature of a wizard's existence except –'

'Exactly what problems are there?' my master interrupted.

'Oh, certainly,' Snorphosio murmured. 'Forgive my digression. But is not digression itself a problem that wizards must –' He stopped and cleared his throat self-consciously. 'Yes. Pardon. The problems. First, it appears that during Vushta's recent trip to and from the Netherhells, the weapons storeroom got jumbled about a bit. We opened the door to find everything in incredible disarray. On first sight it reminded me of the chaos that is the core of all our existences and the problems I had mentioned before that dog a wizard's every waking –'

'Indeed,' my master interposed. 'So something is wrong with the weapons?'

'With the weapons themselves, no.' The scholar shook

his head. 'As far as we know, they are in prime working order. Of course, we cannot tell for certain if they are working properly –'

'And why is that?' Ebenezum jumped in before his fellow could begin another digression.

'All the weapons seem to have lost their labels,' Snorphosio replied a bit sheepishly. 'We can't quite tell what does what anymore.'

'Doom.' I noticed then that Hendrek had silently lumbered up behind us.

'Indeed?' Ebenezum frowned and pulled on his beard. 'Does anyone have a knowledge of the storeroom?'

'Not a very complete one, I'm afraid.' Snorphosio shrugged. 'I'm sure you know how it is. Things pile up, you get way behind in cataloging. Again we return to the nature of life, don't we, and man's feeble attempts to extract order out of chaos? But what, exactly, is the true nature of order? What right have we, as magicians, to impose –'

'What can we do to find magic weapons for the quest?' my master retorted.

'Well,' Snorphosio admitted, 'that's another problem. None of the wizards have been able to reach very far into the storeroom. The sneezing problem, you see. We did manage to drag out one chest full of smaller weapons, however.' The scholar patted a huge strongbox whose top reached up to his waist. 'There may very well be something of value herein.'

'May very well?' Ebenezum exploded. 'Can't you tell?'

'Well . . .' Snorphosio hesitated. 'No. The label problem, you know. One has to be careful around unlabeled enchanted weapons. Besides the sneezing problem, some of these things are quite powerful, capable of warping the fabric of the universe and ending life as we know it.' The mage cleared his throat once again. 'However, we don't think any devices with that kind of power are that small.' He tried to smile and failed. 'At least,' he added, 'we hope not.'

'Hope?' My master seemed to be trembling with anger by now. I had hardly ever seen him so upset. He wasn't using any 'indeeds' at all.

'Oh, we have not been sitting idly with this problem on our hands,' Snorphosio assured him. 'In fact, one of the younger magicians among our number boldly volunteered to test the weapons enclosed to see what might be useful.'

'A bold mage indeed,' Ebenezum remarked, his anger momentarily subdued. 'And what were the results?'

'Well . . .' The scholar tapped the box. 'Our suspicion is that the young fellow's still in there somewhere.' He sighed, but then smiled. 'However, before he disappeared he did manage to give us this!'

His smile broadened as he held aloft a thin sliver of wood.

'This, gentlebeings, is Gllzbchh's Toothpick.'

'Doom,' Hendrek remarked in awe. 'I have never seen a weapon so small. How deadly is it?'

'Deadly?' Snorphosio frowned. 'Well, it is not exactly deadly.'

'Doom,' Hendrek replied. 'Then the weapon is truly dangerous?'

'Well,' the scholar allowed, 'in point of fact, you couldn't even call it exactly dangerous. You can take my word for it, though, that it is very, very annoying.'

'And that is all you have found?' my master demanded.

'No, no, of course not!' Snorphosio insisted. 'Well, actually, in point of fact, yes, it's as far as we got when our poor compatriot disappeared. However, we do have a few more weapons we can offer. Such as this!' He decisively pointed at a nearby oak.

'And what, precisely, is "this"?' Ebenezum asked with some disdain.

'Why, it's a magic tree of course.' The scholar sounded somewhat hurt that my master had not instantly recognized the enchanted vegetation. 'And let me tell you, I got an extremely good price on it, too. Bought it from a renegade demon, actually, fellow in a bright checked suit who sold weapons slightly used.'

'Indeed,' my master responded, making a visible effort to calm himself. 'And how would my apprentice be expected to carry a tree?'

'Carry it?' Snorphosio mused. 'Why would he need to – oh, dear, he is leaving the vicinity, isn't he? What to do?' His tentative fingers prodded the oak's unyielding trunk. 'Maybe we could break off a magic branch?

'Wait, wait!' the scholar continued when he saw the look and the color of my master's face. 'All is still not lost. We have not considered the weapons left over from the last quest!'

'Doom,' Hendrek remarked for us all.

'Now, now,' Snorphosio insisted, 'they are perfectly serviceable. Well, more or less. We have been having some trouble with Cuthbert. The sword claims to have been traumatized by all that battle. Refuses to come out of its sheath. I'm sure all it needs is a good talking to.'

No one commented. Snorphosio quickly continued: 'Then, of course, there is Wonk, the Horn of Persuasion.'

'No, no!' everyone cried in unison. 'Anything but Wonk!' I still remembered the effect the horn had when it was blown, and would do anything to see that it was *never* blown again. I had to face it. There were some weapons just too horrible to use.

'So there are no weapons my apprentice can take with him?' my master demanded.

'Well, no, not exactly.' Snorphosio handed me the enchanted toothpick. 'Well, actually, that is more or less correct.'

'And so Wuntvor must go off to face the unknown with nothing but his wits and my assistance?' My master sighed. 'Oh, well. He has done it before. Come, we had best pick companions before something else happens.'

That's when the earth began to shake again.

'Doom!' Hendrek intoned. 'I shall show you my prowess against the Netherhells. You are bound to take me on the quest!'

'I will surely be among those chosen,' a magnificently modulated voice remarked. The glorious beast pranced forward in the afternoon sun. 'Who can say no to a unicorn?'

'Quick, damsel!' Hubert rejoined. 'We will confuse the enemy with our dancing and snappy patter! Then we shall be the quest's Official Entertainers!'

'I will show my fellow demons exactly how unwelcome they are!' Snarks added. 'And I'd be glad to do it anywhere, especially anyplace without Brownies!'

'More demons?' Tap laughed delightedly. 'Bring them on! I will tell them all the truth about shoes!'

'Even I will not desert you!' my beloved Norei added. 'And you can tell that to Wuntvor when you get the chance!'

'Eep! Eep! Eep!' my legion of ferrets added, eager for the coming fight.

My master nodded to the other wizards, who formed

a circle around the center of the quake.

The table with the five demons erupted again from the earth. Everyone paused for a long moment. I noticed the magicians close by me were holding their breath, perhaps to give them a few minutes longer in the face of this demonic enchantment.

'Quick, my fellows!' I shouted as I gripped my stout oak staff. 'Forward to the attack, before they have a chance to vote!'

The gavel demon at table's center smiled evilly. 'You are too late! We voted this time before we came to the surface so there would be no dissent. Prepare, pitiful mortals, to have your blood boiled!'

'Now!' Ebenezum shouted as he removed his fingers from his nose.

And all the wizards sneezed as one.

'Point of – glub!' a demon shrieked as he was swamped by nasal effluvium. The entire table seemed totally undone by the sudden shower.

Without another word the dampened demons disappeared beneath the earth.

'Master!' I cried. 'You have beaten them again!'

'Only by surprise,' Ebenezum replied when he was done blowing his nose. 'I fear it was our last guaranteed strategy. Next time the demons shall win.'

I looked about me. All was confusion. Hendrek pounded Headbasher against the spot where the demons had sat but a moment before, while Damsel and Dragon tap danced close behind. Snarks beat a hasty retreat, pursued by the Brownie. The other wizards had fallen to the ground, all lost to their sneezing. The unicorn seemed somehow above it all, looking down at the proceedings from behind the length of its golden horn. The ferrets were everywhere, eeping merrily. And Norei, my beloved Norei, was nowhere to be seen.

'It will take far too long to choose companions,' I remarked grimly.

'Indeed,' my master replied. 'It seems to take far too long to do anything.' With that, Ebenezum once again succumbed to a bout of sneezing.

'Then I shall go alone,' I stated, though no one was particularly listening. 'I shall bring help from the Eastern Kingdoms. Do not worry, master. I shall not fail.'

Having said what was necessary, I grabbed my stout oak staff and my pack, which contained both Snorphosio's map and the home study course. No one seemed to have heard my speech, and no one seemed to notice my leaving. Still, I was glad I had spoken.

I would have been happier still if I truly believed what I had said.

EIGHT

'When traveling alone through a deep, dark, possibly enchanted and potentially dangerous forest, it is best to take someone with you.'

– SOME THOUGHTS ON APPRENTICESHIP,
by Wuntvor, apprentice to Ebenezum,
greatest mage in the Western Kingdoms
(a work in progress)

Nothing would stop me now. There was no reason to look back. My beloved Norei apparently no longer needed me. Besides which, I had a world to save.

I left Vushta the way I had entered, through the adjacent town of East Vushta, where I had first fought side by side with the members of the Wizards College Extension Program to save their neighbor city from the clutches of the Netherhells. From there, though, my path was different, leading me away from the shores of the Inland Sea into parts of the world entirely new to me.

I refolded Snorphosio's map and tucked it back into my pack. I had passed the East Vushta Extension College some moments before, and here the road split, one fork leading into the hills, the other down to the seashore. I once again shouldered my belongings and headed inland, toward my destiny.

I was amazed at how fast I left the city behind me.

While the buildings and shops of East Vushta were quite a bit smaller than those of the City of a Thousand Forbidden Delights, they were still built close together, the streets surrounding them thronged with people. Once into the hills, however, what cottages I saw grew quickly smaller and farther apart, each one in worse repair than the one before. The last couple of shacks I passed were obviously deserted, at least of human occupants, although great, dark birds made their nests here and there amidst the collapsed walls.

As the homes grew sparser the trees grew thicker and the road, paved with brick where it left East Vushta, soon became naught but packed earth. A scant few minutes walk beyond that, it had deteriorated to two wagon ruts between tufts of sickly yellow grass. I paused to again look at Snorphosio's map, but according to the scholar's drawing, there was no way I could have made a wrong turn. There was but one road to the Eastern Kingdoms, and I was on it.

Still, I was happy to be on my way. My life had a definite goal once again. I had not realized how much I wanted this kind of purpose until it had been offered to me. I wondered, absently, if questing was habit forming. My pack again on my back, a firm grip on my stout oak staff, I found myself taking broad strides down the rut that passed for a road. I began to whistle one of the little ditties I had learned from Damsel and Dragon.

Something whistled back.

At least that was what I thought at first. But what initially had sounded like a whistle soon became a low moan, then rose in volume, transformed to a howling gale. The wind was upon me all at once, as freezing as it was sudden, as though it had appeared from the worst day of winter, rather than the late summer day around me. The gale hit with such force that I could no longer move forward, but had to struggle merely to remain standing.

Then the wind was gone, as quickly as it came, and the forest grew still once again. I thought for a second that I heard faint laughter in the far distance, but decided after a moment that the sound was more likely the aftereffects of the winter wind upon my ears.

I brushed the ice crystals from my shirt and continued on my way. I wondered if this sort of thing happened all the time in this particular forest. With such weather conditions, I could understand the lack of local habitation.

I walked on for some moments without further incident. Perhaps, I thought, I had just been the victim of some freak late-summer squall, the kind that brings hailstones to shine brightly for a moment before they melt under the summer sun. The trees, rather than blocking my view of the sky, seemed to be thinning hereabouts, and I thought I saw a clearing just ahead.

I began to whistle once again.

Once more my whistle was answered. This time the spot where I stood seemed somehow protected from the main force of the gale, but the wind whipped savagely overhead, almost bending the trees in two. I was inundated by torn leaves and small branches and, as the great oaks and maples groaned above me, I feared that the larger boughs might break off and rain down on me as well.

The second wind vanished as quickly as the first. The trees seemed to shake a final time, then resumed their still and silent vigil.

Did I hear laughter again?

It had to be my imagination.

For the first time since I had begun my journey, I considered that perhaps I should have waited for companions after all. I had gripped my stout oak staff so firmly during the second windstorm that my fist ached. But my staff seemed scant protection against a phantom wind with the full force of winter behind it. What else could I do?

It was then that I remembered the Home Study Course in my pack.

I could not restrain the slightest of smiles. So I was not defenseless after all! I had merely to look up, say, 'Winds from Nowhere' in the index, and all would be explained, including, I imagined, a magical remedy or two. Perhaps they would even have a listing for 'Winds from Nowhere, Caused by Whistling'!

I whipped the pack quickly from my back, almost losing my balance in my enthusiasm. I would prove more than a match for whatever force or being was creating these bizarre weather patterns. Still, I hesitated as I glanced briefly overhead. Perhaps it would be best if I moved out from beneath these trees.

Once in the clearing, a beautiful little meadow dotted with wildflowers, I again set about my task. I placed my pack on the long grass and knelt down beside it, quickly thrusting a hand inside to locate the home study tome.

I drew my hand out just as quickly. My fingers had found something else in the pack, something unexpected, something that didn't feel like a book, or a map, or an enchanted toothpick. Not only that, when I touched it, it moved.

Had whatever caused the wind placed another surprise in my pack? Visions of miniature demons equipped with two or more sets of teeth flitted through my frightened brain. Cautiously, I threw back the flap that had sealed the bag so that I might see the contents in bright daylight. I was no longer on my knees, but balanced on the balls of my feet so that I might make a quick retreat if whatever I found inside proved to be particularly nasty.

I slowly leaned forward, peering into the pack's dark recesses.

There! Something moved again, a dark body darting behind the massive Home Study Course. Did it gibber at me as it fled my grasp? I took a ragged breath. There was nothing I could do but reach in to move the book.

I did just that, cautiously, with exceeding patience, ready at any second to feel tiny, dire fangs piercing the skin of my knuckles. But the stowaway remained hidden. I swallowed. I had faced worse threats than this from the Netherhells. And should I rescue the Home Study Course, I would have a means to banish this problem as well.

It was The Moment of Truth.

I grabbed the book and whipped it from the pack. Now!

Two small brown eyes met my astonished gaze.

'Eep!' the ferret cried.

I laughed. So I had not managed to leave Vushta unaccompanied after all. My new companion was small, even for a ferret, probably not yet fully grown.

'Hello, there,' I remarked to the newcomer. 'Decided to come for a ride, did you?'

'Eep!' the ferret replied joyfully. I stroked its tiny head with my thumb. I realized I was smiling. For some reason, having this small furry fellow around made me feel that half of my troubles had vanished into the air.

Still, if half my troubles were gone, that meant that the other half remained to be dealt with. That's why I held the Home Study Course in my hand. It was time to look up 'Winds from Nowhere' and face my problem directly.

I opened the tome to the index at the rear, flipping rapidly to the W's, eager to find an answer. The last page began 'Wombats, use in potions.' Too far. I would have to backtrack. I turned back a page. Here it was:

'Winds (see also breezes, gales, hurricanes, storms, tornadoes –'

I never realized the entry could be so long! I whistled softly to myself.

And my whistling was answered.

This time the gale came low. My head and arms were still warmed by sunshine, but my legs and feet were frozen where they stood. The wind roared over the meadow. Wildflowers froze and crumbled, while the grass turned from brilliant green to a dead, lifeless gray. And the wind was followed by laughter, much louder this time, and even colder than the gale that preceded it.

I glanced quickly back at the book, doing my best to ignore my frostbitten lower extremities. My eyes rapidly scanned the entries:

Wind charms, simple and complex
Wind chills, their cause and prevention
Wind chimes, their use in spells –

The entries were even longer than I first imagined. My gaze darted more rapidly still, past entries on wind choirs and wind chores, and on to how to make winds churn. The entries seemed to go on forever! My palms sweated where I held the book, despite the freezing gale. What could I do?

'You won't find anything in there,' whispered a voice twice as chilling as the wind.

I looked up into a face I knew, if you could call it a face.

I would know those dark robes and that grinning skull anywhere. I was looking at Death.

'So pleased to see you again.' Death's voice was the sound of brittle leaves blowing in the wind. 'Did you like our little game?'

'G-game?' I whispered back.

Death softly whistled, and the winds howled all around. He laughed, and the air was still again, but it no longer seemed to be the air of summer. It was replaced by the winter chill which nipped at my fingers and set my teeth to chattering.

'You do remember,' Death replied, 'how fond I am of games?'

I did indeed. My master and I had first met Death in the cursed Valley of Vrunge, where we had been surrounded by ghosts not only dragging chains and moaning, but doing all the things they had done in life, from fighting wars to making love. All of that cursed night we spent in the valley, in fact all of life itself and death beyond, was a game. Or so said the creature Death.

'So glad you remembered.' Death spoke as if he could read my mind. 'It makes what I have to say next so much easier.' He pointed a bony finger at my chest. 'For you see, apprentice, I have wished to speak to you for ever so long.' The creature laughed again, a dry chuckle like the sound of crumbling stone.

'Everyone dies,' Death continued, his skull-grin somehow even wider than before. 'And everyone should come to me. That is the natural order of things, after all. But . . .' He paused, and I thought I saw a flash of red deep within his night-black eye sockets. '. . . there are some meddlers who like to change what is natural, who like to create heroes who are eternal and forever beyond my grasp!' Death paused again, smoothing his robes with bony fingers. 'This, however, I have accepted with time. Perhaps people need their eternal heroes. It makes everyone else's deaths so much more poignant, and so much more hopeless. But there is one other I shall never accept, one the gods have created to mock me for all eternity!'

Death swept his arms wide toward the meadow. A few flowers and blades of grass had survived the winds. They all perished in that instant, rotting and falling into dust as I watched.

Death turned back to gaze at me. I looked away, afraid that I might be drawn within those dark sockets and find myself falling for all eternity. The creature spoke again, his voice louder and tinged with anguish.

'Why could I have not seen that time before who you truly were? It would have been so easy to dispense with you in the Valley of Vrunge had I but known your true identity' – Death's voice had become as shrill as the howling wind – 'THE ETERNAL APPRENTICE!'

I turned back to the apparition. What had he called me?

'The eternal apprentice,' Death repeated – more, it seemed, to himself than to me. 'Forever aiding heroes in his bumbling, well-meaning way, and forever accompanied by any number of magical companions. As long as he is with these companions, he is beyond my grasp. I cannot even have him when he dies, for he is immediately reincarnated into another bumbling form!'

The apparition's bony hand grabbed my tunic. 'How unfair it all is! But one day as I was reaping souls, I had an idea. The eternal apprentice is always snatched from my grasp the moment he dies. But what if I could somehow get him alone when he was still alive?'

Death's hand pulled me closer. His breath smelled of decay. I turned my head away, trying to draw untainted air into my lungs.

But Death would not be deterred. 'So I made a point to join your little group, very discreetly, of course. Don't look so surprised! I am always with you. After all, people die a little every day, sometimes in body, sometimes in mind. I only needed to speed the process a bit, to wither a little here, rot a bit there. I will admit, there was dissension among your fellows before I came. Ah, but how a little Death can improve the quality of that dissension.'

The apparition grasped my chin with his other bony hand. He drew my face to his again.

'No one has escaped my effect.'

So that was Death's game! He had worked his discontent among my fellows, as when he sent the Brownie against Snarks, ten times worse than they had been before, somehow undermining the demon's confidence in the process. In smaller ways he had set Snarks against Hendrek, the Dealer of Death against Ebenezum, even, I remembered now, Damsel against Dragon. Then there was the spread of the malady among the wizards! Was the creature before me responsible for that as well?

And what of Norei's reaction to me? I was chilled by the thought. How insidious was Death!

'And so all in Vushta became Chaos.' The apparition chuckled, his spirits renewed. 'What could a poor apprentice do if he wanted to save his master, but leave the chaos behind and strike out alone for the cure!'

Death threw his head back and laughed so hard that his bones rattled.

'And now, at last, I have you alone.' He dragged

me forward, until my chin was almost touching his chest. 'At last, accursed apprentice, you are mine, for all eternity!'

I felt the pack shift on my back.

'Eep!'

Death recoiled in horror. 'What is that?'

The apparition had loosed its grip on me! I staggered back, gasping the chill but untainted air. And with that breath came a rush of emotions that had been somehow suppressed. Death had mesmerized me. I had listened to his explanation as if I were in a trance, beyond fear, even beyond reason. Now, though, my tiny friend had startled him. Now I had a chance.

'I am never without companions!' I said boldly. 'You are wrong, Death. I am not alone. I have brought a ferret!'

'Eep!' my companion added.

Death screamed. His voice echoed the final agonies of countless souls, a sound so horrible that it almost caused me to lose my newfound resolve.

'Will you never be alone? I had some doubts before. I feared you were perhaps a bit too bumbling for the one I seek. But now I know.' His skeletal hand shook as he pointed at me. 'You are truly the Eternal Apprentice!'

'Eep!' the ferret retorted.

'But wait . . .' Death paused, instantly composed. 'Who stands in the way of my goal? Only a dumb animal. And a ferret at that! After all, who can say if a ferret could even properly be called a companion?' Death's skull leered at me. 'I think I shall take you after all. People are said to cheat death all the time. Who will know if Death cheats just this once?'

Death made a fist, and I felt icy fingers around my

heart. I couldn't catch my breath. Was this the end? I thought, one final time, of Norei.

'Eternal Apprentice!' Death crowed. 'You are mine at la –'

There was a small explosion by my feet.

'Hey, guys!' an equally small voice piped. 'It's Brownie time!'

And I heard a scream so intense that Death's earlier cry seemed but a whisper.

NINE

'Even wizards must deal with unwelcome visitors. They eat your food, interrupt your spells, perhaps even criticize your conjuring. What's a poor wizard to do? A mage can, of course, use his other magic to banish these guests, or perhaps even better, turn them into some less offensive form of animal or vegetation. In fact, many beautiful tower gardens have been begun by such a happy accident.

'Unfortunately, by the very nature of his or her occupation, the average wizard will sometimes attract company that is just as magical as the mage, say a rival sorcerer or some form of enchanted creature. These unwelcome guests are somewhat more problematic. They tend to frown on being changed into a harmless herbivore, and become absolutely livid at the suggestion that they might look good as a hanging vine on the veranda. Besides this, they might have the additional audacity to actually change the spells their host wizard conjures, as well as calling up any number of other troublesome residual magicks as they settle in for what seems to be the remainder of the host wizard's lifetime.

'But even though one may not at first be able to rid oneself of such unwanted companions, the resourceful wizard should not despair. In fact, should the wizard simply be prepared to instantly change name, occupation, and country of residence, that *wizard should probably have no further trouble whatsoever.'*

–THE ONE MINUTE MAGICIAN – A
WIZARD'S GUIDE TO BETTER
MAGIC MANAGEMENT
(fourth edition) by Ebenezum
Greatest Wizard in the
Western Kingdoms

'Did I interrupt something?' Tap inquired.

I stared at the Brownie. Hadn't he heard Death's ear-piercing scream? And the words that followed still in my ears with a chilling clarity:

'I will get you yet, apprentice. The next moment you are truly alone, you are mine!'

Tap frowned up at me. 'You seemed distracted. If I'm in the way, just let me know. Brownies never stay where they're not wanted.'

I hastily assured him that he had done no harm. I glanced around quickly, concerned lest Death have one more game to play. But the spectre seemed to have vanished. Only the ravaged hillside, devoid now of all the colorful plantlife that had graced it but a moment before, attested to the fact that he had been there at all.

The Brownie followed my gaze. 'Do you like to stare moodily at piles of dirt? While it is generally not in a Brownie's cheerful nature to criticize his companions, I must say that I could think of better places to stop by the side of the road than this creepy corner.

'But enough of this gloom and doom!' The little fellow jumped happily around so that he stood between me and the barren hill. 'That's one of the reasons I'm here, you know – to help you on your quest with one of those things we wee folk are best at: Good, down-to-earth Brownie advice!'

Down-to-earth Brownie advice? The joy I had felt when the Brownie first arrived seemed to be draining rapidly from me. It didn't help that Tap had begun to hop about again, giggling merrily as he bounced. Perhaps, I thought, there might be some way to reason with the small fellow, if only he would stand still long enough.

'Um . . .' I began. I waved my hands at him, hoping the gesture would quiet him down.

'And a happy Brownie hello to you, too!' Tap waved back. His moving hands seemed to make his jumps even higher. 'That's more like it! I knew a little hopping about would cheer you up immediately. That's Brownie Power!' After a few more ecstatic leaps, the little fellow paused to add: 'I am here, of course, for other reasons as well.'

There was a distant crash in the forest. I turned, full of trepidation. Was Death coming back? I put a finger to my lips in an attempt to caution the Brownie to silence.

'And what are those other reasons?' Tap continued as if he hadn't heard anything but the sound of his own voice. 'First, of course, is the might of Brownie-know-how! We little folks have hundreds of years of shoemaking experience. And let me tell you, that really counts for something in the know-how department!'

There was another crash in the forest, both louder and, I imagined, closer. I failed at that immediate moment to comprehend exactly what connection shoemaking had to our present situation. I cleared my throat in an attempt to interrupt the small fellow.

'Nasty cough you have there,' Tap remarked. 'But

speaking of counting for something, Brownies do count,
you know. We may be small, but we think big! That's
another thing you have in your favor – the joy of Brownie
enthusiasm!'

The smashing and crashing was definitely closer now,
and accompanied by guttural screams. Another thought
chilled me to the bone: Maybe it wasn't Death at all. Maybe
it was demons, come to stop me from getting help for
Vushta!

'But basic Brownie protection doesn't stop there,' Tap
continued merrily. 'For at its center is the greatest gift of
all, the thrill of Brownie magic; a wizardry that shines like
bright leather, full of spells laced with the best intentions!'

The commotion in the forest was becoming louder still.
Besides the crashing, I could now hear the sounds of
rending and tearing, as if some force was demolishing the
very trees and bushes that made up the woods. The guttural
screams continued as well, although now I could also hear
the somewhat lesser cries of terrified forest creatures as they
rapidly fled the scene. And the noise was close enough now
so that I could clearly tell where it came from – directly in
front of me, behind the barren hill.

'And then, of course, there is one more reason for
believing in Brownie Power . . .' Tap continued, but
paused when he saw the look of extreme consternation
upon my countenance. The rending and screaming continued unabated, loud enough so that the Brownie had to
shout in order to be heard.

'Um,' I said, glancing above the Brownie to the far side
of the hill. 'Don't you think we should do something?'

'Well, if you think it's time.' Tap did a small dance,
limbering himself up for the magic to come. 'But why so
upset? Is it that little noise in the woods? Brownies are

ready for everything! You never have to worry when there's Brownie Power around!' The little fellow sighed. 'We'll pause then, and deal with the commotion. I guess I'll just have to wait to tell you about how I'm supposed to transmit messages between you and Ebenezum.'

'What?' I shouted at the small fellow. Then the wizard had sent the Brownie! Perhaps I was glad to see Tap after all.

'Well, tell me –' I began.

My question was interrupted by the loudest shriek I had heard so far.

'Oops,' the Brownie remarked as he stared at the top of the hill. 'Then again, maybe Brownies aren't ready for *absolutely* everything.'

I followed the Brownie's gaze to the summit of the barren rise before us. There stood two demonic figures. Much worse, they were demons I had met before.

'There they are!' The creature on the left pointed and waved. He was wearing a checkered suit. 'I told you our magical weapons wouldn't let us down!'

Brax the salesdemon turned to his companion. The other demon grunted, a guttural sound not unlike the screams we had heard but moments before.

It was this second fiend whose appearance caused my blood to freeze, whose immense size, immense claws, and immense teeth, led one's gaze away even from the other creature's extremely loud attire.

The second demon was Guxx Unfufadoo. Guxx, the fiend who had given my master Ebenezum his sneezing malady, and who had, until recently, been involved in a plot for the Netherhells to subjugate the surface world to his demonic administration! He had almost won, too, for the demon had only been stopped when I managed to capture a

strand of his nosehair and return it to Ebenezum and his
fellow wizards for them to effect a counterspell.

So, if you looked at the course of events in a certain way,
I was the only reason Guxx was not now ruler of both the
world above and below. I was the only reason he had not
retained the exalted title of Grand Hoohah (whatever that
was; I had been told not to ask) and was instead wandering
upon the surface world with but a single companion instead
of his usual retinue. I was the only reason that he did not
have fantastic amounts of gold and jewels at his disposal as
well as all of humanity as his slaves, but instead seemed to
be a penniless outcast far from home.

I took a moment to swallow, although my throat was far
too dry, and wondered if Guxx Unfufadoo might be the
slightest bit annoyed. I wondered if the demon had indeed
sought me out for a purpose, perhaps as a practice ground
for his amazingly sharp claws and incredibly sharp teeth, so
that they might not fall into disuse. Or perhaps Brax, who
made his demonic living selling slightly used enchanted
weapons, had come along with the express purpose of pro-
viding Guxx with the nastiest of his wares for my disposal.

Both demons smiled at us and waved. They began to
descend the hill.

Whatever the two had in store, I had no doubt it would be
fiendishly hideous. Not to mention very, very bloody.

I drew myself up to my full height, my stout oak staff
firmly in my hands. It was not much protection against
rending claws and teeth, but it was the best I had, and I
would use it to my fullest. I had often feared the worst in my
encounters with the Netherhells. Now that the worst was
here, I was ready for it.

'Yes!' Brax called down to us. 'You are the very creatures
we were seeking. No, no, don't run away! Demons are very

fast, it would be completely useless. In fact, we want to be your friends!'

Friends? I lowered my staff to stare at the two demons. Maybe there was something worse than the worst.

Guxx grumbled darkly as they approached. His voice sounded like gravel being ground to dust. He flexed his claws and gnashed his teeth. I could see the dark glow of the fires of the Netherhells in his eyes. I attempted to swallow again, and wondered exactly what kind of friendship they were looking for.

The two demons paused as they reached the bottom of the hill a scant few feet away. They were so close that I could smell the brimstone on Guxx Unfufadoo's breath.

'Now!' Guxx intoned.

Brax quickly reached into a large, leather bag he carried and drew out a tiny drum. He began to beat upon it with a regular rhythm. With that, Guxx stepped forward and began to intone:

> 'Guxx Unfufadoo, noble demon,
> Wrongly shunned by Netherhells traitors,
> Forced to walk the surface pathways
> Until he can regain his kingdom!'

The large blue demon nodded at his smaller companion.

'That is why we are here,' Brax added. 'Banished from the Netherhells because of Guxx's failure.'

The larger demon's claws snaked out to snag the fabric of Brax's suit.

'Again!' Guxx ordered.

Brax hastily returned to beating on the drum. The larger demon began anew:

'Guxx Unfufadoo, never failing,
Greatest of demonic heroes,
Those that scoff at his great prowess,
Will find they will soon be eaten!'

Brax paused in his drum beating to add. 'Well, failure wasn't the exact word I meant. The real word I meant to use was, um –'

'Continue!' Guxx commanded. Brax went back to his drum.

'Guxx Unfufadoo, hungry demon
Has a plan for those who mock him,
Has these claws, so good for rending,
And these teeth so good for chewing.'

'I meant setback!' Brax hurriedly amended. 'That was it. Not failure! No, no. Never failure! Nothing but a setback!'

This time Guxx's clawed hand lifted Brax completely from the ground.

'Again!'

Still aloft, Brax beat on the drum as Guxx intoned:

'Guxx Unfufadoo denies setbacks,
He will destroy those that bring them.
Guxx the mighty he will beat them,
Tear off all their limbs and eat the –'

A look of horror spread across the large demon's countenance. He tried to stop himself, but it was already too late. He began to sneeze.

He dropped Brax in the process. The smaller demon

sighed and readjusted the jacket of his checkered suit. 'You now know of Guxx's fate. At the end of the battle he caught your master's malady. Once, his fearsome rhymes gave him ever greater power. Now, whenever he rhymes, even if it should be by accident, he sneezes.'

'Buckles and laces!' exclaimed the Brownie, whom in the excitement I had almost forgotten. 'So his magic has been turned against him!'

''Tis true,' Brax concurred. 'This misfortune has forced Guxx Unfufadoo into talking nothing but blank verse.'

So that was what you called what the large demon had been spouting. I agreed that it certainly was a tragedy. Guxx sneezed again, a truly horrible sound from such a demonic nose.

'Well,' Brax said, 'at least now he'll stay quiet for a while.' He took a further moment to straighten his checkered creases. With Guxx temporarily indisposed, he seemed much more his old salesdemon self.

'I suppose you want an explanation,' Brax ventured with a laugh. 'I understand that humans are like that.'

'Brownies are like that, too,' Tap added from where he now stood by my side.

'I'm sure you are!' Brax replied jovially, quick to include another potential customer. 'I suppose it is only fair. And while I explain, you'll have the opportunity to learn about some prime, previously owned weapons that I luckily thought to bring along. And all I need is your signature in blood. Only a formality, really. You'll heal in no time, and a magic weapon will be yours! Just think: no money down, a lifetime to pay!'

So Brax had weapons? Well, we could certainly use them, what with the unknown Eastern Kingdoms before us and a committee of demons likely to show up at any moment to

Dvote on the best manner for our demise. And then there was Death, who wanted me for his very own. But what weapon could one possibly use against the creature that embodied the end of life itself?

'No rush,' Brax added cheerfully. 'Guxx Unfufadoo and I plan to be with you for quite a while, and you may purchase a weapon at any time during that period! You see, that's why we came here – to be your companions on your forthcoming quest!'

'Buckles and laces!' the Brownie exclaimed.

I was somewhat taken aback by this information as well. Until his defeat, Guxx Unfufadoo had been our direst enemy, ready to destroy us by any means possible. Our first encounter with the fiend had caused my master's malady, and further, altercations had led to no end of bloodshed and destruction of property. Now this foul creature, risen from nocturnal slime pits hidden deep beneath the earth, wanted to be my ally?

'Um . . .' I ventured.

I remembered then what Death had said about companions. If I was who the spectre said I was, I always had to have them. Maybe Guxx and Brax couldn't help themselves. Because of my nature, they had to become my companions. They had no other choice. I marveled at my newfound power. To attract such otherworldly creatures as these, I must be irresistible.

'It is no wonder that you are at a loss for words,' Brax added quickly. 'What a surprise to be joined in your quest by the greatest of all demons. And what an honor!' He shook the bag by his side. 'Now, admit it! How much better you would feel with a new weapon the equal of your newfound companions!'

It was true. A formidable weapon might make me feel

better. Especially a weapon that would protect me against demonic teeth and claws.

'Interested, hey?' The salesdemon tugged at my sleeve. 'Well, wait just a second while I fetch a contract. . . .'

Tap the Brownie tugged at my other sleeve. 'Think carefully about this. What need have you of weapons from the Netherhells when you have Brownie magic!'

I remembered Brownie magic from some of our prior battles. The weapons began to sound better all the time. But Tap's interruption reminded me that the Brownie had said he was in contact with my master. Perhaps it would be prudent to contact and speak with Ebenezum before I entered into any sort of a bargain with demons.

'I've got the contract right here.' Brax had reached into his bag and pulled forth a sheaf of parchment almost as large as my Home Study Course. 'Yes, it does look a little imposing, doesn't it? Just a lot of Netherhells legalisms, I assure you. Nothing to worry about at all, at least not in this lifetime. And you only have to sign it once, for a weapon that might even protect you against whatever you're looking for on this quest!' The demon smiled as he flipped to contract's end.

'Um . . .' I replied. This was all going too fast for me. There seemed to be no time to contact my master, even if I knew how to use the Brownie to do so. Still smiling, Brax waved a sharp-edged pen in the direction of my index finger. What should I do?

There was a great sneeze, and the contract went flying from Brax's hands. Guxx Unfufadoo had regained his feet.

'But –' Brax cried, but his protestations died with a single glance from the larger demon.

'Begin!' Guxx Unfufadoo demanded.

Brax shuffled through the bag quickly to find his drum. As soon as it was in his hands, Guxx chanted:

'Guxx Unfufadoo, great companion,
Joins the noble surface heroes,
He will make their quest successful
For the glory of demonkind!'

Brax shrugged his checked shoulders. 'I guess we'll have to talk about the weapons later.' He glanced up at the larger demon, who glared back at him.

'Oh, that's right!' Brax said nervously. He drew a piece of parchment from his sack and read it without inflection: 'Excuse me, but since we are going to be your companions on this venture, I hope it isn't too impudent to ask exactly where we are going?'

'Why,' Tap chirped, 'to the Eastern Kingdoms, of course!'

'The Eastern Kingdoms?' Brax hesitated, the parchment falling from between his fingers, and turned pale (in actuality, he turned a much lighter shade of green). 'Isn't that where they take heroes and bake them into loaves of bread?'

I assured the demon that I had discussed the matter with my master, and Ebenezum had said the tales were greatly exaggerated.

'Exaggerated?' Brax retorted. 'What does that mean? That they only bake heroes into rolls and muffins? I had no idea that when you set out on a quest you were going to –'

Guxx raised one of his clawed hands above his head, instantly silencing his lackey.

'Again!' Guxx stated. Brax picked up the drum and began to beat.

'Guxx Unfufadoo, fearless demon,
Accompanies them to the East.
Enemies shall know no quarter!
He shall rend them, man or beas –'

The large demon started to sneeze before he had finished
the last syllable, falling instantly to the ground.

'Alas.' Brax shook his head sadly. 'The big fellow has
rhyming in his blood. Now where did that contract go?'

'Hold!' I demanded. I had had enough for the moment
of epic verse and Netherhells contracts. Of course, the fact
that Guxx Unfufadoo was temporarily indisposed didn't
hurt, either. I would get some answers!

I asked why the two demons were really here.

'Well . . .' Brax looked over his shoulder at the indisposed Guxx. 'He can't hear a thing while he's sneezing.
Very well. We are genuinely here to help you on your quest,
for that is the best way for Guxx to gain revenge on those
who banished him.'

Really? The demon's honesty took me by surprise.

'Um . . .' I began. But no, if I were to be master of this
situation, I would have to think clearly. How would my
master handle a situation like this?

'Indeed,' I began again. 'And then, I imagine, Guxx will
eat me.'

'Oh, on the contrary,' Brax replied, somewhat taken
aback. 'I don't think Guxx plans to eat you at all. That is,'
he amended, 'at least not in the near future.'

'Indeed?' I asked. 'But isn't he mad at me?'

'He's probably furious, but that's beside the point. It's
all a matter of priorities, you see. First he must destroy his
opposition in the Netherhells, then return there to
reestablish his rule.' Brax smiled his best salesdemon's grin.

'You will be happy to know that then and only then will he come back and eat you.

Somehow, I did not find this particularly reassuring.

'So we will come with you on your quest,' Brax continued. 'Or you can refuse our help, and Guxx could simply eat you now. That's one thing about having a demon of his magnitude as an ally. You always know exactly where he stands!'

I also knew exactly what he ate. It didn't help.

Brax frowned. 'Now where is that contract?' He peered around in the gathering gloom. Our encounter with the demons had taken the final hour of daylight, and night was rapidly coming upon us.

'Indeed,' I said a final time. 'So you think it is convenient to join me in order to serve your own ends?'

'Yes, more or less,' Brax reiterated, somewhat distracted. 'That, and the rumor that you're the Eternal Apprentice.' He glanced back in my direction. 'You, I know it's silly – well, let's face it, it's ridiculous – actually, its's more ludicrous than anything. Anyway, Guxx is not one to discount rumors. Any rumor!' Brax smiled at me and shook his head. 'You?' He snickered softly.

The salesdemon turned to regard the barren hill, now a black shape against the starlit sky.

'How am I supposed to find my contract in the dark?'

I wished him luck, and told him that I would be retiring for the night. I walked away, motioning Tap to follow. The Brownie and I would need to have a discussion.

And there was one more thing I had to do before I went to sleep: consult my Home Study Course. There might be nothing in there to prevent one's meeting Death, but there surely must be a spell or two for exorcising demons.

TEN

*'One should never attempt a spell without sufficient
practice. Then again, one should never get eaten by
demons, either, or have to go without a date on
Saturday night.'*

> – SOME THOUGHTS ON APPRENTICESHIP
> by Wuntvor, apprentice to Ebenezum,
> greatest mage in theWestern Kingdoms
> (a work in progress)

'We have to talk.' I whispered urgently to the Brownie.
'How do we get in touch with my master?'

'Have no fear!' Tap reassured me heartily. ''Tis as easy as
making shoes.'

'Say!' Brax called cheerfully across the field. 'I think I've
finally found the contrac –' The salesdemon's voice was
abruptly cut off as he found a set of long, nasty-looking purple claws resting on his shoulder. The claws belonged to
Guxx, who seemed to have stopped sneezing for the time
being.

'Begin!' Guxx bellowed in the other demon's ear. Brax
hastily dropped the contract and picked up his drum.

Guxx took a deep breath and recited:

'Mighty Guxx, the best of demons
Has no fear of this Duck's ovens!

We shall join you, boldly, bravely:
All will flee, in fear before us!'

The demon raked his claws through the air for emphasis.

'Indeed,' I replied when I realized that the former Grand
Hoohah was waiting for a reaction. 'Nice to have you along.
Now if you'll excuse me –'

'Continue!' Guxx roared. Brax beat his drum.

'Mighty Guxx says we should hurry!
There are many who would stop us;
Traitor demons, down below here,
Who want this world for their foul reason!'

'Indeed,' I answered again. 'Um . . . indeed.'

Apparently it was going to be more difficult to quiet Guxx
down than I had first imagined. Still, there must be some
way I could get a moment free to talk to the Brownie. I
decided to try another strategy.

'Good advice, I am sure,' I called to Guxx as I continued
to walk away. 'And we will hurry, I assure you, as soon as we
get a good night's sleep.' I paused to yawn and stretch.
'Now, if you'll excuse –'

'Persevere!' Guxx screamed. Brax continued to beat.

'Guxx Unfufadoo, never tiring,
Guides our heroes into battle!
Who needs sleeping? Who needs eating?
When this great demon leads us onwards!'

I cleared my throat. 'Indeed,' I murmured. Guxx seemed
to be a demon used to getting his own way. What could I do?

Tap looked up at me with some consternaton. 'Is it time
for Brownie Power?'

I glanced at the little fellow. What did I have to lose?

'Indeed,' I asked. 'What kind of Brownie Power did you have in mind?'

'It's a challenge, all right,' Tap agreed, glancing at the heavily clawed and muscled Guxx. 'But Brownies are always ready for a challenge. How do you think we came up with high-buttoned shoes?

'What if –' The Brownie shook his head. 'No. The demon would slice through any shoe I could conjure. Even a really big shoe.' He paused a moment in thought. 'How about . . .' The little fellow's frown deepened. 'No, that thing wouldn't even notice a rain of buckles and laces.'

'Does all your magic have to center on shoes?' I asked with a hint of hysteria.

'I beg your pardon!' Tap replied, a hurt edge in his voice. 'Brownie magic may be specialized, but what we do, we do with style.'

I quickly apologized, explaining that there was a certain set of sharp, purple claws too much on my mind. The Brownie said he quite understood.

'I know!' Tap clicked his heels together and began to dance. 'You have given me the answer, apprentice. Style is the key. Brownie style! All our problems are solved. I will show them the wisdom of the Brownie Way!'

'In – deed,' I replied slowly. Brownie style? Still, after my initial shock, I realized the little fellow's idea had a certain merit. After all, I knew from my own encounters with the wee folks' ideas that getting a lecture on Brownie philosophy would probably slow the demons down far longer than any physical force we could possibly imagine.

I told Tap to go ahead. He skipped merrily over to the demons whilst whistling a happy tune.

Now was the time for me to get to work. While the others were occupied, I would at last have a minute to look through the Home Study Course. My first priority was to find a spell to banish demons. Once I had accomplished that, I could contact Ebenezum and get on with my quest.

I hunched down, careful that my back was facing the others, and rummaged quickly through my pack. After taking a brief moment to pet my ferret, I pulled forth the Course and turned rapidly to the index, anxious that I should find the spell before the rapidly fading daylight vanished entirely.

I found 'demons' in the index almost immediately. It wasn't at all difficult; the entries went on for pages. I quickly looked down the left-hand column.

Demons, summoning for special occasions, page 612
Demons, summoning on short notice, page 623
Demons, summoning multiples thereof: odd
    numbers, pages 634–6; even numbers, pages 637–9
Demons, summoning specific colors, page 944

I turned back a page, searching the 'Demon, B's for 'banishment.' My gaze jumped at random among the entries:

Demons, bathing habits, see Slime Pools; Uses and
    Abuses
Demons, brandishing as a form of warning, page 326
Demons, cuddling with, some words of caution, page
    945

This was taking forever. I flipped the page again, and there it was, at the top of the right-hand column.

I stopped reading, and rapidly turned to page 487. There was the heading, in bold letters:

BANISHMENT
THE ALL-PURPOSE REMEDY

'This spell,' the book went on, 'is particularly effective in dealing with demons, and so simple and direct that even beginning wizards can accomplish it with ease.'

I couldn't help but grin. Effective? Simple? Direct? This was the very thing I had been looking for.

'Shoes?' I heard Guxx bellow behind me.

'Yes!' Tap yelled back with almost equal force. 'Shoes are the answer; the only answer! Let me explain . . .'

The Brownie's voice thankfully lowered to a more conversational level which I could no longer understand. I returned to the Home Study Course and the spell that I would accomplish with ease.

Spell Variation No. 1: Banishing Demons.
Just follow the few simple directions below, and any demon in your vicinity will instantaneously be banished from the surface of the world.

Oddly enough, the next paragraph was printed in bright red:

WARNING: FOLLOW THESE DIRECTIONS EXACTLY. SUBSTITUTIONS CAN LEAD TO DISASTER!

Why did they print a warning if the spell was so easy? Perhaps it was explained in the introductory portions of the book, somewhere 'in the four hundred eighty-six pages preceding this one. Maybe I should try to read a little bit more.

'More shoes?' Guxx screamed from halfway across the field. I turned to listen. 'Brax!'

Brax pounded on his drum as Guxx intoned emphatically:

'Guxx Unfufadoo, peerless demon
Has heard enough of Brownie prattle,
Has waited long enough for humans,
And will lead us into batt –'

Great clouds of dust rose about him as Guxx succumbed to a sneezing fit.

Brax sighed. 'It's a shame when a natural rhyming talent like that has to go to waste.' He paused a moment to straighten the lapels on his checkered suit. 'Now, if you'll permit me to change the subject –'

Tap tried to continue his lecture, but Brax was too fast for him.

'No, no, my good Brownie!' Before the Brownie could protest, the demon quickly retrieved the sheaf of parchment from where it had fallen in the grass. 'I'm sure "Stitching techniques for proper heel placement" is a fascinating subject. But we do have this contract here, and we all know from experience that Guxx will only sneeze for so long.'

I looked back at the salesdemon, waving his contract above the faltering Brownie. It appeared, at least this time, that Brownie Power had failed.

'Wait!' Tap interjected hastily. 'It's, uh – time for a demonstration!' He jumped into a speedy dance.

The demon's feet were suddenly covered by shiny brown shoes.

'Not bad,' Brax murmured, temporarily distracted from his salesmanship. 'Do they do anything?'

'Do they *do* anything?' Tap replied with the slightest of hurt tones. 'These are shoes!'

Brax stared at his newly covered feet. He did not seem that impressed. 'So?'

'Don't you know about the joy of shoes?' Tap asked in astonishment. 'They are an art form, and one of the great inventions of the modern world!'

'Really?' Brax nodded solemnly. 'But they don't do anything?'

'Of course they do things!' Tap seemed to be getting a tad overexcited. He paused to catch his breath. 'I mean, they keep cold air away from your feet, for one thing. And you know those little sharp rocks that hurt the soft undersides of your feet? Well, now that you have these . . .'

I turned back to my book. It didn't look like Tap could keep Brax distracted much longer, and Guxx was likely to stop sneezing at any moment. I had to banish this pair before they interfered any further with my quest. Warning or no warning, this spell would have to do. I had no time to worry.

I quickly read the spell.

make sure you have sufficient quantities of all the following before you begin:
1/2 batwing, crumbled
One left eye of newt
1/4 cup dried duckwort blossom
One medium toad gizzard
One pinch salt (to taste)
Mix the above ingredients in a large cauldron . . .

I stopped reading. Cauldron? Toad gizzard? Left eye of newt? Follow these directions exactly?

How could I? I didn't have any of those things!

'And look at those laces!' Tap continued quickly, his voice rising again. 'Why, the practice you can get tying knots . . .'

The demon casually kicked the shiny brown shoes off his feet, sending them sailing high above the cloud of dust that encased the sneezing Guxx.

Tap was horrified.

'I'm through fooling around,' Brax said with a smile. 'Let's talk contracts. I already know about shoes. In fact, I have a pair just for you. A pair that does more than keep your feet warm. That's right, Brownie, I'm talking about a pair of – magic shoes.'

'But you threw away – I mean, those were perfectly good . . .' Tap's voice faltered. 'M-magic shoes?'

'Absolutely correct.' Brax patted the little fellow's pointed cap. 'I could tell from the first time I met you that you were the kind of Brownie who likes to step ahead of the pack. And how better to do that stepping than in a stunning set of enchanted footwear?'

Tap, eyes and mouth both opened wide, took a step toward the demon. 'En-enchanted footwear?'

Oh, no! Brax had found the Brownie's weakness. Soon Tap would be laboring under a Netherhells contract probably even worse than the one that doomed Hendrek.

I had to banish the demons now! The general spell I had found would do me no good. But the index had been full of others.

I looked up 'Demons, banishing on short notice':

There will often be times when demons will not have the courtesy of allowing you the time to perform one of the more intricate and civilized banishment spells found elsewhere in this tome. At this point, you have two options: to run, screaming, from the demons until you find some spot you might perform those civilized spells, or use the short, dirty little magick that follows. PLEASE NOTE: BE SURE TO FOLLOW THE DIAGRAMS EXACTLY!

The warning at the end was, again, printed in red. Still, there didn't seem to be any arcane ingredients necessary to the spell that followed, only a series of hand and foot gestures. I should be able to handle this one easily.

'What – what kind of enchanted footwear?' Tap asked dreamily.

'Only the very best, I assure you,' Brax replied heartily, 'with firm leather soles and bright blue tassels!'

'Blue tassels?' Tap responded, a beatific smile spreading across his face. 'Bright blue tassels.'

There was no time to waste. I began to follow the instructions in the Home Study Course – exactly.

'First,' I said aloud, 'perform the rite of the Mystic Rooster, to notify the spirits that you command their attention.'

I placed my right hand above my head as the book indicated and crowed.

'What's that?' Tap yelped, his trance temporarily broken.

'Only the young human, clearing his throat,' Brax assured the Brownie. 'That's not important now. We were talking shoes.'

Tap nodded. 'Shoes.'

I crowed again, but neither Brownie nor demon took further notice.

'They'll make you a Brownie among Brownies, and all you have to do is sign on this dotted line.' Brax riffled the contract before him. 'Don't worry about all the fine print. Merely Netherhells' legalities, of interest only to the demons who enforce these things. One small signature and the shoes are yours.'

'Small?' Tap blinked. 'Are you saying that Brownies are small?'

'Why not at all!' Brax assured him. 'Once you have these shoes, you'll be a big man in the Brownie set. Here, let me show them to you.'

The demon opened his sack and looked inside.

'I think they're right over here, below these magic false teeth and this magic imitation housefly.' He rummaged deeper still. 'Oh, yes! And this magic antelope's horn. Unfortunately, it only works on other antelopes. Ah, I think I see them towards the bottom.'

It was time to proceed with my spell. I quickly read the second set of directions: 'Next, perform the Rite of the Mystic Sparrow, to instruct the spirits to fly to your aid.'

I spread my arms to my sides, as instructed, and waved them up and down, while at the same time bending my knees and emitting a high, chirping sound from between my teeth.

'No, I'm sorry,' Tap said, looking back at me. 'That doesn't sound at all like clearing a throat.'

'But who knows what he got in there?' Brax murmured. 'Besides, we have a contract to sign.'

I chirped again. I didn't see any sign of spirits. Was this thing working?

'Might be the hiccups,' Tap ventured.

'Yes, it might!' Brax replied with the slightest bit of irritation. 'But what does that matter when we're talking about *magic* shoes?'

I chirped again for good measure, hoping the spirits could hear me.

'Whooping cough?' Tap mused. He glanced back into the demon's gaze, and the questioning look dulled in his eyes.

Brax stared at the Brownie. The smile reappeared on Tap's tiny face.

'Yes,' he whispered happily. 'Magic shoes.'

'That's a bit more like it,' Brax replied merrily. 'Once we get the contract signed, we can ask the young human what he's doing. Maybe it's a hobby of some sort.' Brax went back to searching in his bag.

Perhaps it was time to go on to the third part of the spell, I decided.

The demon dropped his sack as purple claws surrounded his neck.

'Begin!'

Even in Guxx's stranglehold, Brax managed to pick up his drum. The blue and purple demon chanted:

'Guxx Unfufadoo, Mystic Demon,
Knows when he sees magic brewing,
Sees when humans give him trouble,
Says that wizards soon get eaten!'

The Brownie shook his head as if to clear it.

'Him?' Tap pointed at me. 'A wizard? If he was a wizard, why would he need Brownie magic?'

Guxx glowered at me, flexing his claws.

'Yeah,' Brax added. 'The little fellow's right. I mean, what kind of magic can you make by clearing your throat? It's easier to bclieve this guy's the Eternal

Apprentice than' – he snorted – 'a wizard!'

Both Brax and the Brownie had a good laugh.

Guxx still glowered, but the other's arguments seemed to have kept him, at least for the moment, from attacking and eating me.

If I was going to banish them, there would never be a better time. There was nothing to do but finish the spell.

I glanced quickly to my Home Study Course: 'Now it is time for the Mystic Warthog, to instruct the spirits to banish the demons from the surface world.'

I quickly curved my hands to either side of my nose, like tusks, and began to snort, stamping my feet in the described rhythm.

'Magic!' Guxx screamed, and leapt for me, claws extended.

Somehow, I managed to stand my ground and finish the spell, although the sight of an onrushing demon somewhat unnerved me.

And then I thought: I had stomped my foot seven times. Hadn't I? Guxx was still rushing forward to rend and tear. I had lost count.

I stomped once more to be sure.

And Guxx froze in mid-stride.

The spell was working! Brax seemed frozen as well, drum in one hand, contract in the other. The spirits must be at hand. I snorted a couple more times for good measure. Soon the banishment would begin.

The ground began to shake. What was going on? The Home Study Course had said nothing about this.

The quake beneath my feet intensified. It took me a moment to realize that I hadn't banished anyone.

Instead, I had summoned the Netherhells!

ELEVEN

'The professional magician must always be ready for the unexpected, for who knows what magic might bring? Thus, one should always be prepared when performing sorcery, and have on hand a full knowledge of all the latest banishment spells, a good half-dozen well planned escape routes, and perhaps most important, a constant supply of clean linen in the guest room.'

– THE TEACHING OF EBENEZUM, Volume IX

Oh, no. What had I done?

The shaking earth before me tore asunder, and from that rift in the ground rose a great oaken table, complete with five demons. This was far worse than I had thought. I had somehow summoned the entire dread legion of the Netherhells' Conquest by Committee!

'Point of order!' the small, somewhat sickly looking demon at the end cried.

The much larger demon at table's center pounded its gavel. 'Yes, yes. What is it this time?'

'Beg pardon,' the small, sickly demon remarked in a voice so brash that no one, anywhere, at any time, would ever pardon anything it said. 'Look around us. We don't appear to be where we should be. I really thought someone should mention that.'

'What do you mean?' the gavel demon demanded. 'We followed the most recent burst of wizardly energy, and here we are.'

The gavel demon was so busy glaring down at its shorter committee member that it had not bothered to study the surroundings. This, I thought, might be my chance. If the demonic committee was going to pause for a discussion, maybe there was time for a counterattack after all!

'Beg pardon,' the small sickly demon continued, 'but there don't appear to be any wizards.' The demon smiled, totally self-satisfied. 'I thought someone should mention that, too.'

The gavel demon looked about in astonishment. 'By the Netherhells! For once our small, sickly member is correct. There don't appear to be any wizards! Is this not then Vushta after all?' The demon paused to look about suspiciously. 'Careful now! This could be some sort of surface world trick.'

Oh, would that I did have a trick! Maybe, I thought, if I looked quickly, I might find something in my Home Study Course. But what?

'Point of order!' the small, sickly demon screamed.

The gavel demon looked at the other fiend with half-closed eyes. 'You've already had your point of –'

Small and sickly shook its head emphatically. 'This is an entirely different one.' It pointed its diminutive and pale hand across the field. 'Isn't that the former Grand Hoohah standing yonder?'

They had spotted Guxx! I would have to act quickly. I opened the Course to the index. But what to look under? Mayhaps 'Demons, immobilized by magic'? I flipped to the back of the book.

'Oh, my,' the gavel demon murmured, nodding at the silent Guxx. It coughed politely, a truly unpleasant sound. 'Excuse us, your immenseship.' The gavel demon tried to smile. 'Didn't mean to bother you. Just passing through, don't you know.'

Guxx, frozen immobile by magic, did not reply. I scanned the pages quickly, searching for 'Demons, immobilized . . .'

'Your magnificenceship?' the gavel demon ventured. 'Surely you understand.'

Guxx stood there like a statue. The gavel demon began to sweat. I looked down at my book again. I spied an entry for 'Demons, immersed in syrup.' I was getting close.

'Your superiorship?' The fiend fell to its knees. 'Please give us a chance to explain!'

I quickly scanned the next entry. 'Demons, immodesty at parties.' But 'immodest' came after 'immobile'! That meant the entry I was looking for did not exist!

I stared blankly at the book. The answer had to be in there somewhere. Didn't it?

'Point of order!' the small demon yelled. 'The Grand Hoohah hasn't moved –'

'So what if the Grand Hoohah hasn't moved?' the gavel demon screamed hysterically. 'If the Grand Hoohah doesn't want to –'

'Beg pardon,' the small fiend continued. 'I believe he hasn't moved because he cannot move. See how the birds flutter about him, as if he were a tree or standing stone. He appears to be frozen, perhaps by some diabolical surface spell.'

'What are you . . .' The gavel demon paused to peer at the immobile Guxx. At that very instant a sparrow alighted on the former Grand Hoohah's nose.

'Frozen?' the gavel demon whispered.

Frozen! I thought. Of course! I quickly thumbed through the index to F.

'I just thought someone should mention that,' the sickly demon added with a grin.

'Frozen. You don't say. Frozen.' The gavel demon wiped its brow and pounded its gavel. 'Who cares about the old Grand Hoohah anyway? It is time for the committee to rule!'

Here it was! 'Frozen demon, on a stick, page 212.' On a stick? Somehow, that didn't sound right. Still, it was my only hope.

The large demon pounded the gavel again. 'All in favor of attack?'

Four of the five demons raised their sharp and ugly claws. I would have to hurry before my blood was boiled!

'Very well,' the gavel demon rapped. 'Majority –'

'Point of order!' the small, sickly, dissenting demon shrieked.

It appeared that I might still have a moment. I quickly turned to page 212.

'I am sorry,' the gavel demon said in a very loud voice that didn't sound sorry at all, 'but the vote does not have to be unanimous in a case like this.'

The sickly demon pulled a huge tome from beneath the table. 'But it says right here in the Netherhells bylaws . . .'

I had a tome of my own to look through. I found page 212 and quickly read through the text. Here it was!

'FROZEN DEMON ON A STICK: For the wizard that enjoys entertaining, here's the perfect end to a delightful meal –'

I stopped reading. This wouldn't do at all.

'But there aren't any wizards!' the gavel demon

screamed. 'You said so yourself! Surely the rules are different when there aren't any wizards!'

'Point of –' the other demon began.

'Oh, no, you don't!' the gavel fiend exclaimed. 'The rest of us are going to attack without you!'

So this was it. There'd be no more time for the Home Study Course. I dropped my book and picked up my stout oak staff. I knew it wasn't much protection against the might of the committee, but it was all I had. I hoped that with the help of the Brownie, who now stood on one side of me, and my ferret, who had emerged from the pack to stand on the other side, that we, together, might make an accounting.

'Come, fellow demons,' the gavel demon extolled. 'It is time to boil blood!'

'Oh, no, it isn't!' another voice boomed, high above me.

Who could it be? Demonic reinforcements, wishing to boil our blood even more efficiently than before? With some trepidation, I looked aloft.

'Look out!' cried the voice, both loud and deep. 'Make way! Clear a path! Watch your heads!'

The voice belonged to Hubert the dragon, who carried the damsel Alea upon his back. The two of them appeared to be landing in our midst.

The demons scattered. Three of them took their table with them.

'Thank you,' Hubert said, once he had settled his huge dragon bulk on the ground. 'We always do like to make an entrance.'

'Point of order!' the sickly demon interjected.

The gavel demon ignored the other's cries, turning instead to the newcomers, its gavel raised above its head like a weapon. 'How dare you tell the Committee of Conquest it isn't time to boil blood!'

'Simplicity itself,' Hubert replied. 'No matter what the occasion, without Damsel and Dragon it simply doesn't happen!'

'Doesn't . . . happen?' If the gavel demon had seemed upset before, now it was absolutely livid, the once rich blue of its scales turned a shiny purple. I had to admit that even I was taken aback by Hubert's remarks, perhaps because I had never thought of boiling blood as an 'occasion.' Still, the arrival of Damsel and Dragon had, at the least, temporarily stopped the demonic attack. Perhaps I should give the Home Study Course another try.

'I'll show you what doesn't happen!' the gavel demon shrieked after it had managed to control its breathing.

'Of course. Certainly,' Hubert replied affably. 'But first allow us to introduce ourselves. Damsel, if you would get me my hat?'

Alea reached into the satchel strapped to Hubert's back and extracted a cylindrical purple hat with a snappy brim. She placed it firmly on Hubert's head.

'But –' the gavel demon began.

'No buts about it,' Hubert replied. 'We have to get to know each other. And what better way to get acquainted than with a little song and dance?'

'What?' the gavel demon bellowed. 'Don't –'

Damsel hopped down off the dragon's back and Hubert began to sing:

'The trouble with demons, as everybody knows,
Is when you stomp them, they squish between your toes.'

'Between your toes!' Damsel chorused.
Hubert continued:

'The trouble with demons, as everybody sees,
Is when you kick them, they splatter on your knees.'

'Right on your knees!' Damsel echoed.

The demons stared at them, open-mouthed, their yellowed teeth glinting in the sun. I would never have thought to neutralize a Netherhells attack with song and dance, especially a song and dance about squishing demons. Still, Hubert had told me many times: 'There is no such thing as a hostile audience, only inadequate performers.' Now, it seemed, he was out to prove his point.

The strange thing was, the song and dance worked. Maybe it was the newness of their performance, the incongruity of song and dance just before battle, the true horribleness of the dragon's singing voice, or perhaps simple shock. Whatever combination of factors neutralized the demons, they only sat and stared, stupefied.

Let's face it. Even I was dazzled by Damsel and Dragon's fancy footwork. Mesmerized like the others, I completely forgot about my Home Study Course.

Damsel and dragon sang together:

'They're not much of a treat
Because they're no good to eat.
Too spicy! And their claws,
Will give your stomach pause.
But the trouble demons do
Is when a demon troubles you!'

'Yeah!' Damsel and Dragon shouted. 'So let's give a little advice.'

Hubert waved his tail in Alea's direction. 'Take it, damsel!'

Alea launched into a series of complicated dance steps, much like I had seen the Brownie use when he was performing his magic.

'Say, big fellow,' she called out to Hubert. 'Do you know why demons don't accept jobs from dragons?'

'Why, yes, Damsel!' Hubert blew a smoke ring. 'They're always afraid of getting fired!'

They danced together for a moment, the dragon's footsteps shaking the earth.

'But tell me, Damsel,' Hubert said at last. 'I understand you'll never date anyone from the fiery pits of the Netherhells.'

'Yes, it's true,' Alea sighed. 'It's just that they keep reminding me of old flames.'

The two danced some more.

'Say, Damsel,' Hubert began.

'Yes, Dragon –' Alea replied.

'Do you know demons don't like the surface world?'

'No, but if you hum a few bars, I'll fake it!'

When I look back on it now, I realize that line was where Damsel and Dragon went wrong. That final joke was far too old and far too horrible. It snapped the spell their impromptu show had cast. The demons simply couldn't take it anymore.

'Boil the dragon's blood!' they chorused as one.

'I'm pretty hot-blooded already,' Hubert quipped. 'Comes from having a forest fire in your lungs.' But the demons had all gathered behind their table and were staring intently at their adversary.

Hubert stumbled and almost fell on top of Alea. The Committee's concentration was too much for him. His top hat fell from his head. He gamely tried to finish his routine, but his movements seemed to have more stagger and less dance in them with every passing moment.

I had to do something. But what? I had learned from bitter experience that the Home Study Course might not be the best resource when one was hurried. And I could think of no better reason to hurry than what was transpiring between Hubert and the demons.

'Is it time for Brownie Power?' Tap asked.

'It's time for anything!' I cried. 'Anything you can think of.'

Tap nodded grimly. 'You want the works, you got it!' He began to dance with purpose.

A dark brown cloud rolled in to fill the sky. The smallest demon shouted 'Point of order!' but the others were too busy boiling blood to listen.

Then it started to rain slippers, directly over the demonic committee.

'Not enough!' Tap grimaced. 'Brownies do it better!'

He danced faster. The rain turned first to sandals, then to shiny shoes with buckles. A couple of the blood-boiling demons glanced up.

'You're getting to them!' I shouted encouragingly.

Tap shook his tiny head. 'Still not enough. Brownies do it best!' He danced so fast that I could no longer see his feet.

The rain turned to thick, heavy boots.

The committee cried out in alarm, shielding their heads and staring up at the boot-laden sky. Hubert stood up and shook his large body. The spell had been broken!

'All right, Damsel,' he began. 'Time for another chorus. A-one and a –' The dragon gasped.

I glanced back at the committee. They were once again concentrating their collective will on the dragon, the boots bouncing harmlessly from their brightly scaled bodies. Their demonic hides were too thick. Once the initial surprise was gone, they had returned immediately to boiling blood, knowing the shoes would do them no harm.

With a final groan, Hubert sank to his reptilian knees. Alea ran quickly out of the way as the dragon's great bulk crashed to the ground.

'Not enough,' Tap gasped. 'Brownie Power not . . .' And he, too, fell to the ground, beyond dancing another step. The boots stopped falling. The demonic committee stood behind their table, directing their unanimous blood-boiling stare at the quickly fading dragon.

The Brownie had failed. It was up to me. If Hubert was to live, I would have to distract them. Somehow. I ran towards the table, the loudest scream I could muster upon my lips.

'Die, fiend!' I shouted as I swung my stout oak staff.

'Beg pardon,' the small, sickly demon replied as it deftly ducked beneath my blow, 'but I think not.' And it picked up the huge volume of Netherhells bylaws to defend itself.

I backed away from the massive weight swinging in the demon's hands. Would that I had brought my own Home Study Course and we could have fought book to book. As it was, my stout oak staff was no match for the heavy tome. One swing of the bylaws and my weapon snapped in two!

'Point of order!' the sickly demon screamed as it leapt atop me to press the amazingly heavy tome against my chest. I was pinned instantly against the ground, as if I had the bulk of the mighty Hendrek pushed into me. I couldn't breathe! I would be crushed to death by the Netherhells bylaws!

The demon on my chest cackled. 'The vote is unanimous, and the final results are dea –' The demon's sentence ended in a surprised screech.

'Eep! Eep!' came the answering screech of my ferret, who leapt straight for the fiend's astonished countenance. The demon fell backwards in shock, and the bylaws slid from my chest.

I did not move for a moment, attempting to regain my breath. I turned my head and saw that Alea kneeled by the fallen Hubert.

'Oh,' Alea sobbed. 'What can we do?'

'I will die . . . performing!' Hubert replied with a groan. 'It is the way . . . it should be! Hit it, Damsel!'

Alea began to dance before Hubert's prostrate body as the dragon sang as best he could:

'The trouble with . . . demons,' Hubert gasped, 'as . . . everyone believes, is that . . . they don't go well . . . with crackers . . . and they don't . . . go well . . . with . . . cheese.'

'Not good with cheese!' Alea chorused with tears in her eyes. Hubert would go to his death a showdragon!

The demons chortled behind their table. They knew when they were winning. And Hubert was by far the strongest among us. Only his dragon fire had any hope against the combined demonic might of the Netherhells committee. With Hubert defeated, they would destroy the rest of us in less time than it took to say 'Point of order!' Nothing could save us now!

Then Guxx Unfufadoo began to sneeze.

TWELVE

'Demons are sadly lacking in the social graces. They are just as likely to eat you with the salad fork as with the proper utensil, and after they've gobbled up two or three humans, they seldom even cover their mouths when they belch. Still, if you insist on inviting a demon to your next gathering, it will make for a fascinatingly different party, especially if you seat some of your least favorite guests on the demon's side of the table.'

— Ask Ebenezum: The Wizard's Guide
to Perfect Etiquette, fourth edition

It took me a moment to comprehend what had happened. Guxx had suddenly, miraculously, recovered from his frozen state. At first I had no idea why. Then I realized that the former Grand Hoohah only sneezed when exposed to poetry. And that, after a fashion, is just what Damsel and Dragon had given him in their 'Trouble with Demons' song.

Damsel and Dragon had assaulted Guxx's frozen ears with rhyme after rhyme, so that at last his sorcerous malady had overwhelmed whatever spell I had laid upon him, the stronger magick winning out in the end. I was sure, though, that the crucial moment came during the dragon's last verse, the one that paired 'believes' with 'cheese.' Almost a good rhyme, but not quite; the sort of poetry Guxx used to thrive on!

'Point of order!' the small demon screamed as it pointed at the sneezing Guxx.

'I see it!' the gavel demon replied. 'I think this situation calls for a brief conference.' The five demons huddled together.

Slowly Guxx was recovering. The sneezes were becoming fewer and further between. The former dictator of all the Netherhells staggered over to the still-frozen Brax.

'Begin!' Guxx rumbled in the other's ear.

Brax blinked, and began to beat his drum.

> 'Guxx Unfufadoo, noblest demon,
> Greets this group of demon traitors,
> Has one question for these demons:
> How would they like to be murdered?'

'Murdered?' the small, sickly demon ventured. 'How about "Not very much"?'

Guxx pointed a quivering claw at the small demon and yelled again in Brax's ear: 'Continue!'

Brax beat and Guxx intoned:

> 'Guxx informs you: He can eat you;
> He can rend you; he can tear you;
> He can squash you; he can stomp you.
> "Not very much" is not an option!'

'All in favor of retreat!' the gavel demon exclaimed.

The Committee disappeared before they could even take a vote.

Quiet descended over the field, the only sound the muted beating of Brax's drum.

'They're gone?' Hubert sniffed. 'Oh, well. They weren't

much of an audience.' The dragon tipped his hat in my direction. 'Still, you can't say we didn't give them their money's worth.'

'Oh, Wuntie!' Alea ran towards me across the field, her long blond hair streaming behind her in the wind. 'You were so brave, facing those demons all by yourself!'

'Hey!' a weak voice said by my feet. 'What about me?'
The Brownie seemed to be recovering, too. 'Don't I count for something? Well' – the small fellow paused, then added in a whisper – 'maybe I don't.'

'Eep eep!' my ferret commented.

But Alea only had eyes for me. She was approaching rapidly, her arms outstretched to embrace me. My throat suddenly felt very dry.

'It certainly was dramatic there for a few minutes,' Hubert mused. 'What do you call that staring routine of theirs?'

I told the dragon they referred to it as boiling blood.

'Boiling blood?' Hubert nodded his approval. 'It has a ring to it. I wonder if we could incorporate "the dying dragon" into our act. What pathos!'

And in that instant Alea was upon me.

'Oh, Wuntie!' she whispered as her form pushed against mine.

'Um,' I replied. Before I could say more, her lips were covering my own.

'You were so brave back there,' Alea gushed between kisses. 'So bold, so . . . so foolhardy!' Her lips swept in for another attack, but I managed to dodge them long enough to wriggle from her grasp.

'Alea!' I gasped. 'Please!' I did my best to catch my breath. 'We are on a quest!'

'But that's just it!' She smiled fiercely. 'There's something about a man who . . . who . . . *throws* himself at danger!'

I saw fire in the damsel's eyes. I took a step away. Alea managed to reach out and catch my wrist anyway. This was too much. Didn't she realize the importance of our mission?

'I'm sorry, Alea,' I insisted, disentangling myself again from her embrace. 'Whatever you have in mind, the quest must come first.'

'Is that so?' She smiled meaningfully at me as she stepped even closer than she had been before. 'Well, my bold' – she paused to ruffle my hair – 'quester. Perhaps while we are' – she paused to rub her shoulder against mine – 'questing, we will at last get a little time to spend' – her hand drifted down from my head, grazing my neck and spine – 'together.'

'Um,' I remarked. 'Uh . . . indeed.' I had the feeling that her definition of questing might be somewhat different from my own.

'Now that I'm with you,' she added, 'I'm not even afraid of being baked into bread.'

'Baked into bread?' a small voice piped from near my feet.

Alea nodded. 'That's what they do to you in the Eastern Kingdoms.'

'Why would they do that?' Tap inquired.

'So that the giants can eat you,' Alea answered.

'Oh,' Tap replied. Somehow, he didn't seem to be his old self. The smile was gone from his voice, the bounce from his step. And perhaps most shocking of all: since his shoe defeat, he hadn't even referred to Brownie Power.

'Recommence!' Guxx shouted from the spot where he stood, halfway across the field. Brax rebeat his drum.

'Guxx Unfufadoo, noble leader,
Tells you "Have no fear of giants!"
Follow me to Eastern Kingdoms,
And my claws will shred their ovens!'

Guxx roared as he finished the verse, sweeping his extremely long, extremely sharp claws through the air for effect. I knew what this meant. He wanted to take over the quest!

Guxx glowered meaningfully in my direction. What could I do? I no longer had even my stout oak staff for protection.

'Uh,' I remarked. I wondered if there might be a way I could quickly glance through the Home Study Course without raising the demon's suspicions.

A great shadow fell over me. I looked up to see Hubert, who casually blew a smoke ring in Guxx's general direction.

'I think not,' the dragon replied softly. 'Wuntvor is the leader of our quest. We follow him.'

'Reassert!' Guxx screamed. Brax continued his rhythmic accompaniment.

'Guxx Unfufadoo, natural leader,
Does not follow any human,
Leads the bravest into battle,
Eats any who disobey him!'

The demon paused to show his teeth.

'I trust that is your final word.' Hubert coughed gently, then inhaled and removed his top hat.

'Proceed!' Guxx added. Brax took his drum and proceeded.

'Guxx Unfufadoo, never beaten,
Leads no matter what the dragon –'

Two great gouts of flame burst from Hubert's nostrils, searing a patch of ground mere inches from Guxx's toes. Brax lost the beat, jumping away from the fire with a yelp. Guxx stared down at the charred earth for a moment before concluding his verse.

'. . . Then again, there is no reason,
Not to hear some more discussion.'

'Bravo,' the dragon replied. 'And our reasoned discussion should begin with our leader, Wuntvor.' He glanced down at me. 'Well, Wuntvor? Anything you want.'

Guxx grumbled darkly, but made no further move. Hubert had given the quest back to me, and I knew exactly what I wanted. No, as much as I yearned to rest and put a good meal in my belly, there was something we all needed more:

I had to contact Ebenezum!

'I must be alone for a moment,' I said, much more solemnly than I felt.

Guxx glared again at the scorched grass, then paced away from the others. Brax followed at a distance, obviously fearful of his master's mood. I turned to Hubert and thanked him for his efforts.

'Think nothing of it,' the dragon said with a toss of his head. 'We know where our interest lies. After all, when was the last time you saw a demon applaud?' He chuckled derisively. 'They have no appreciation at all of the vaudevillian arts.'

The vaudevillian arts? I wasn't too sure if I had any appreciation of those myself, but I thought it rude to mention that thought to a dragon who had so recently saved me. Instead I asked Hubert and Alea to leave me with the Brownie.

Damsel and Dragon readily agreed.

'Come on, Tap,' I said to the small fellow by my foot. 'It's time for Brownie Power.'

Tap frowned up at me. 'Are you sure?'

This was far worse than I thought. I had to be careful not to frown back at the Brownie. How would my master handle something like this?

'Certainly,' I replied with a cheerful smile. 'Don't you remember, Brownies do it better?'

Tap turned to stare at the ground. 'Do they?'

This was not going to be as easy as I had hoped.

'Of course they do!' I knelt down and patted the Brownie's back with my index finger. 'Didn't you tell me that Brownies have it all?'

'All of what?' Tap looked up at me and sighed. 'Somehow, none of it seems to matter anymore. I failed. I . . . I couldn't save you with my shoes.'

'Indeed?' I replied. 'But we are still here and safe, aren't we?'

Tap nodded mutely.

'And we're here in part because of your brave efforts. Your shoe attack gave Hubert enough time to sing his final verse, the verse that reawoke Guxx and, ultimately, saved us all.'

The Brownie paused in thought. 'Then Brownie Power didn't fail you?'

'No, it just worked in a way we didn't expect.' Like everything else that has happened to me since leaving the Western Woods, I added to myself. I remembered what Ebenezum had said about my leading a charmed life. I thought again about what Death had told me abut the Eternal Apprentice.

'So you see,' I added aloud, 'now you have saved my life more than once.'

'I . . . I have, haven't I?' Tap's voice was filled with wonder.

'Indeed,' I added. 'Never fear. Brownies have their proper place in the scheme of things.'

'And an important place it is, too!' Tap added, the

old verve back in his voice. 'That's Brownie Power!'

'Indeed it is,' I coaxed. 'The same Brownie Power with which we're going to contact Ebenezum!' –

'You need to contact Ebenezum?' Tap laughed. 'Well why didn't you say so? 'Tis time for Brownie magic!'

'Indeed,' I replied.

Tap began a dance even more complicated than the one he used for the rain of shoes. A breeze sprang up from nowhere, lifting the dirt and dead leaves into a tall, brown cloud that circled around us like a wall so that we were hidden from the eyes of others. But the cloud kept its distance, so that I had no trouble breathing and Tap could continue his dance.

Tap winked up at me. 'Are you ready?'

Somewhere in the far, far distance, I heard a sneeze. A wizardly sneeze.

'Indeed!' my master's voice called, faint but clear. 'Be with you in a second!'

The wall about us intensified, turning from the color of yellow mud to that of dark, rich earth. Then suddenly, directly in front of the spot where Tap was dancing, there appeared a point of light upon the wall. The Brownie whistled and cheered as his feet flew from step to step.

The light grew, filling fully half the circle in which we were enclosed, and I realized I was looking at the courtyard of the Wizards College at Vushta, just as I had left it, except for one thing.

In the center of the yard was a giant shoe.

'Now that's Brownie Power!' Tap exclaimed.

'Indeed?' the shoe replied. 'You wished to speak with me, Wuntvor?'

It was my master, the great wizard Ebenezum!

THIRTEEN

*'What happens when you encounter a gigantic and
hideous creature who sports huge fangs and claws and
breathes great streams of flame? May I suggest that
you make friends as quickly as possible.'*

– THE TEACHINGS OF EBENEZUM, Volume XXIIV

It took me a moment to collect my thoughts.

'I'd appreciate it,' Tap mentioned as he madly moved his
feet, 'if the two of you would communicate. I've already
learned once today' – the Brownie gasped in air – 'that I
cannot dance forever.'

'Certainly,' I replied, a bit abashed. I realized I was
having some trouble addressing the wizard in his shoe dis-
guise. I shouldn't have been surprised, really. Ebenezum
and the Brownie had used the protective abilities of the
giant shoe once before, when the wizard and I found ourselves in the midst of a union meeting of mythical monsters,
a magical situation my master could only survive from
within the protective shoe leather. Now Ebenezum was
called on to confront magic from a great distance. Under
the circumstances, the enclosing shoe made perfect sense.

Still, I had looked forward to seeing my master's long
white beard and stately robes, tastefully embroidered with
silver moons and stars. Somehow, talking to a shoe was
nowhere near as reassuring.

'Um . . .' I began.

'Yes, Wunt?' my master-inside-the-shoe prompted. Where should I start? So much had happened since I had left Vushta. Perhaps I should begin with the attack by the Netherhells. Or mayhaps it was more important to reveal Guxx's startling turnabout when he joined the quest.

Instead I decided to tell him about my meeting with Death.

'Indeed?' my master remarked when I was finished. 'That could explain a great many things. When you left Vushta so suddenly, I felt there must be some deeper reason. That was why I sent the Brownie after you. But Death called you the Eternal Apprentice?'

The shoe paused and rocked back on its heel. 'Death is an enigma, Wunt. His power is one of the most natural things in the world, the ending of life. Still, few wizards of repute have endeavored to study Death's power, for fear of what that knowledge might bring. Thus, while Death is with us every day, we know little of his true nature. However, the very concept of an Eternal Apprentice is a fascinating conjecture.' The shoe's laces wriggled as if the wizard was moving about inside. 'Indeed. I will have to think on it. In the meantime, Wuntvor, you seem to be following the best path. Do you wish any further advice?'

I wished any and all advice the wizard could give me, so I told him about Guxx, and our recent altercation with the Netherhells.

'I see.' The whole shoe appeared to nod solemnly. 'It sounds like an uneasy alliance at best. And yet if Death is correct in his accusations, Guxx has joined you as another companion, a situation that could work to your advantage.'

The shoe creaked as Ebenezum no doubt leaned forward

against the leather. Did I see his steel-gray eyes studying me through the eyelets?

The Brownie waved his tiny hands in my direction. 'I hate to bring . . . this up, fellows,' he managed, breathing heavily, 'but this Brownie's power has . . . almost worn . . . through.'

Now that he mentioned it, I noticed that Tap's once fancy footwork was becoming more of a shuffle than a dance. The magic image of Ebenezum's shoe flickered and began to grow indistinct around the heel.

'Very well,' my master continued. 'We shall hurry. Wuntvor, one part of Death's story seems to be correct, and that is his information about companions. According to what you have told me, you left Vushta hurriedly because it seemed that the entire town wanted to accompany you. That was apparently the case, for moments after we realized you had disappeared, everyone who desired to join your quest had disappeared as well. I fear, Wuntvor, that half of Vushta is following you upon the road, wishing to be your companion.'

I was quite taken aback. It appeared that this quest might get somewhat larger than I had at first anticipated.

And then the true meaning of the wizard's statement sank in.

'Everyone?' I breathed, almost fearful of considering the possibility. Could my master mean that Norei was rushing to join me as well? I had almost given up hope, but now –

Tap stumbled and almost fell. He slowly dragged his feet back and forth, as if they were made of lead. The shoe was fading.

'Whoever plans to meet you, I am sure you will see them soon enough,' Ebenezum continued quickly. 'We need to discuss strategy, and I fear that the Brownie cannot dance forever. I believe that my fellow wizards have recovered sufficiently to best that demonic committee one more time. We shall try to draw the next Netherhells attack here, a ploy that, if nothing else, will serve to further confuse them and give you time to finish your quest. That's the advantage to fighting committees, you know; the chance of confusion increases in direct relation to the number of committee members. But make haste, Wuntvor. Enlist Mother Duck to our cause and we will be able to defeat the Netherhells forever!'

'That's it!' the Brownie gasped, falling on his face. Ebenezum disappeared, and the brown dirt wall settled to the ground. That meant it was time for action.

I cheered heartily. My companions all looked at me with some surprise.

'No time for sleeping!' I scooped the Browne up in my palm and beckoned with my free hand to Guxx and Brax, Damsel and Dragon. 'Onwards, fellow beings. We seek the Eastern Kingdoms!'

I quickly gathered up my pack, once again containing both ferret and Home Study Course. I left the remains of my stout oak staff behind; I would find a replacement along the way. I began to whistle one of Damsel and Dragon's ditties. All was right with the world. Norei was following me!

I heard a rustling in the bushes behind me. Could it be? Would my prayers be answered so soon?

I turned and walked quickly toward the dense underbrush. 'Is it you?' I whispered.

I got no reply, save the sound of heavy breathing. It did not sound like Norei. And yet, what if she had run all the way from Vushta to be with me? Would not her breath be labored as she tried to draw air into her sweet lungs?

Perhaps she was afraid to step out and meet me when she was not yet at her best. But now that she was so close, I could not bear to wait another moment without her! I would have to coax her out of hiding.

'Are you in there?' I murmured softly.

Was it my imagination, or did the breathing get louder?

'If you've come all this way, why not come out and see me?' The bushes rustled again. Was she coming out at last?

'Come on, now,' I prompted. 'You know how much I've missed you.'

And with that, a head forced its way through the undergrowth; a head topped by a golden horn.

'How long I have waited for you to say that!' The unicorn stared at me with its large, limpid eyes. 'Others of my kind might have scoffed at me, for galloping after you all the way from Vushta. But you should know by now that you are one of the few mortals for which I would' – the unicorn paused, tossing its splendid head so that its horn shone in the sun – 'work up a sweat.'

'Well,' I replied, a bit taken aback. This had not quite worked out as I had planned. 'But you don't understand. You see, I thought –'

The unicorn glanced past my shoulder at my other companions, who had turned to watch us.

'I see now,' the magnificent beast whispered conspiratorially. 'You're shy about sharing your feelings in front of all your friends. I understand perfectly. Unicorns know all about shyness.' It nudged me gently with its golden horn. 'We'll talk about this later' – the beast snorted briefly in the direction of the others – 'when we're alone.'

'Indeed.' I cleared my throat and turned to face the others. 'The unicorn has volunteered to join our quest!'

No one seemed particularly excited by the prospect of the

unicorn ally, but then no one objected, either. I turned east and waved for the others to follow.

'What we need,' Hubert called from where he lumbered along behind me, 'is a good marching song. The sort of thing to lift the spirits and make the miles fly by!'

Alea looked up at him: 'Were you thinking of singing number 126?'

'A perfect choice!' the dragon agreed 'Shall we? Once you learn the chorus, everyone, feel free to join in.'

Damsel and Dragon began to sing:

'If we are bold, if we are brave,
If we believe in true romance,
If we are questing, with a world to save,
We'll save it all with song and dance!
If we are mighty, if we are true,
If we are to win the battle long,
How can we conquer? What can we do,
Unless we do it first with dance and –'

Guxx ran in front of the singing, dancing couple, dragging Brax behind him. 'Now!' he screamed above the din of the song.

Brax regained his feet and started to beat.

'Guxx Unfufadoo, reasoned demon,
Asks that you would cease your singing,
Asks if you could stop your rhyming,
Asks if we might walk in silence.'

The demon blew his nose for emphasis.

'What?' the dragon cried happily. 'But you just haven't

gotten into the spirit of the thing. It gets better as it goes along. Listen to this.'

Damsel and Dragon sang together:

'If we are brave, if we are bold,
If we believe that truth just grows,
Then come on and do what you're told.
Bring a song to battle and tap those toes!'

'Continue!' Guxx screamed in response. Brax pounded on his drum.

'Guxx Unfufadoo, annoyed demon,
Demands you stop this caterwauling,
Demands you spend this trip in silence,
Or there will be some retribution!'

'Did someone say something, Damsel?' Hubert inquired.

'Not that I heard, Dragon,' Alea replied as she pirouetted.

'Oh, well.' Hubert blew a smoke ring in the shape of a fly. 'Must have been an insect somewhere. But we have another verse!'

'We have hundreds of verses!' Damsel added. And they sang again:

'If we are true, if we are mighty,
You'll hear us singing down the street,
Come on now and don't be flighty,
Just come with us and slap those fee –'

'Overwhelm!' Guxx shrieked in a voice so loud that it shook the trees.

Brax pounded on the drum with renewed force.

'Guxx Unfufadoo, enraged demon,
Informs those who still are singing,
Soon enough they'll find those voices,
Stomped to bits by feet of demons!'

'Damsel?' Hubert remarked. 'I feel another verse coming on.'

'Indeed!' I yelled over everyone. 'I've had enough . . .' I paused and coughed to get my voice back down to a reasonable level. 'I've had enough of your petty arguing. This is a quest, and we're all on it together. Therefore, for that period of time remaining before we reach the Eastern Kingdoms, I demand that there be no more vaudevillian singing or Netherhells declaiming! Anyone who doesn't agree is free to leave the quest. Is that understood?'

Guxx and Hubert glowered at each other, but both continued to walk with the rest of our party.

The unicorn trotted up to my side and tossed its magnificent mane.

'I've never seen this side of you before,' the golden horned beast murmured close to my ear. 'It's quite a revelation.' Its dark, soulful eyes looked deep into my own. 'Oh, I love it when you talk tough!'

I noticed that all the others in our band were watching me again.

'Maybe,' Alea nodded to Hubert, 'he's going to be a wizard after all.'

I walked on ahead. The others followed. They were beginning to truly accept my leadership. Alea said I would be a wizard after all. And for a minute I believed her, at least until we came to that next clearing; the one with the big painted sign:

> You are in the vicinity of
> THE EASTERN KINGDOMS
> Are you sure you want to be?

The Brownie climbed onto my shoulder to get a better look. 'What does that mean?'

'I think,' Alea answered, 'it has something to do with giants baking bread.'

'Nonsense,' I replied. I didn't want their spirits to plummet now, when we were so close. 'There could be any number of meanings to that sign.'

'Like what?' the Brownie asked.

I couldn't think of an answer.

From deep within the trees behind the sign, another voice spoke.

'Doom,' it said.

FOURTEEN

*'Why are wizards your friends? Surely it is because
they are reputed to be able to create vast sums of gold
from the empty air. You do not agree? Then it must be
because they can predict with astonishing accuracy
the next visit of the royal tax collector or the royal
mother-in-law. Still no? Then you must certainly
agree that it must be that they have been rumored to
take those people with whom they are not friendly,
and turn those individuals into mice and swine?
Surely you see my point of view by now. Let me put it
to you this way: Would you rather oink for a living?'*

– excerpted from the lecture series 'Why Wizards
Are Your Friends,' given in part by Ebenezum,
greatest wizard in the Western Kingdoms.
(See footnote)

'Doom.'

I would know that deep, resonant voice anywhere.

'Are we just going to stand around in the bushes all
day?' another, infinitely more grating voice added. 'I
didn't come on this quest to spend my days standing
in shrubbery!'

I knew the second voice as well.

Footnote: The above lecture was, unfortunately, never completed, due to an altercation in the audience, some of whom had
been turned into swine.

There was a great crashing and banging in the bushes. I saw the doomed warclub Headbasher flash through the green.

The warrior Hendrek emerged a moment later. 'Doom,' he remarked. 'I cleared a path.'

The truth-telling demon Snarks followed him out. 'I don't see why you bother using that club of yours. Why don't you just push your way through? Any bush would have to yield to your greater size.'

'Doom,' Hendrek replied.

'Indeed,' I interjected. 'I am glad to see you as well. You have come to join our quest?'

'Well, it was better than spending all our time around a bunch of sneezing wizards,' Snarks answered. 'Plus, this questing thing tends to get in your blood. Hendrek and I both felt it was time to go out and rescue something. It's much better than sitting on your hands in Vushta, especially considering the unwelcome small fry that have been showing up lately. Any chance to get away from –' Snarks stopped and stared. 'What's that on your shoulder?'

'Brownie Power!' Tap called out.

The demon turned a slightly lighter shade of green. 'Maybe I enjoyed standing in the bushes after all.'

Tap, seeing the demon's distress, hopped off my shoulder and skipped toward Snarks. 'I haven't been feeling quite myself lately, either,' the Brownie admitted. 'Now that you're here, though, everything's going to be as happy as a Brownie jamboree!'

'I was afraid of that,' Snarks moaned.

For once I sympathized with the demon. As much as it pleased me to see Tap's spirits returning, I feared that even I would not be capable of surviving a Brownie jamboree.

'Doom.' Hendrek lifted his dread warclub Headbasher. He had seen Guxx.

Guxx had seen Hendrek and Snarks as well. He poked at Brax with a pointy claw.

'Begin!'

'Indeed,' I remarked as Brax picked up his drum. 'You remember what I said about anybody who sang or declaimed on the quest?'

Brax stopped beating. Guxx glared at me for an instant, then whispered in the other demon's ear.

Brax cleared his throat when the former Grand Hoohah was done. 'My ruler would like to tell you the following.' Brax smiled uneasily. 'Let's see. Guxx Unfufadoo, noble demon . . . um, that he certainly is . . . um, sought to greet our new companions, sought to tell them he was friendly . . . and, uh . . . oh, he sought to welcome them to questing.'

Hubert snorted derisively. 'That sounds an awful lot like declaiming to me.'

'Indeed!' I exclaimed, before this could go any further. 'This arguing is going to get in the way of our quest. Perhaps I have been too harsh. A little modest declaiming might be in order after all.'

'Agreement!' Guxx shouted. Brax began to beat his drum.

Hubert snorted a short burst of flame. Brax stopped beating, glancing apprehensively at the vaudevillian lizard above him.

'No,' the dragon insisted. 'If he gets to declaim, we get to sing and dance.'

Alea looked up at her partner. 'What did you have in mind?'

Hubert paused a minute to consider. 'How about number 216?'

' "The Demon Slaughter Polka"?' Damsel nodded approvingly. 'Well, it's certainly bouncy enough.'

'Indeed!' I interrupted quickly. Somehow, this was getting out of hand all over again. 'No singing, no declaiming. The edict stands.'

Snarks and Hendrek both looked at me.

'Doom,' the large warrior whispered. ' "The Demon Slaughter Polka"? I thought we were all supposed to be friends on this quest.'

'How can you possibly make friends with a dragon who sings?' Snarks asked. He glanced at the former Grand Hoohah. 'For that matter, who could possibly trust a demon politician?'

I told Snarks and Hendrek how Guxx had come to join us. I also mentioned that Guxx and the dragon had had a small difference of opinion. But I also thought again about what Death had told me when we met. He had sent friend against friend back in Vushta to get me to meet him alone. Now I heard dissension all around me once more. Could Death be intensifying our quarrels to ruin our quest? If so, he must still be following our progress, something that I should never forget, even when we were being attacked by demons.

I shuddered to think what would happen if Death did get me alone.

'Wait a moment,' Snarks queried. 'Guxx joined you because he thought you were the Eternal Apprentice?'

'Doom,' Hendrek remarked.

'It is a frightening thought,' Snarks echoed. 'Eternal Apprentice, huh? Does that mean you'll have those same pimples throughout the rest of time?'

'Indeed,' I remarked, somewhat distracted. 'I think not.' I was their leader now. I would have to act like one. How would Ebenezum handle this? I stroked my chin in thought.

'Indeed,' I said again. 'What we really need here is some strategy. The Brownie and I recently contacted Ebenezum –'

'That's Brownie Power!' Tap exclaimed from where he ran by our sides. I looked down at the little fellow. He seemed to be his old dancing, smiling self at last. Both my talk with the Brownie and his summoning of Ebenezum seemed to help him, although for a while he looked as if he might still slide back into despair. Now, though, the arrival of Snarks seemed to have revived his spirits completely.

The demon Snarks shivered visibly as the Brownie approached. I ignored both of them and continued. '. . . and when I spoke with Ebenezum, the wizard told me that many of our allies in Vushta are coming on their own to join this quest.' I nodded first towards the unicorn – keeping its distance from the others, but still a member of our party – then at Hubert, Alea, and the Brownie. 'Of course, we have also been joined by two denizens of the Netherhells, but it is almost impossible to even approach Guxx and Brax without being assaulted by unrhyming verse. Talking strategy is completely out of the question. Damsel and Dragon, I am afraid, are almost as hopeless –'

'Theater people,' Snarks agreed.

'Doom,' Hendrek added.

'But now that I have been joined by those who were my companions on our successful campaign to rescue Vushta, I feel strategy is a priority. Especially because we are already on the edge of the Eastern Kingdoms.' I nodded at the large warning sign.

Hendrek read it. 'Doom,' he concurred.

'But come, we must resume our march. It grows dark.

We should get as close to our goal as possible!' I waved for the others to follow us, and they did so. There were enough of them by now to form a substantial line. I led them down the trail into the next wooded area, with Snarks and Hendrek still by my side.

I realized, then, that they had accepted me as their leader. But why wasn't I happier about this turn of events? As soon as I asked myself the question, I knew the answer. I would not be happy with anything until I knew the whereabouts of one more traveler from Vushta – one who was dearer to me than all the others I had left behind. Still, how could I broach the subject without letting my emotions interfere with my leadership? But I must know!

I would ask, I decided, but I would do so casually.

'Now, as to strategy,' I continued, the soul of casualness. 'Our first priority, I would think, would be to assess our strengths. We have gathered quite a complement together on this march, and we may even be joined by more. Tell me' – my voice caught in my throat for a second as I asked the next question – 'is anyone else coming from Vushta to join us?'

Snarks and Hendrek both shook their heads.

'No one?' I prompted easily. How could they have forgotten Norei?

'Doom,' Hendrek replied. 'We are the slowest of those to follow you. We are the last.'

'It wouldn't have happened if this large fellow had followed my diet and exercise guides,' Snarks added. 'But he won't listen to me. Nobody listens to me. And we could only lumber so fast after you.'

It occurred to me, then, that perhaps Norei hadn't followed after all. But that couldn't possibly be!

'Are you sure there was nobody else?' I insisted.

'Planning to join you here?' Hendrek shook his massive head with finality. 'None that we passed.'

This was terrible! After what Ebenezum had said, I had simply assumed that Norei would join us, and looked forward to at last explaining those few small misunderstandings that had happened between us recently. But what if she truly did not want to see me again? Would I never get the chance to tell her that I might be the Eternal Apprentice?

But I had to get hold of myself. This wasn't the way for a leader to act. I had no time to pine for lost love. I had to stride boldly forward, vanquishing foes and righting wrongs, making the world safe for Vushta and magicians everywhere. So what if Norei was gine from my life forever?

'Indeed,' I said one final time. 'Are you sure there was *absolutely* nobody else?'

'I think it's time for a new question,' Snarks retorted. 'Something that relates more to the quest, like, "What's your favorite color?" '

'Doom.' Hendrek looked back at me and frowned. 'Why do you keep asking?'

'Indeed,' I replied to give myself a chance to think. Despite my best efforts, my feelings about Norei were taking their toll on my supervision of the quest. Would it weaken my leadership even further if I were to admit how much I missed her? Perhaps I was becoming too strident in my questioning. I recalled that when I first decided to broach this subject, I had resolved to be as easygoing as possible.

So far I had failed miserably.

I took a deep breath. I would simply have to appear even more casual, and everything would be fine.

I looked casually at Snarks and Hendrek. 'I don't know,' I began, scratching casually behind my ear. 'I was just . . .

curious.' I yawned even more casually. 'There were some others we might be able to use. For example, how about' – I paused, casually picking a name out of the air – 'Norei.'

'Oh!' Snarks exclaimed. 'That's right! Your heartthrob. How could we forget –'

'Doom,' Hendrek interrupted the demon. 'Norei will definitely not be joining us.'

What? Norei not joining us as at all? All casualness left me as I demanded how Hendrek could be so sure.

Snarks spoke up first. 'I'm afraid this is one time the immense one here is right. We passed her on the way here.'

So they had seen her. That meant she was on the road to the Eastern Kingdoms! But what they said made no sense. Why had they told me –

'Doom.' Hendrek spoke before I had a chance to frame a question. 'She has too much pride to join you. Not after, as she told us, what happened in Vushta. She will, however, follow at a respectful distance in case you get into trouble.'

'Indeed?' I said. I did not know what to feel. One part of me was overjoyed that she cared enough about me to hover near, ready to protect us should disaster strike. But another part of me despaired of ever speaking to her again. And if I never spoke to her again, how could I possibly explain what had really happened?

'Doom,' I whispered.

'Hey!' a gruff voice retorted. 'Watch where you're going!'

'What?' I said. It was hard to make out shapes in the gathering gloom. But it was true that in my grief over losing Norei, I had not watched my feet, and thus had walked into and toppled what appeared to be a pile of short pieces of wood.

'Who's there?' I called.

There was no further response. The woods around us were deadly still.

'Doom,' Hendrek explained. 'It appears to be another sign.'

I realized the large warrior was not speaking metaphorically when I looked where he pointed with his club. While I wasn't paying attention, we had walked into another small clearing. In the center of that clearing, just beyond the lumber I had disturbed, was another large expanse of white wood. The light was fading around us more rapidly than I had realized, but I could still barely make out the words:

It's not all that far to
THE EASTERN KINGDOMS
Sure you don't want to turn back
now?

'Friendly sort,' Snarks remarked.

'Doom,' Hendrek added again.

'But we're not turning back. We are almost to our goal.' I glanced at the woods around us, completely black in the descending darkness. 'I think – it is time at last to make camp. It is too dark to go farther.'

'Doom,' Hendrek repeated, glowering out at those same woods. 'There is something out there.'

He was right. We had all heard the gruff voice in the dark. I kicked at the wood by my feet. 'Use this to build a fire. We will take turns at sentry.'

I scanned our surroundings once again, but could see nothing but the forest, close to us on every side and far too quiet.

'Gentle beings!' I turned to the rest of our party. 'We camp here tonight, sleeping close together. We move again at first light. We are at the edge of the Eastern Kingdoms.'

I paused. Did I hear something move out in the woods? It was my imagination, wasn't it?

I cleared my throat and added: 'I fear that tomorrow the quest begins in earnest!'

FIFTEEN

'The sages say that under certain circumstances, extensive traveling in strange lands can be both entertaining and educational. This is true, for there are few things more educational than putting one's hand or foot too close to a ravenous demon or mythological beast met in these same travels. And what of using what limbs you still possess to escape from said hungry creature? Well, let me assure you that that escape will be far more entertaining than the alternative.'

— THE TEACHINGS OF EBENEZUM, Volume XXXV

So we would camp at last. Unlike the last time I had made this suggestion, when Guxx had first decided that he was going to lead our party, there were no protests from any of our group. Besides having to inform Alea that when I spoke about sleeping close, I did not necessarily mean her and me, we settled down without further incident.

I realized that I had brought no food in my haste to leave Vushta earlier, but everyone else, apparently, had not been so shortsighted. Hubert had brought an immense amount of supplies (it is amazing how much a dragon can carry on his back), and Hendrek had brought a sizeable sack as well, although the large warrior seemed intent on consuming as much as he had contributed. Guxx and Brax elected not to eat with us, something that, quite frankly, I was perfectly happy with, being a bit afraid of finding out exactly what the demons *did* eat. But the rest of us sat down to a filling meal around the camp fire we'd built from the pieces of the warning sign.

Our bellies full, the rest of our party settled down to sleep. I had elected to take the first watch. There was some thinking I had to do, some things I had to work out if I were going to successfully lead these others to brave the perils before us. I threw another bit of wood into the fire and stared at the flames. Somehow, I could not keep the quest foremost in my mind. Another thought kept driving all others away:

How could I get Norei to speak with me again?

I turned from the flames. The fire didn't hold any answers. The ferret nuzzled my knee as it finished off the scraps I had saved for it. At least this little animal still had some affection for me. But it wasn't the same. The night was growing cold. Soon the ferret would retreat to the warmth of my pack, and I would be left here, all alone.

Of course! I was astonished how simple the answer was when it came to me. The pack! The Home Study Course was in my pack! That was the answer to my problems with Norei. For had not even my master, the great wizard Ebenezum, mentioned that the book contained love potions?

That was it! How simple! How perfect! I would use my magic to bring her back!

I quickly pulled the tome from my pack and turned so that I could read it by the light of the fire. I turned to the index, under L. Here it was!

'Love potions, all purpose, page 33'

All purpose? What need had I to go any further? I flipped rapidly to the proper page.

'What kind of idiot did this?'

I looked up from my reading. It was the gruff voice, calling from the woods.

Somebody coughed. I looked around the fire. It didn't seem to be one of my compatriots; they all were sound asleep. I heard the cough again. It came from the forest as well, on the opposite side of the clearing from the gruff voice.

Whoever was out there, I was surrounded.

I closed the book. Love potions would have to wait. There was something out there, something from the Eastern Kingdoms; maybe even something that wanted to bake me into a loaf of bread. Oh, how I wished I still had my stout oak staff!

'You'd better watch out.'

That voice was right behind me! I spun quickly, clutching the Home Study Course as a shield.

It was Brax.

'I couldn't sleep,' the demon said. 'I heard voices. I came over to warn you. The situation looks pretty tense.' He paused a moment to straighten his checkered lapels. 'A weapons salesdemon *lives* for times like these. In fact, I just might have a little something here . . .' He let the rest of the sentence hang in the air.

So Brax wanted to sell me weapons? 'Sorry,' I replied. 'Not interested.'

'That's all you have to say?' The demon looked grieved. 'Not interested? I tell you, I'm losing my touch.' He dropped the heavy sack he was carrying. It fell to the ground with a clank. 'Oh, how being Guxx's rhythm section cramps a salesdemon's style!'

I told the salesdemon to be quiet. There was something out there.

'There certainly is!' Brax whispered. 'And how much better you'd feel facing it with one of my previously owned weapons!'

'No, I wouldn't,' I replied.

The demon sighed. 'My timing is gone completely!'

'You're in a lot of trouble!'

Brax and I looked at each other. It was the gruff voice from the woods!

'Mayhaps I should answer it,' I ventured.

'Mayhaps,' Brax agreed. 'And don't forget, I have a sack full of weapons. No down payment, easy terms, at least one lifetime to pay.'

I decided to ignore the demon and respond to the voice instead.

'Hello!' I called to the night. 'And a good evening to you!'

'What's it to you?' the voice yelled back.

Well, whatever the thing was, it was talking to me, even though it didn't sound very friendly. I decided to try again.

'I merely thought that, if you had a problem –'

'Who asked you anyway?' the voice interrupted.

'Well,' I continued, trying to keep a cheerful tone, 'it's just that you shouted at us, and I thought you wanted to communicate, like any civilized being –'

'So's your old man!' the voice rejoined.

My mouth snapped shut. I was at a loss for words.

'I think you'd get much better results with a previously owned weapon,' Brax whispered.

I was beginning to agree with the salesdemon. But obnoxious as the voice was, how could I slay what I could not see?

'Doom,' a voice rumbled at my side. 'You have no need of previously owned weapons.' I looked over and saw that Hendrek watched us from a sitting position.

'Indeed,' I said to the large warrior. ' 'Tis true that I have you and the others in our party to protect me from harm. Still, there may come times when I must fight on my own and need a weapon to help me survive.'

'Doom.' Hendrek nodded his head. 'We have brought your weapon.' He reached over to shake Snarks.

'I'm awake!' the truth-telling demon grumbled. 'How could anybody sleep with all this shouting going on!'

'Doom,' Hendrek replied. 'Give Wuntvor his weapon.'

'All right! All right!' The demon sat up with a groan. 'That's the problem with questing; it doesn't give you any leisure time. It's just quest, quest, all the time quest.' He rummaged through his own sack. 'Here it is!' He pulled something long and shining from the sack and threw it in my general direction. 'Now can I go back to sleep?'

I recognized the weapon in its dark blue scabbard before I had even caught it. It was Cuthbert.

I looked to Hendrek. 'But I thought the sword refused to come out of its sheath?'

'Doom,' the warrior answered. 'We persuaded it.'

Snarks laughed. 'If it didn't come out, we were going to melt it down into ornamental paperweights.'

The sword almost sprang from its sheath as I pulled it free.

'Can you imagine?' Cuthbert cried. 'Ornamental paperweights? The very idea. A sword has some pride, you know!'

'Indeed,' I remarked, wondering how much I should agree with the weapon. Even with my substantial magical background, I always found it a little difficult to converse with a sword. Especially a sword like Cuthbert, who was a bit of a coward, particularly when it came to anything even potentially violent.

'So,' I added after a second's pause, 'you are prepared to do your duty?'

'Well . . .' Cuthbert paused in thought. 'You can use me to threaten. Any blood, though, and we will have words!'

'I am certain we will,' I agreed. 'But you shine in the dark as well.' In fact, Cuthbert had done that very thing in our quest through the Netherhells, lighting our way through countless caverns.

'Oh, certainly,' Cuthbert responded jovially, quite pleased that I had asked. 'And I shine very nicely, too.'

'Quite true. And that is the very thing we need now!'

'Why didn't you say so? Having me go on and on about bloodletting! I should have known you wanted much more civilized magic. Give me but a second while I brighten up!'

The sword glowed, first a dull red, then orange, then yellow, then blinding white.

'How's that?' Cuthbert asked.

'Perfect!' I answered. I held the sword before me and marched toward the spot where I had last heard the gruff voice.

'No fair!' the voice yelled. A short figure, perhaps half my size, leapt from the shadows and ran back into the trees. I heard other running feet as well. And one of the runners was coughing.

I stood at the edge of the clearing, listening to the fading sound of feet scambling over broken branches and dead leaves. It was far too dark to follow them, even with a magic sword. Besides, I had a feeling we'd meet again, soon enough.

'Indeed,' I said to the sword.

'That's it?' Cuthbert said in relief. 'I feared, when we went running toward the woods – well, never mind. That's fine. Any time!'

I sheathed the sword and returned to the camp fire.

'Doom.' Hendrek nodded. 'I will take the next watch.'

I didn't argue, but settled down with the Home Study Course to read myself to sleep.

The morning was magnificent. The sun was golden as it peeked through the trees, turning the leaves a bright, translucent green. Even the moss-covered rocks seemed to glow in the gentle morning light.

Alea rushed around the dying campfire to my side, her pale blond hair attractively mussed from sleeping.

'Oh, Wuntie!' she thrilled. 'Isn't it wonderful?' She waved at the scenery around her. 'It's like we woke up in some fairy land!'

'Hey!' a high voice yelled by my feet. 'Watch your language!'

We both looked down at Tap the Brownie. The little fellow shrugged defensively.

'Well, no one ever calls it Brownieland, do they?'

'It doesn't matter what you call it,' a beautifully modulated voice said from just past my shoulder. 'This is a magic place. We have entered the Eastern Kingdoms.'

I turned to look at the unicorn, and it was as if I had never seen that wondrous beast before. Its white coat and mane were blinding in the morning light, the color of newfallen snow in the high mountains. And its golden horn shone as if that gold were molten and the horn itself held the light of the sun. It pranced upon the bright green sward, beneath a sky the color of a brilliant robin's egg.

When I had first seen the unicorn, it had taken my breath away to see such magnificence in our everyday world. Now, though, the unicorn was even more incredible, surrounded by a world as beautiful as the beast. It was enough to stop your heart and be overjoyed that this might be the last thing your eyes beheld before you went to the grave.

This was where the unicorn belonged. I had no need to ask why the creature knew this place was magic. These Eastern Kingdoms, this 'fairy land,' as Alea had called it, was where the unicorn must have been born.

'Come,' the unicorn said. 'I will lead you.'

I quickly instructed the others to gather up their belongings and follow us.

'Do you know the way to Mother Duck's?' I asked the unicorn as I shouldered my pack and the Brownie once again climbed onto my other shoulder.

'I know much about this place,' the splendid beast answered. 'For many years it was my home, until I found a reason' – the beast glanced significantly in my direction – 'to seek other things outside. There are all sorts of sights I might show you.' It lowered its wondrous eyelids, halfway closing its soulful eyes. 'I know private places as well.'

'Indeed,' I replied. 'I am afraid that our need to meet with Mother Duck precludes any extensive side trips.'

'As you wish.' The unicorn sighed. 'I only pray that when our business is done, you spare some small thought for those of us with . . . other needs.' With that, the wondrous creature turned and walked down a trail into the woods. I beckoned for the rest of our group to follow.

Our first hour or two was uneventful. We traveled slowly but steadily through the Eastern Woods until we heard the hammering.

'Doom,' Hendrek commented behind me.

I cautioned the others to be quiet. Perhaps we might be able to sneak up on the noisemakers. Normally, the tremendous racket my own group caused would have made this quite impossible. However, the hammerers were so incredibly loud that I felt we might still have a slight chance.

Cautiously, the unicorn led the rest of us down the trail. Hendrek walked up to my side.

'Doom,' he whispered. 'Who could they be?'

'Well they certainly aren't Brownies!' Tap retorted. 'Listen to that noise. No technique at all!'

I motioned both of them to be silent. I thought I heard voices. And sure enough, as we walked I could hear the rudiments of a distant conversation.

'What do you think you're doing?' The voice was the same gruff one I had heard the night before.

'Why are you picking on me?' a somewhat more high-strung voice replied. 'Why does everybody always pick on me?'

Someone else yelled something incoherent. Then somebody coughed. I would recognize that cough anywhere. We were approaching whatever had surrounded us the night before!

I walked into the rear end of the unicorn. It had stopped to listen to the voices. I apologized to the magnificent beast, and it said it understood perfectly, especially since we were in public.

'Why did you stop?' I asked the beast.

The unicorn tossed its mane distractedly. 'I know those . . . individuals up ahead. I was thinking about taking another route. One that would avoid them.'

'Doom,' Hendrek remarked. 'Are they dangerous?'

'Well' – the unicorn considered – 'no, not really. But they're very, very unpleasant. Why don't we take another trail? It will only add on half a day's march.'

I told the unicorn we couldn't afford the time. We would have to march toward the hammering.

The unicorn sighed. 'If they won't listen to me, what can
I do?' Reluctantly, it led us down the road once again.

We turned a bend in the path and there they were, hammering together another sign:

> You are now entering
> THE EASTERN KINGDOMS!
> Don't say we didn't warn you

But who were they?
Or, more specifically, *what* were they?

SIXTEEN

'When meeting happy woodland creatures
Be careful what you do,
For many woodland creatures
Are only happy eating you!'

> – 'Woodland Wonderland' (verse six), excerpted
> from THE DAMSEL AND DRAGON SONGBOOK
> (still awaiting publication)

'Oh, no! Not you again!'

One of the hammerers scowled in our direction. The other half dozen or so turned to look at us as well.

'See?' another of their number shrieked. 'I told you they were picking on us!'

'Oh . . . wow,' a third added. Still another one coughed.

I wondered again exactly who, or what, these fellows were. They were short, about the size of Snarks, although their features were not demonic in the least. They had large, round heads, and bushy brows that seemed to accentuate their emotions, so that the fellow who scowled at us seemed the very picture of disgust.

There was an uncomfortable silence, broken only by one of the fellows' continued coughing. Very well. This situation called for leadership. More than ever before, it was time for me to live up to my position on this quest.

'Indeed?' I queried. 'I am afraid we cannot "pick on

you," as you put it, until we know who you are.'

One of the small fellows jumped down from where he had been working on the top of the sign, wringing his hands as he approached us.

'Oh, certainly, certainly, most honored sirs,' he began. 'Please take no offense from the manner of my fellows.'

'They cannot be Brownies,' Tap asserted: 'No manners at all.'

'Oh, might I please beg your pardon?' the hand-wringing hammerer pleaded. 'Oh, noble sirs, who are obviously far more knowledgeable than myself and my poor companions –'

'Speak for yourself!' the scowling fellow interjected.

The hand-wringer smiled apologetically and continued. 'But as I was saying, although I am sure that we are as mud beneath your feet –'

'Oh, yeah?' the scowler retorted.

The fellow of the wringing hands smiled even more apologetically '. . . indeed, some of us are more like the worms in the mud beneath your feet . . . but as unworthy and pitiably valueless as we are, I believe you should know the smallest bit about us before you pass judgment.'

'Indeed?' I prompted.

'Certainly! Oh, incredibly so, most valued sirs. And so, as inconsequential as we may be' – he glanced at his fellows. 'Please! No further comments!' He cleared his throat – 'I thought that I might introduce us. Of course, as you worldly-wise travelers have no doubt already surmised from our compact stature and industrious work habits, we are dwarves.'

'Industrious work habits?' Tap began. 'They couldn't buckle a shoe, much less hammer –'

I instructed the Brownie to quiet down.

'Dwarves?' I asked instead. This was interesting. I had heard of a group much like this one in an old tale, back when I was a boy. Could such stories be true in the Eastern Kingdoms? I decided it would do no harm to inquire.

'Could you be –'

'No, no, most esteemed sir!' the hand-wringer interjected before I could finish my sentence. 'Although that would be an excellent guess, I fear it is incorrect. You see, we are the other ones.'

'Indeed?' I replied. 'The other ones?'

The fellow nodded rapidly, overjoyed that I understood.

'Yes, we are the Seven *Other* Dwarves!'

Snarks stepped to my side. 'Other dwarves? You mean there's more of these things around here?'

'What's it to you?' the scowling fellow inquired.

'Doom,' Hendrek replied, the enchanted warclub Headbasher swinging free in his enormous hand.

'Now, now,' the hand-wringer hastily interposed, 'most incredibly intelligent and well-mannered visitors – to whom we are but the blemishes upon the worms crawling in the mud beneath your feet – I beg of you to but allow me to introduce my poor and most certainly overrated companions, and I shall be eternally grateful.'

'Indeed?' I said again. I had my doubts if I wanted this fawning fellow to be eternally grateful (or eternally anything else) on my behalf. However, I had the feeling that if we did not suffer through his introductions, we might never find Mother Duck.

I asked the dwarf to proceed.

'Oh, bless you!' the hand-wringer cried. 'I grovel at your feet in thankfulness. Even though I am no more than the dirt on the blemishes on the worms in the mud – but no, let my pitifully inadequate words introduce my fellows –'

'You can say that again!' the scowler barked.

The hand-wringing dwarf pointed to the fellow who had just spoken. 'This is Nasty. As you remarkably fine gentlemen can certainly ascertain, he lives up to his name.'

'I suppose it has to be me next!'

The hand-wringer nodded to a dwarf to the left of Nasty. 'Touchy,' was all he said.

'Do you have to be so abrupt?' Touchy wailed.

'I'd ignore them, if I were you,' said the dwarf to Touchy's left. 'I don't intend to have anything to do with them!' The speaker turned away, his nose in the air.

'And Snooty,' the first dwarf added.

Another dwarf wandered into Snooty's backside.

'Why don't you look where you're going?' Snooty yelled. 'Oh, why do I have to put up with such a lowlife?' The dwarf lifted his nose even farther aloft, imploring the heavens.

The fellow who was performing the introductions placed a hand on the bumper's shoulder. The other dwarf blinked repeatedly, as if he couldn't quite focus his eyes.

'And this,' the first dwarf continued, 'is Spacey.'

'Oh,' Spacey remarked, somewhat distracted. A moment later he added: 'Wow.'

The first dwarf waved his hand to include those fellows in the background. 'And here, of course, we have Dumpy, Noisy and Sickly.'

Dumpy moaned, Sickly coughed, and Noisy dropped something.

'Oh!' the first dwarf exclaimed, as if the thought had just occurred to him. 'But most esteemed sirs, I have neglected to introduce my own ridiculously deficient self.' He bowed low, kissing the dirt before my feet. 'Most wonderful, most magnanimous, most enlightened gentlemen, who are so high above me that I am but a pinprick on the ground beneath your eyes; nay, even more, a pinprick upon a pinprick –'

'Get on with it!' Nasty yelled.

'Oh.' The dwarf stood again, still all smiles, but also still not quite looking me in the eye. 'Certainly. I, honored sirs, am Smarmy.'

'There's no doubt about that,' Snarks remarked.

'Indeed,' I replied. 'Very nice to meet you. Now, if you will excuse us, we must be on our way.'

'Oh, no!' Smarmy cried. 'A hundred thousand pardons, most incredibly wondrous sirs, but that would never ever do. Now that you are in our less than worthless company, I am piteously afraid that this is where you must stay.'

'Doom.' Hendrek raised his club above his head. 'Are you trying to take us prisoner?'

'Oh, most certainly not!' Smarmy pleaded. 'We would never use force against such honored gentlebeings as yourselves. However, as lowly and degenerate a speaker as I am, might I ever so gently *suggest* that you become our prisoners?'

'Indeed?' I replied, restraining Hendrek from using his club. 'And why would you make that suggestion?'

'A million pardons that I should be so presumptive, oh astonishingly insightful travelers, but my humble suggestion, though probably barely worth your consideration, is in every likelihood a thousand times better than the alternative.'

'Indeed?' I queried. 'And just what is the alternative?'

Smarmy smiled even more apologetically than before, but his reply was only two words:

'Mother Duck.'

'Where?' Touchy screamed.

'Oh, that I would have to deal with such people!' Snooty added haughtily.

'Oh . . . wow,' Spacey remarked.

Sickly coughed. Dumpy moaned. Noisy dropped something.

'Doom,' Hendrek murmured.

'Very probably,' Smarmy agreed. 'Especially if Mother Duck catches you wandering around alone in the Eastern Kingdoms without her authorization. I sincerely believe that your chances are far better if Mother Duck catches you wandering around the Eastern Kingdoms with us.'

I felt two small but strong hands grip my shoulders. An incredibly worried face framed by blond hair thrust against my nose.

'Oh, Wuntie, I told you!' Alea whispered. 'We'll be baked in the giant's ovens!'

I gently moved Alea to one side, whispering back that we would talk once I had learned all our options.

I nodded again to Smarmy. 'Indeed. In both your scenarios, Mother Duck catches us. Is there no other alternative?'

Alea clung tight to my arm. 'We'll be mixed with flour and yeast,' she murmured half to me, half to herself, 'and baked into bread!'

Smarmy shook his head grimly, as if he were telling me the saddest thing in the world. 'Alas, not in the Eastern Kingdoms. Mother Duck catches everybody.'

'It's not fair,' Alea continued. 'My mother didn't raise me to die being mixed with yeast.'

Guxx Unfufadoo stepped forward, dragging Brax by his side.

'Commence!' he shrieked. Brax positioned his drum and commenced.

'Guxx Unfufadoo, demon leader,
Does not care who this Duck catches,
Has no fear who this Duck threatens,
Rather fancies Duck for dinner!'

'Is that so?' Hubert retorted. 'To my side, Damsel! Number 341!'
Alea left my side at last to rejoin the dragon.
They sang:

'We've got a toast of just one kind,
For those we know with a ruling desire.
You might possibly change your mind,
When you've been toasted by Dragon Fire!'

'Indeed!' I shouted at the top of my voice. 'You've both had your say! You are now even. There will be no further singing or declaiming. The truce goes back in effect *now*.'
Hubert and Guxx glared at each other, but neither spoke further.
I spoke again to Smarmy, 'Still, the two of them do have a point. I doubt Mother Duck has ever encountered anything like us before. After all, we have demons and a dragon on our side.'
'Not that it's going to do you any good!' Nasty sneered.
'Why do I have to always be around when these unpleasant things happen?' Touchy demanded of no one in particular.
'Oh . . . wow,' Spacey added.
'I know that if I had my way, I wouldn't be with any of you!' Snooty exclaimed distantly.
Noisy dropped something. Sickly coughed. Dumpy moaned.

'Oh, most nobly deluded sire,' Smarmy replied when his fellows were finally done, 'the remarkable show of force that you mention might work elsewhere, but not with Mother Duck.'

'Indeed,' I answered. Somehow, this was going all wrong. We were on a mission to save the surface world, not start a war. I would simply have to explain myself better. 'But you realize that a show of force is the last thing on our minds. We come in peace, to tell Mother Duck of a great threat that affects the Eastern Kingdoms as well as our homeland.'

Smarmy wrung his hands in agreement. 'All the more reason to join with us. When Mother Duck finds you, which she will whether you are with us or not, she will assume you are with our unworthy band for a purpose. She will then at least wait a few seconds for an explanation before deciding your fate.'

'Doom,' Hendrek interjected. 'Deciding our fate?'

'Yeah, bumpkin!' Nasty added. 'Or you could say "choosing your death" instead!'

'Who are you calling a bumpkin?' Snarks demanded.

Nasty pointed at the warrior. 'This blimp over here!'

'That's going too far!' Snarks rejoined. 'Wuntvor, lend me your sword. Only I can call Hendrek a blimp!'

'Doom,' Hendrek agreed. He swirled Headbasher through the air above Nasty's head.

'Indeed!' I called again. 'Put down your weapons and lower your voices. There is no need for battle. In fact, a fight might keep us from our goal of meeting Mother Duck.'

'How right you are, learned young master!' Smarmy chimed in. 'That is why you must stay.' The Dwarf stopped wringing his hands, and wiped them nervously on his worn, brown leggings. 'But to be totally frank, honest, and candid with you, there is a further reason as well. You see, if we do not capture you, Mother Duck will "decide our fate" as well.'

'She's like that!' Touchy agreed. 'Oh, why do I always have to get into the middle of these things!'

'Indeed?' I replied. 'Then perhaps we should travel with you. And as we travel, perhaps you can tell us something about this Mother Duck.'

'Then you will be our prisoners?' Smarmy shouted gleefully. 'Oh, a thousand thousand thanks. You have no idea what this means to my humble band, especially in terms of continued longevity.'

'Fine,' I said. 'Now that we are under your care, what do you wish us to do?'

Smarmy frowned. 'Oh, dear. We're supposed to do something? Yes, that would be a very good idea, wouldn't it? Mother Duck is very big on that, calls it "advancing the plot," she does. Oh, deary dear. Most of the time we simply hammer, you know, and put up these warning signs. Oh, my.' The dwarf paused, frowning, then smiled for an instant before shaking his head and frowning again.

'I'm afraid I haven't the faintest idea,' he said at last.

I told the dwarf it might be something to think about. He agreed wholeheartedly, said that he would consult with the other dwarves and definitely have a plan by morning.

I turned to my companions and instructed them to make an early camp. Mother Duck sounded like a very difficult character indeed. I had to do some thinking as well, or we might all wind up as some giant's dinner.

'Oh, Wuntie!' Alea trailed after me. 'Something is wrong,' she called. 'You are so preoccupied these days. Have your feelings changed for me? Has the magic gone from our relationship?'

I turned back to stare at the damsel as she rushed forward to fling her arms around me.

Of course! That was the answer!

SEVENTEEN

' "'Tis as plain as the nose on your face' is another annoying remark that sages make. Think on it. When was the last time you went walking down the street, looking at your nose?'

– THE TEACHINGS OF EBENEZUM, Volume I

Magic!

It was so obvious, I didn't know why I hadn't thought of it before. I felt like kissing Alea, but stopped myself for fear it might lead to other things.

The only way we were going to survive the Eastern Kingdoms was through magic. But exactly what magic?

I thought at first of contacting Ebenezum. Yet what could he do at this great a distance? Besides, with what the Brownie had already been through, I doubted he had the energy for anything pertaining to Brownie Power. And even if the Brownie could manage to contact my master, it was the kind of magic, what with a dancing Brownie and a great cloud of dust, that rather called attention to itself.

But perhaps most important of all, I did not yet know the Seven Other Dwarves' true intentions. Even without talking to Ebenezum, I realized it was important to keep our various magical abilities to ourselves until I knew a little better what they had planned for us.

That was the real problem – just when should we use our

magic? Perhaps it would be best to wait until we confronted Mother Duck. Then, if need be, I could resort to the Home Study Course. True, many of the recent spells I had attempted from that tome had not worked out quite as I had planned. Still, the law of averages demanded that I would eventually get a spell correct. Didn't it?

But no. I realized that the less time I had to master a spell, the more chance I had of it going awry. Handling emergencies with the Home Study Course would have to remain a last resort. I needed someone here with a real mastery of magic.

It was then I knew. My heart quickened with the realization. We truly needed Norei.

'Wuntie?' Alea whispered huskily in my ear. 'When you squeeze me like that, all my doubts are forgotten.'

'Um?' I said. 'Oh.' In my enthusiasm for my new plan, I had forgotten that I had a young, attractive blond woman in my arms – a young, attractive blond woman who was looking very fixedly into my eyes. What could I say? 'Indeed. Well, I'm afraid we don't have time for any of that right now, Alea. I must make plans.'

'Oh, I'll forgive you this time,' Alea said throatily as she stroked my arm. 'When you hug that *recklessly*, I can wait.'

'Yes . . . well,' I replied. 'Indeed.' I shook the young woman from my arm and shrugged the pack off my back.

'Why don't you watch where you're throwing things?' Touchy demanded from somewhere behind me. The pack seemed to have landed in the vicinity of his head.

'Um . . . indeed,' I began, somewhat distressed by this turn of events. 'I beg your pardon –'

'You should beg our pardon for ever crossing our paths!' Snooty demanded.

'Oh, why bother with them!' Nasty remarked to his

fellows. 'They're all going to be eaten by giants anyway!'

Sickly coughed in our direction, and Dumpy's moan had a sinister undertone. Nasty told Noisy to walk over to me and drop something on my foot.

This seemed to be getting out of hand. Without Smarmy here to act as spokesbeing, the other dwarves were becoming definitely hostile. And where was Smarmy? Before he disappeared, didn't he say something about deciding our fate?

Maybe I should talk to Ebenezum after all. But where had Tap gotten to?

Noisy stumbled toward my pack. Was the dwarf going to attempt to drop it on my foot in retaliation?

'Watch out, Noisy!' Touchy screamed. 'He's got a weapon!'

Who had a weapon? Where they talking about me?

Then I remembered I was wearing Cuthbert. Perhaps I should draw the sword and confront the dwarves with naked steel. That would certainly end all this confusion for good. Still, I wanted to avoid violence if I possibly could. Oh, why did everything always have to get so complicated?

I really wished I could talk again with Ebenezum. If only there were some way. . . .

Noisy once again trundled in the direction of my pack. I placed my hand on Cuthbert's hilt as a warning.

It was then I remembered.

Of course! Cuthbert was more than your everyday sword. Not only could it talk, but the sword had other magical properties as well. I had used it repeatedly to contact Ebenezum when I was in the Netherhells.

Then that was the answer! I had no need to wait for the Brownie; I would use Cuthbert instead. I looked around me at the glowering dwarves. Perhaps it would be best to talk to my master now, before the situation got any worse.

'Stand back, varlets!' I called as I attempted to pull the sword from its sheath.

The sword didn't budge. I tugged at the hilt with both hands, but it made no difference. It appeared to be stuck.

'Cuthbert?' I inquired with the slightest edge of desperation.

'I'm not coming out,' the sword replied, its voice muffled but distinct. 'I can hear raised voices. I know when there's going to be bloodshed.'

'The only blood shed around here,' Snooty remarked disdainfully, 'will be yours.'

'Eaten, eaten, eaten!' Nasty added.

'See?' Cuthbert retorted. 'It's quite cozy in my sheath, thank you very much.'

Snarks rushed to my side. 'Ornamental paperweights,' he whispered to the sword.

'Is – is that so?' Cuthbert replied, obviously wavering. 'Well, maybe holding down paper wouldn't be such a bad job after all.'

Noisy leaned down to pick up my pack, then stomped towards me with a smile. Hendrek stepped to my other side, Headbasher in his hand.

'Doom,' the large warrior remarked.

Snarks leaned even closer to the sword. 'Ornamental paperweights sculpted to look like me.'

'A sword has some pride!' Cuthbert sprang from its sheath. 'Stay away, now! Don't force me to do anything rash or' – I felt the sword shudder in my hands – 'messy.'

Noisy paused, looking doubtfully down at the pack in his hands. And then the pack moved.

Dumpy moaned uneasily. Sickly coughed a warning.

'Watch out!' Touchy shrieked. 'It's one of those Western Kingdom tricks!'

'Eep!' the ferret screamed in Noisy's face. The dwarf dropped the pack and ran.

'Indeed!' I called, wishing to stop this nonsense as soon as possible. 'We come in peace. We wish you no harm!' Mayhaps, I thought, I should resheathe the sword I now waved in my hand as a sign of my good intentions. And yet if I restored Cuthbert to its sheath, I somewhat doubted my chances of getting it to come back out again.

The dwarves continued to scowl at me, believing my brandished sword rather than my words.

'You just wait for the giants!' Nasty exclaimed.

I replied that it might be far better if both our parties waited for a while and settled down for the late afternoon and evening as we had first intended. The dwarves grumbled and walked off to eat on the far side of their newly erected sign. I told my companions that we should settle down as well, and added that I would take the first watch. I needed time for quiet contemplation.

Our current situation was becoming more unpleasant with every passing moment, and it promised to get much worse. The dwarves were not quite openly violent, but I had met friendlier demons in the Netherhells. I knew I had to take some action, but I thought it best if I tried something quiet. I feared that even contacting Ebenezum with the sword might draw too much attention. It would do me no good to speak to my master if, as a by-product, I managed to start a riot.

'Doom.' Hendrek approached me. ''Tis not a good situation for a trained warrior.'

'Hey, Hendy,' another voice said behind me, 'this is not a good situation for anybody. Especially those among us not now equipped with high-quality, previously-owned magical weapons.'

I did not have to turn around to identify the speaker.

Brax, straightening the lapels of his checked suit, strolled around in front of us. Hendrek lifted his enchanted club Headbasher as I hefted Cuthbert, showing Brax that we, at least, both had our magical weapons.

'No bloodshed!' Cuthbert squeaked.

'Now, now,' Brax quickly added. 'There is no need for a show of force. Our current situation constrains all of us. Yonder dragon cannot sing, my master Guxx cannot declaim, and I can find little time to ply my sincerely honest and valuable trade. We must do what we can to keep our spirits up.'

'Doom,' Hendrek agreed, eyeing Brax meaningfully. 'How much better I would feel if I could bash something.'

'Come now, Hendy, I haven't demanded payment on your high quality warclub since –'

'Something in checks,' Hendrek interrupted.

'Now, just hear me out,' Brax replied. 'You may not like your payment schedule, but you have to admit that your dread Headbasher has given you first-rate magical service.'

'Doom,' was Hendrek's only reply.

Brax nodded briskly. 'And that's exactly what you'll have if you can't properly defend yourself against whatever's going to happen here in the Eastern Kingdoms.'

He lifted the bag he carried with him and shook it. The bag clanked significantly.

'Do you know what this bag is filled with? That's right – magical weapons; practically every weapon you'll ever need. We have broadswords, rapiers, daggers, penknives, letter openers, and corkscrews. And that's not all! Also in this pack you'll find powders, poisons, philters, and potions, and a surprise or two besides! And I'm willing to give it all to you for a special group rate! That's right, all the weapons in this sack can be yours for one low price, payable with the simplest Netherhells contract imaginable!' He hefted the clanking sack again. 'How much would *you* pay . . .'

He paused, smiling up at me as if expecting an answer. He wanted to sell me all those weapons? I swallowed hard. What should I do? If he were to offer me only one or two, I definitely would have refused, fearing the Netherhells contracts. But all of them? What power they would give us! Maybe they were the magic we needed.

'Uh . . .' I began.

'Don't answer yet,' Brax interrupted, whipping still another weapon from behind his back, 'because you also get this enchanted battle ax at no additional charge! That's right, this cleaver goes through your enemies like a knife through butter. And it also slices vegetables!' He removed a carrot from his coat pocket and tossed it in the air. The battle ax neatly cut it in two. 'It's great for making tasty snacks!'

'Quiet down over there!' Nasty yelled from the other side of the sign.

'Dwarves would probably make tasty snacks,' Brax added, tucking the ax once again behind his coat. 'Well, what do you say?'

'No bloodshed!' Cuthbert warned.

I looked at Hendrek.

'Doom,' the warrior remarked.

Hendrek and Cuthbert were right. Upon sober reflection, I realized that stockpiling weapons was not the answer. From all I had heard of Mother Duck, I felt we had more of a chance convincing her through reasoned discussion than with a show of force.

'Sorry,' I told Brax, 'but your weapons do not fit in with our plans.'

'Plans?' Brax asked. 'We have plans?'

'Well, we will have plans,' I assured him. 'They will definitely be completed by tomorrow.'

'Oh, but do we have plans for you!' Snooty called from beyond the sign.

'Should we' – Sickly coughed – 'let the giants' – he coughed again – 'get them?'

'Nah,' Nasty replied. 'I think we should save them for Mother Duck!'

They all laughed and coughed together.

I told Brax and Hendrek to ignore the derisive dwarves and get some rest. I tried to remain as calm as possible, casually flexing my sword arm as my companions turned back to our half of the campsite. I decided that at least for now, it wouldn't do any of them any good to see how truly concerned I was. For I felt this was one of the most serious situations I had faced since I had begun to quest. Whether we were going to encounter giants or Mother Duck, we needed all the magic we could muster. And not the blunt, brute-force magic of Brax's slightly-used weapons. We needed thinking magic.

I had to get Norei to join us.

But how could I contact her? And even if she knew of my problem, how could I be sure she would respond to my request? Once, not so long ago, we had been as close as two could be. Now I feared she would never talk to me again. Oh, if only we could start anew, like the two lovers we were meant to be!

I stared at my pack. But there was a way to start anew!

I reached inside and, briefly petting the fertet, lifted out the Home Study Course. I would have to consult it one more time after all. But I would do it slowly, carefully, not allowing any mistakes. I had to succeed, if I were to gain Norei once again by my side.

My heart pounded in my ears as I turned to the index. My decision was made.

I would have to use the love potion.

EIGHTEEN

'What, exactly, is love? Why it's the most wonderful, even greater than the most wonderful – no, it's the greatest, even greater than . . . no, that still doesn't quite explain it. Rather, it's like the dawn light shining over a field of the most beautiful wild – but perhaps that is too metaphorical. But you know the feeling? Yes! Is there anything better? There's no need to answer. I'm glad I was able to explain.'

– SOME THOUGHTS ON APPRENTICESHIP
by Wuntvor, apprentice to Ebenezum,
greatest mage in the Western Kingdoms
(a work in progress)

Here it was, on page 44: 'The Universal Love Potion Spell.' To my surprise, it was the least complicated spell I had found in the entire Home Study Course, full of simple ingredients and simple gestures. In a way, though, that made sense, for what could be more pure than love? I quickly set about locating the ingredients: fresh spring water, green leaves and wildflowers, as well as a few dried twigs for a fire. I then moved to the farthest edge of the clearing so I could pursue my magic without interruption.

I checked the incantation a final time. There was still one ingredient missing! I quickly ran and fetched Cuthbert.

'What are we doing?' the sword demanded as I picked it up. I assured it that I would do nothing violent in nature. I simply needed its sharp edge to cut off a lock of my hair.

'So I've been reduced to barbering?' Cuthbert replied, obviously not happy with the situation. 'Don't you think a pair of magic scissors would be better for that kind of work?'

I asked him if he'd rather help out on a spell that required blood.

'Now that you mention it, you are getting a little shaggy around the ears,' the sword allowed. 'Would you like me to take a little off the top, too?'

I laid the suddenly subdued sword to one side and began preparations for the spell. First the making of the fire, then the burning of a leaf and a flower, then a spray of water into the flames; all performed, of course, with the proper incantations. Now it was time for the fresh-cut hair. I waited for some new remark from Cuthbert, say how my hair oil would dull its blade, but the sword only whimpered as I sawed.

I tossed the hank of hair into the flames. The fire burned bright blue. Now I would only have to say the final words and the spell would be complete.

But my concentration was broken by a noise, a rustling in the bushes just opposite where I stood. What could it be? Perhaps another visitor from Vushta? I realized I wasn't breathing. Could the spell have worked before I had even completed it?

'Why, look who we have here!' a distinctly male voice called.

'Yeah,' another voice mocked. 'Here.'

I knew who it was even before I felt the knife at my throat. Grott, Slag, and Vermin, the three representatives of the Vushta Apprentice Guild, had found me.

'Thought you could get away from us by simply going on a quest to the Eastern Kingdoms?' Grott drawled as he emerged from the bushes. 'How foolish that was, especially since your solution to our little problem is long overdue!'

'Yeah,' Slag added as he, too, stepped into view. 'Long.'

Vermin's blade pressed against my throat.

'Um,' I said. I had completely forgotten about these three and their demand for a cure for their masters by moonlight tomorrow. Except by now their deadline had come and gone; it would have been moonlight yesterday. I thought my forgetfulness was understandable, considering what had happened since my last meeting with the apprentices. But I wondered if there was any way I could get them to agree with me.

Still, I could not help but be impressed with their dedication in their search for me. If only they would use that fortitude in our cause! Unlike myself, who had spent most of the last months caring for a sneezing wizard, they had probably been learning magic from their mentors! If they could but put aside their quarrel with me for a time, what allies they would make!

'Indeed,' I replied. 'So you have followed me all the way into the Eastern Kingdoms. But things are different here from the safe streets of Vushta. In these strange lands we are all in peril for our lives. Under these circumstances, don't you think we could forget our little differences and all work together, for the good of Vushta and the surface world?'

'You have no cure, then?' Grott growled. 'Well, perhaps we will forget after all, once Vermin has carved himself a small memento from somewhere on your chest. But remember, there is still a better way.' Grott's smile turned positively jovial as he added: 'Our forgetfulness can be bought, for a mere thirteen hundred pieces of gold.'

'Thirteen hundred?' I blurted. Their price had gone up yet again.

'Uh –' Slag interjected.

'Oh, did I say thirteen hundred?' Grott waved his hand apologetically. 'So sorry, a slip of the tongue. I meant to say fourteen hundred.'

'Fourteen?' I exploded. 'Where –'

'Uh, Grott,' Slag interrupted, pointing past the other apprentice's shoulder.

'Not now,' Grott replied curtly. 'We are doing business.' He nodded pleasantly in my direction. 'Where will you find those fourteen hundred and fifty pieces of gold? Why, you're a magician's apprentice, after all. We thought you could come up with something.'

'Indeed,' I answered. This particular conversation was getting me nowhere. While I admired my fellow apprentices' single-mindedness in pursuing their goal, I felt their talents could be put to much better use in our present situation. But how could I convince these three to join us?

'I do not have the gold,' I told the grinning Grott. 'Nor do I have a cure for the malady that afflicts all our masters. However, if you were to stay and work with me in the Eastern Kingdoms, we will certainly encounter many wonders. Who is to say if, among those wonders, we might not find a cure? And who can say how much gold we might find besides?'

'Stay?' Grott replied. 'Well, we will not go very far. After all, we have an investment here.'

'Yeah,' Slag hastily added. 'Here. Uh. Listen, Grott –'

'Not now, Slag. You're ruining my timing!' Grott turned back to me and nodded sadly. 'Poor Wuntvor. We do think it is a shame that you have neither the cure nor the gold. And just so you remember how important our business dealings are, I think it's time that Vermin took his little souvenir. That way, you'll be even more eager to have the fifteen hundred pieces –'

Grott broke off abruptly. A strained look came over his face.

'Vermin, is that you?'

But, of course, Grott's knife-wielding companion still had his blade at my throat. Grott's back was pressed against the bushes. He reached a hand around to feel behind him.

'Slag?' Grott inquired.

'Yeah,' Slag replied. 'Unicorn.'

'I certainly am,' a magnificently modulated voice spoke from the bushes. 'And a more wondrous and deadly beast you will never meet. Now, if you would please move yourselves into the middle of the clearing, where we can see what everybody is doing . . .?'

Grott and Slag both obliged. The unicorn followed, his horn pressed into Grott's spine. Vermin pulled the knife away from my throat to warily study the mythical creature.

'Don't even think about it,' the unicorn stated, 'unless you want to become part of a picturesque tableau.' The splendid beast snorted, the sound like the ringing of deep and sonorous bells. 'You know, the kind of tableau that features great gouts of blood flying everywhere and poor humans writhing in their death agonies as the unicorn rears triumphantly, dark blood-stains tastefully mottled on its shining golden horn? Surely you've seen the scene. It's on thousands of tapestries.'

'But you mistake our intentions!' Grott exclaimed hurriedly. 'After all, we are but poor apprentices, just like Wuntvor here. We only wanted to have a little talk.'

'And I imagine you like to talk with knives?' The

mythical beast pawed the ground meaningfully. 'Well, I like to talk with my incredibly sharp, glowing golden horn.'

Grott's smile seemed a bit forced, 'Vermin,' he remarked between clenched teeth. 'Why don't you put away your knife?'

The other apprentice sheathed his blade.

'Now, we were discussing the best way for Wuntvor here to furnish us with fifteen hundred and fifty pieces of gold.'

'I think it might be time,' the unicorn replied, 'to discuss instead where you would like the holes gored in your body.'

'Yeah,' Slag said. 'Good-bye.' Both he and Vermin ran for the underbrush.

'Wait for me!' Grott bolted away from the unicorn with a speed I had never seen in him before. 'Remember!' he called to me over his shoulder. 'Sixteen hundred pieces –' And then he, too, was lost in the bushes.

I told the unicorn that I didn't know how I could express my thanks.

'I have an idea or two,' the incredible beast replied. 'My head's gotten awfully heavy after all that threatening.'

'Indeed,' I responded, 'Perhaps later. Unfortunately, at this moment I am in the middle of a spell.'

'Sorcery?' The unicorn sniffed. 'But aren't *I* magic enough?'

I apologized again. The unicorn walked slowly back toward camp, a broken mythical beast.

But what had happened to my spell? I turned to my fire, but the flames had gone out. There was nought left but a few glowing embers. And I was so close to success! I had completed all but the very last portion of the spell. What should I do?

Someone stirred among the sleepers. I thought I heard a muffled 'doom.' My altercation with the apprentice guild must have roused some of my fellows. I had no doubt that one or more of them would be joining me momentarily. That made my decision easier. I did not have time to entirely begin the spell again. I would have to complete it as quickly and best as I could.

I piled what twigs and leaves I still had atop the fire's remains and blew on the embers until flame started to lap around the dry wood. I would have to finish my incantation speedily and hope for the best. I looked at the flames. The fire was the wrong color, bright yellow flames where they should be blue.

Well, that was easily solved. I reached for Cuthbert.

'Now what?' the sword demanded. 'You can't fool me! I heard the threats!'

'Indeed,' I answered. 'I assure you that we are now quite alone. I only need you to cut a bit more hair.'

'Barbering again?' was Cuthbert's response. 'Is this going to be a regular activity? I mean, things like this get out, they could ruin a sword's reputation. I can hear the other magic swords now. "So how you doing, Cuthbert? Shave any faces lately?" Oh, the shame!'

I ignored the sword and used its edge to chop off another chunk of hair.

'It's not that I don't have dreams,' Cuthbert continued as I worked. 'It's all this traveling around. It gets so wearing, especially when your owner won't put you back in your scabbard. Oh, would that I could settle down, away from all this bloodshed and strife. Perhaps a nice wall somewhere, hanging half drawn from my sheath so that I might watch the hustle and bustle around me. But no. I am forced to lead the life of a vagabond sword, traveling through whatever bloodstained region my master –'

I put the sword back in its scabbard. I had to concentrate.

I looked a final time at the spell in the Home Study Course.

'Having done all these things' – the book said – 'the final step is most important. Taking a hank of fresh-cut hair from your head, plunge it into the fire and recite the words below. Remember, as you recite these words, place in your mind the image of the loved one you wish this spell to affect. The fumes of this potion will then reach out to your beloved, wherever he or she may be. Again we emphasize, concentrate on your beloved, for the strength of this spell will vary with the purity of your thought.'

I threw my hair into the fire and the flames again burned blue.

'Norei,' I whispered, then began the incantation.

'Doom!' boomed from the campsite.

'Now that's Brownie Power!' Tap answered.

'Let me go,' Snarks retorted, 'or we'll have Brownie Power for breakfast!'

'In my humble and most likely worthless opinion,' Smarmy added, 'the little fellow is completely correct.'

Then everybody started to talk at once. I glanced back at the fire, but the blue flames were gone. And what of the love spell? I would have to hope that my incantation had worked before I was interrupted.

The voices back at the camp were growing louder by the moment. My companions and all the Seven Other Dwarves seemed to be shouting at once. I supposed I would have to go back and quiet things down.

'Indeed!' I called out as I walked towards them.

'Wuntvor?' they cried in unison. A sudden silence fell among them. That was odd. Maybe they were accepting my leadership at last.

But why were they all looking at me so strangely?

NINETEEN

'There are many definitions of love. The starving man, about to chew greedily on a roast chicken leg, is sure to give you one predictable view. The recently cooked chicken, however, may be of a different opinion.'

— THE TEACHINGS OF EBENEZUM, Volume LVIII

'Oh, Wuntie!' Alea screamed. 'At last we can be together!' She ran towards me, smiling as though she hadn't seen me in weeks.

'Oh, no, you don't,' the unicorn thundered magnificently. 'I saw him first!' And with that, the mythical beast also galloped in my direction.

I stopped, open-mouthed. What was happening here?

Guxx stepped forward, dragging Brax after him.

'Elucidate!' the chief demon cried. Brax winked at me and began to beat on his drum. Guxx bellowed in my direction:

'Guxx Unfufadoo, heartfelt demon,
Wants to speak of admiration,
Wants to pledge his faith undying,
Wants to get to know you better!'

'Oh, yeah?' the dragon bellowed. 'Well, you ain't heard nothin' yet!' He began to sing:

'Here's an apprentice that's just the nicest,
You want him there in any crisis,
Even though he's kind of awkward and shy.
His adolescent charm is so revealing
How could clumsiness be so appealing?
You could say that Wuntvor's my kind of guy!'

This was getting stranger by the moment. And Guxx and
the dragon were once again ignoring my edict about
declaiming and singing. Perhaps an 'indeed' would be in
order here.

But before I had a chance to utter a single word, Alea
was upon me. Literally. She threw herself against me, and I
could not keep my balance. Then, once I was down, she
covered me with a barrage of kisses.

'Uh,' I began. 'Al –' I found that I didn't have enough
time between kisses to speak her full name, '. . . eee . . .'
Instead I was reduced to uttering but one syllable at a time
'. . . a!'

'That's my name,' she purred, 'and from your lips it
becomes music!'

'Alea!' I repeated, trying to take advantage of this few
seconds' reprieve 'Would you please' – she started in
again – 'let' – I tried to struggle, but it was no
use – 'me' – her grip was like iron – 'breathe!'

She lifted her lips from my own, a look of concern on her
countenance. 'Oh, forgive my ardour, most dear Wuntvor.
It's just that I have missed you so.'

She missed me? But I had only been standing on the
other side of the clearing! What madness was this?

'Stand away from that innocent lad, you hussy!' a
magnificently dynamic voice demanded. 'You are not
worthy to kiss his toes!'

'What?' Alea stood up and glared at the unicorn.

'Yes,' the unicorn sighed, 'and what wonderful toes they are! Not to mention his legs, his arms, his shoulders, his ill-cut hair! And' – the splendid beast paused, somewhat overwrought – 'what of his lap?' A small groan, half despair, half desire, escaped from between the unicorn's pearly teeth. 'I dare not speak of it, lest the thought drive me wild!'

But Alea was ready to speak and more. 'What do you mean, I'm not worthy of Wuntvor's toes? I'll have you know that I'm one of the most sought-after performers in all of Vushta.'

'My point exactly,' the unicorn replied dryly.

'Hah!' Alea retorted. 'Look at this hair' – she grabbed two great handfuls of glistening blond strands – 'these lips' her exquisite mouth pouted tantalizingly – 'this exquisite womanly form!' She proceeded to pat other parts of her anatomy. 'This is what Wuntvor desires! Not some over-stuffed horse with a bump on his nose!'

'Overstuffed!' the unicorn responded, pawing the ground. 'Bump on my nose? I would be offended, if those words had not come from an *actress*!'

'How dare you!' Alea demanded. 'I'll act all over *you*, you big, stupid –' She sputtered, waving her fists at the magnificent beast.

I stood up as the two of them argued. They seemed to have forgotten about me completely. I walked past them towards the others.

'Doom,' Hendrek greeted me as I approached. 'But perhaps not, now that you are here.' To my horror, the large warrior smiled.

'Good old Wuntvor!' Snarks shook my hand. 'Why, you're the best clumsy, pimply-faced apprentice with bad posture I've ever had the pleasure to know!'

Snarks had complimented me. I stared stupidly down at the hand he had so heartily shaken. Something was definitely amiss.

'Oh, Wuntie!' Alea called from where I had left her. 'Don't run from me, lover! I cannot exist without you!'

'How can someone like you know what love is?' The unicorn snorted proudly. 'A mythical beast like me *is* love.'

It couldn't be. I felt a cold spot, deep in my innards, as if I had a snowball in my stomach. They were all talking about – but, no. I shuddered to even think of it.

Could something have gone wrong with the love spell?

'Wuntvor!' Alea commanded. 'We must be together always. I must feel you in my arms!' She ran towards me again.

'You cannot fight it!' the unicorn cried as it also galloped in my direction. 'Your lap and my head were destined to be as one!'

'Indeed,' I remarked hastily, glancing at my nearby companions. 'Uh, fellows? Could you keep those two away from me for a little while? I need to think.'

'Doom,' Hendrek grinned. 'Anything for you.'

'Of course!' Snarks skipped after the warrior. 'I tell you,' he said musingly, 'I just want to pinch his pimply-faced cheek.'

Hendrek and Snarks were joined by Guxx, Brax, and Hubert. That was good. The five of them would save me, at least temporarily, from the overaffectionate advances of Damsel and unicorn. I could not doubt that it was the love conjuration. But what had gone amiss?

I had followed the spell exactly as instructed by the Home Study Course; except, of course, that I had let my hair burn before I had completed the magic, and so had added some more. Perhaps I had made the spell too powerful. But I had thought of Norei when I finally completed the spell! At least, I had thought of her for an instant. Then there had been that commotion between my companions and the dwarves, and my attention had been temporarily distracted.

Could it be?

The ball of ice in my belly turned to a boulder. I had turned to look at everybody in mid-spell. Did that mean I had worked my love spell on the entire camp?

The Seven Other Dwarves smiled at me.

'Why, Wuntvor's not such a bad fellow, compared to some I could name,' Snooty remarked.

'Yeah,' Nasty added. 'Actually, he's kind of cute.'

'Why didn't you ask me?' Touchy interjected. 'Anything you want, Wuntvor, we're at your service!'

'Indeed,' I replied. What else could I say? The spell was insidious. Everyone in camp seemed to be affected. Those who hadn't liked me before had become my friends, and those who had previously been attracted to me, I would have to fight off with Cuthbert.

But what of Norei? My magic had originally been meant for her. This, then, was the final irony. In dissipating the spell, had I lost her forever? The ice seemed to overtake my whole form.

'A happy Brownie hello!' Tap called from somewhere near my ankle. 'And may I say it's a pleasure to work for you! It fills my heart with Brownie admiration!'

'That's true,' Smarmy added, stepping up next to the little fellow. 'That's what we call Brownie Power!'

'Indeed?' I said, although my heart wasn't in it. My heart was far away, with a woman I would never see again!

'Yes!' Tap agreed with the dwarf. 'And all that great Brownie Power is here for you, the most worthy of worthies!'

'Oh, dear,' Smarmy interrupted. 'But may this humble and obviously pitiable fellow beg to differ? While this young human is certainly worthy, not to mention lovable as lovable can be, he is most unfortunately completely lacking in Brownie magic!'

'Too true,' Tap agreed sadly. 'But can we fault him for being far too tall and far too human? Remember, we Brownies must be generous with our gifts.'

Smarmy nodded happily. 'That's Brownie Power!'

Snarks returned then. 'We've got the girl and the horse under control, at least for the moment. I just thought you'd like to know. I am at your service.' He eyed the Brownie suspiciously. 'Do you need me to take care of anything else?'

'Oh, most humbly no,' Smarmy answered. 'We Brownies will take care of everything!'

Snarks turned a deeper shade of green. The dwarf's remark seemed to render him temporarily speechless.

'Indeed?' I asked, curious despite my misery. '*We* Brownies?'

'Well, perhaps this worthless individual is counting his dragons before they are hatched,' Smarmy admitted. 'Or at least, I was worthless! But I was fortunate, for Tap took me aside and showed me the way.' Smarmy smiled down at the Brownie. 'I have seen the truth in Brownie Power, and Tap has accepted me as one of their own!'

'I've already made him an honorary Brownie,' Tap added. 'All he needs is ratification from the Brownie Council!'

'I am a little large,' Smarmy explained, 'but Tap

says they will in all probability make an exception.'

'Soon,' Tap piped merrily, 'there will be Brownies everywhere!'

'Doom,' Snarks whispered.

'It has been a dream I've had,' the Brownie continued, 'to show others the wisdom of the Brownie Way, ever since I came here to prepare the way for his Brownieship . . .'

The Brownie paused, turning a shade of green almost as colorful as Snarks.

'His Brownieship!' Tap whispered, true horror distorting his countenance. 'I forgot.' All this talk of guests, and I so wanted to teach Snarks – his Brownieship would go to Vushta, expecting me –' The little fellow hit his forehead with the palm of his hand. 'Oh, dear, is my buckle bent! My lace is frayed for good!'

'Indeed,' I commented. I felt sympathy for the small fellow. As surely as I had forgotten about the Vushta Apprentice Guild and their demands, Tap had not remembered that his Brownieship was still to arrive in Vushta with an important message. And when the Brownie's ruler finally came, Tap would be far away in the Eastern Kingdoms!

'You could always go back to Vushta,' Snarks suggested, 'and stay there.'

'No, my place is here with Wuntvor. A Brownie never backs out on a quest.' Tap paused, his face a mask of anguish.

'Oh, I will never make shoes again!'

'Alea!' the dragon roared behind me. 'Forgive me Wuntvor! I could not fry a dancing partner!'

I turned to see the damsel almost upon me. She grabbed me by the shoulders and wrenched me to the ground.

'They tried to keep me away from you,' she whispered

hoarsely. 'Rather they should try to keep the sun out of the sky!'

'Um,' I replied.

'Or grass from growing in the ground!' the damsel continued, hugging me close. 'Or water from filling the ocean! How can I say it?' She smiled with sudden inspiration. 'I know! I will sing it instead!'

'Must you?' Snarks asked.

Alea ignored him and burst into song:

'He's my apprentice!
He's the only one for me,
And Heaven sent us
To live forever happily!'

'Apparently she must,' Snarks remarked. Across the clearing, I heard Guxx begin to sneeze.

'Oh, Wuntie!' Alea squealed, and launched into the second verse:

'He's my apprentice!
And what am I to do?
The perfect world is lent us,
In love with my little Wuntie-poo!'

'Could this get any worse?' Snarks wailed.

And then the unicorn was in our midst, snorting wonderfully at Alea.

'You think to win this lad's favor with your song?' The beast tossed its splendid head, its mane flowing magnificently in the wind. 'Well, we mythical creatures know poetry as well. Remember, a unicorn *is* art!'

The beast turned to look at me with its large, soulful eyes.

'Oh Wuntvor, do not be forlorn,
For you can stroke my golden horn.'

It tossed its head, its forelocks blowing wonderfully in the evening breeze.

'There's no need to suffer pain,
When you might ruffle my wild mane.'

The unicorn paused, lowering its head so that its wondrous horn almost touched my lower ribs.

'And you needn't wander 'round the map,
For I'll lay my head upon your lap.'

'I was wrong,' Snarks whispered. 'It got worse.'

Alea stood, ready to confront the mythical creature. 'What do you mean,' she demanded, 'reciting poetry for my Wuntie? Don't you know I'm the one that can give him what he needs?'

The unicorn shook its perfect mane. 'All "your Wuntie," as you call him, needs, is a magnificent horned head upon his lap!'

'Is that so?' Alea screamed, rushing the unicorn. 'I'll give you a magnificent horn . . .'

They were at it again. I crept away from them as quietly as I could. Still, escape was only a temporary solution. I knew they would be on me again in a matter of moments. I had to get out of this somehow, and I feared I needed more magic than was at my command.

It was time to call on Ebenezum.

'Tap!' I beckoned to the Brownie. 'I need your help!'

Tap and Smarmy rushed to either side of me.

'At your service, oh glorious leader!' the Brownie chirped.

'I need to contact my master, now,' I informed him urgently. 'Are you up to it?'

Tap hesitated. 'That means talking to Vushta? But what if his Brownieship . . .' He sighed, then grimly straightened his jerkin. 'No, you are right. This is a job for Brownie Power!'

Smarmy applauded. Snarks asked to be excused.

'Yes, we are ready,' Tap answered at last, his tiny voice filled with determination. 'For Smarmy here will help me dance. It will be his first lesson in Brownie magic!'

'Indeed?' I said, wondering if the dwarf were up to it. But I had no time to argue. If I didn't get my master's assistance, I didn't know how I was going to get out of this.

'Very good.' Tap nodded to Smarmy. 'Now follow me. First you move your right foot, cool and tight, then you wriggle to the left and you . . .'

I glanced nervously about as Tap finished giving the honorary Brownie his instructions. Alea was tugging on the unicorn's mane while the beast used its horn to muss the damsel's hair. This was getting ugly. I urged the Brownie to redouble speed.

'For you, anything!' Tap cheerfully agreed.

'That's Brownie Power!' Smarmy added.

All four of their feet began to move so fast that I could no longer follow them. We were surrounded by dust. The world around the three of us disappeared in an instant, replaced by the brown wall on which images of Vushta already flickered.

'Master!' I called.

'Wuntvor?' my master asked just before he sneezed. 'I will be ready for you in but a moment!' I knew that meant he had to reach the protective enclosure of his gigantic Brownie shoe.

The picture on the dust wall began to gain definition and color. It was the courtyard of the Wizards College, with Ebenezum's shoe at the very center. I caught a glimpse of one sleeve of my master's robes, the dark blue tastefully embroidered with silver moons and stars, as Ebenezum lowered himself within his protective barrier. The sight of the robe was oddly reassuring, as though I were looking at a little bit of home. I was doubly glad, then, that I decided to contact my master; I felt calmer already. For the first time in quite a while I felt that perhaps everything would truly work out for the best.

The earth shook.

Oh, no, I thought. Not now! The Netherhells couldn't be attacking again!

But the quake was not repeated, at least not for a moment. And when it came a second time, it was again a single tremor, as if someone had made a mallet from a thousand trees and was pounding it slowly against the earth. It had to be something other than the Netherhells. Didn't it? I could not see or hear outside of the dust cocoon. I hoped that whatever it was, it would allow me enough time to speak with Ebenezum.

The ground shook again, with such force that it knocked all three of us from our feet. Without Tap and Smarmy's constant dancing, the dust cloud began to settle and our surroundings became dimly visible.

I did not at all like what I saw outside.

'Buckles and laces!'

Tap and Smarmy saw it as well, and could do nothing
more than stare, open-mouthed. The dust around us was
almost gone.

'Indeed!' my master called. 'Wuntvor –'

But the spell was broken. And in its place stood the
largest shoe I had ever seen, perhaps five times the size of
the one that contained Ebenezum.

'Is this Brownie Power?' Smarmy said in awe.

Tap shook his head. 'I believe this is even beyond us.'

I decided I should breathe again. But if this wasn't
Brownie Power, what was it? Then I noticed that the shoe
was connected to a pants leg that rose into the sky.

There was another noise. It was either a mountain falling
or the loudest voice I had ever heard, saying 'Oops!'

'What do you mean, oops?' Touchy demanded.

I looked up, and I do mean up, at a figure whose hair
brushed against the clouds. The tallest creature I had ever
seen smiled apologetically and waved to his left.

'I seem to have crushed this half of the forest,' the giant
replied, somewhat abashed.

'Well, if you'd only stop dragging your feet!' Nasty
replied. 'Can't Mother Duck find any better help?'

'Come on, fellows,' the giant chided. 'Is it my fault if
they don't build trees any bigger?'

'The trees are perfectly fine for me,' Snooty insisted.

'Well, you still have all the rest of them. As you see I
carefully placed my right foot in this clearing.' The giant
glanced back at his other foot, which was resting in the
distance on a recently deforested hilltop. 'Oops. Well, I'm
afraid you've lost a few more. If only forests didn't have
trees so close together.'

'So that's why you've come here?' Nasty demanded. 'To
destroy our homeland?'

'On the contrary!' the giant insisted. 'Destruction is the farthest thing from my mind.'

'Pity it isn't the farthest thing from your feet,' Nasty snapped.

'Never mind,' the giant rumbled. 'I am here – on official business. You see, Mother Duck has heard that strangers have entered her domain. Strangers whom I must carry away!'

'Strangers?' Sickly coughed.

'Not here!' Noisy bellowed.

'Begging your extremely enormous pardon,' Smarmy added, 'but we have seen no strangers. Rather, we have only been visited by our extremely close friend and his companions.'

'Is that so?' the giant mused. 'No strangers? Then I suppose I must carry off an extremely close friend and his companions.'

'No!' all Seven Other Dwarves wailed together as they clustered around me. 'You can't take him!'

'Ah.' The giant smiled. 'So this is their leader. That makes things simpler. He will be taken and questioned first.'

'Oh, no, you don't!' Hubert the dragon shouted defiantly. 'I'll make Wuntvor glad that he included us on his quest. Take that, giant!'

The dragon reared to his full height and shot a lance of flame at the giant's knee.

'Oh. That feels good,' the giant remarked as he gently picked up Hubert and placed him to one side. 'Mayhaps when we have a little more time, I will have you play some fire over my sore shoulder.'

The giant reached for me. Each finger was the size of one of the trees he had just crushed. What should I do? I thought of drawing Cuthbert, but even if I could persuade the sword to emerge from its sheath, I doubted that the giant would feel much more than a pinprick no matter how I sliced and cut. He was huge! I had met giants before, but this fellow from the Eastern Kingdoms was three times the size of those we had in the west. Besides that, he was apparently in no mood to talk the situation over.

What could I do? I panicked and ran.

The giant's hand cupped down before me, splintering the outer edge of the woods.

'Excuse me,' the giant apologized as he lifted me aloft, 'but that's what is going to happen if you try to get away.'

It was hopeless, then. I could only wait, a firm grip on my sword and pack so I would not lose them as the giant lifted me aloft between one huge thumb and forefinger. He placed me in the palm of his other hand.

'Comfy?' he asked.

'But you can't take him –' Smarmy began.

'Sorry, but it's been ordered by Mother Duck.' The giant paused, surveying all those who stood in the clearing. 'Would anyone care to question her?'

The dwarves all stared up at me, grim and silent.

'Good. We are off, then.'

In a single stride we were out of sight of the others.

So I had been captured by a giant from the Eastern Kingdoms, to go to who knew what fate? For all I knew, this huge fellow was taking me to Mother Duck, which was where I wanted to go in the first place. Of course, there were those stories about the giant's ovens that everyone kept going on about. Still, Ebenezum had told me to beware of rumors. Perhaps this situation was not as bad as it appeared.

'Please answer one question,' I ventured. 'Does Mother Duck really take intruders and bake them into bread?'

'Oh, that.' The giant coughed gently into his free hand. 'Let me put it to you this way. Which do you prefer, whole wheat or pumpernickel?'

TWENTY

'Before I came to be in the service of the wizard Ebenezum, greatest mage in the Western Kingdoms, I sometimes thought of life as nothing but confusion, with the world a whirling ball of chaos in which anything could happen to you and, given sufficient time, probably would. Since I have become an apprentice, however, I have revised my views, and now consider my earlier worries and fears nothing more than a glimpse at everyday reality.'

– SOME THOUGHTS ON APPRENTICESHIP,
by Wuntvor, apprentice to Ebenezum,
greatest mage in the Western Kingdoms
(a work in progress)

Whole wheat or pumpernickel?

No! It would not be! I rebelled at going to my death, completely powerless.

But I wasn't completely powerless! My sword might not do any good against one so large, but I still had my pack, and within that pack was my Home Study Course! I soon had the pack off my back and the book in my hands. Now all I had to do was look up G in the index.

'Eep!' the ferret cried, jumping out of the pack and onto the giant's hand.

'Eh?' the giant said. 'What's that? Oops!'

The hand fell away beneath me, and I fell with it. The ground rushed toward me with alarming speed. Both book and ferret went flying away.

I landed with a slap in the once again steady palm.

'Sorry, there,' the giant remarked. 'Hope I didn't shake you up too much. Didn't see that cottage. Well, at least it used to be a cottage. But what were you doing? You weren't trying to get away, were you?'

I glanced up at the giant. What could I do now?

I heard a tiny, tiny 'eep' from far below.

I wished there was something else, anything, that would save me from my doom. But the Home Study Course was gone, and my ferret, too. I shook the pack a final time in frustration, as if I might get some magical solution to mysteriously appear.

Into my hand fell a small sliver of wood. A sliver of wood that had been given to me in Vushta!

What could I do? I was desperate. Perhaps I could distract the giant long enough to attempt an escape. I held the toothpick out to him.

'How about this?' I challenged.

The giant laughed. 'How about what? You are actually holding something? I cannot see your threat.'

I placed the toothpick in the palm of his free hand.

'What is this? A tiny sliver of wood? Odds bodkins!'

The wood grew in the giant's hand. It was then I remembered that this was no ordinary toothpick, but a weapon given to me by the wizards of Vushta!

The giant grasped the thing, which had grown to the size of a substantial tree trunk, between two great fingers.

''Tis a magical tooth pick!' the giant cried in surprise. 'Mayhaps I shall use this. I can feel some bread stuck between my molars.'

Smiling, the huge fellow brought the mystic wood to his enormous mouth. But he cried in surprise as the pick leapt from his hand, straight into his mouth!

'What?' the giant mumbled. 'Methinks this wood has a mind of its own.' He wrinkled his brow. 'Oh, that feels good. No, not there! My gums are much too sensitive.' He frowned. 'I'll put a stop to this!'

He reached around his teeth with the fingers of his free hand. 'Where are you?' He grunted. 'Almost! The thing is bewitched. I will have it in a minute.'

He ceased to speak then, for a time, cocking his head this way and that and prodding about his jaws with various combinations of fingers. His movements became more frantic as the minutes passed.

'It is only a toothpick,' he said at last, pausing to calm himself. 'I *will* get it free. If I could just rzzssmm.'

'I beg your pardon?' I asked politely.

The giant pulled his hands from his mouth. 'Reach it. That's what I said. If I could just reach it. But I am afraid I will need bff hrrzmms!'

'I'm sorry?' I asked.

The giant frowned down at me. I could tell he was getting annoyed. '*Both hands*!' he repeated as he once again extricated his fingers from his mouth. 'I will need both hands. Excuse me, I will have to put you down. There! A finger back here will do it. Almost. It's stuck just behind this tooth. I'll just dislodge it here and everything will be frsgglggsm.'

So it was that I found myself back on the ground again as the giant staggered away, both hands stuffed in his mouth. I was free! The weapons of Vushta had once again done their work. And speaking of weapons, I realized that I still carried Cuthbert, thrust through my belt. The sword, which seemed so ineffectual when I was in the grip of the giant, somehow appeared much more useful now that I was back on solid ground.

Now all I had to do was find my way back to my companions and the dwarves. I had no idea how far the giant had carried me, although I imagined he took half a mile in a step. How many steps had we gone? Ten? Twenty? Certainly not more than thirty.

I swallowed grimly. I could be quite some distance from my companions; half a day's march or more. At least I knew the direction the giant had come from. Well, at least I thought I did. He had staggered around a bit as he tried to dislodge the enchanted toothpick. I would just have to make my best guess and hope I came across copses of ruined trees about the size of a giant's footprint. Who knew? If I could retrace the giant's footsteps, perhaps I might be able to regain the Home Study Course, and my ferret, too!

Clutching Cuthbert's handle for reassurance, I set out into the forest in what I hoped was the correct direction.

The woods were thicker here than they had been where we met the dwarves. The trees overhead blocked out what little evening light remained, save for a faint, rosy glow to the west, and I had to be careful not to run into tree trunks or what scraggly underbrush grew in the darkness. I could recognize no landmarks, for the giant had carried me here far above the trees. At last, despairing of having to walk through inky blackness, I drew forth Cuthbert. I would need his light to proceed farther, and with the sun gone, we would have to guess at the direction of our companions.

'Where are we?' the sword whispered once I had drawn him forth.

I told Cuthbert that I did not know exactly. We had to find our companions, and I would need his light.

'A civilized response,' the sword replied as it glowed obligingly. 'There has been so much shouting and movement of late, that it is nice to have a few moments of quiet. It seems as though, lately, every time I've been drawn, it's to fight some sort of monster or hideous demon. I tell you, it's enough to make a poor sword paranoid.'

'Well,' I replied, 'all you have to do for now is light my way. I assure you that we are quite alone.'

But as soon as I finished speaking, a wind sprang up, a chill night wind that turned my clothes to ice against my chest and legs.

'What's that?' Cuthbert cried.

The sword was answered by a chuckle so dry it would drain the water from a stone.

'Yes, Wuntvor,' the same dry voice rasped, 'you are alone, for the first time in ever so long.'

I knew who it was even before I spun Cuthbert about to illuminate his skull-like visage.

'Is that who I think it is?' the sword whimpered.

Death sighed, the sound of winter's coldest gale.

'Ah,' he said, 'alone at last with the Eternal Apprentice.'

What was he talking about? Even now I was not without companions. I held one in my hand.

'No, I am not alone!' I shook Cuthbert at Death. 'I have my sword!'

'Leave me out of this!' Cuthbert wailed.

Death chuckled again. 'Is this what you call a companion? A magic sword? No, I am sorry, apprentice, to escape my touch you will need more than an inanimate object.' Death shrugged back the sleeves of his robes to reveal his white-bone arms. 'But there is nothing I can say today that you have not heard before. You are mine now. Don't you think it's time we went to my domain?'

Death stepped towards me. He reached out a skeleton hand. I took a hasty step away, waving Cuthbert wildly before me.

'There are other uses for a sword!' I cried, desperate for some defense.

Death laughed. 'Poor child. Neither can you hope to kill me. Death, my dear apprentice, holds a monopoly on killing.'

Cuthbert whimpered again, and shook in my hand. 'No, you don't!' I exclaimed, saying anything that came into my mind that might give me another few seconds of life. 'You've called me the Eternal Apprentice! And you know I have companions! And uh . . . I'm sure they'll come and join me any second now!'

'That means we'll have to hurry, doesn't it?' Death grinned. 'Come to me now, and the Eternal Apprentice shall be mine at last.'

But a streak of reddish-brown leapt between Death's bony legs!

'Eep! Eep!' the streak exclaimed. My heart leapt within my chest. My ferret had found me!

'Oh, come now, Wuntvor,' Death remarked, the slightest trace of irritation entering his sepulchral tones. 'You know a ferret is not much of a companion either. If I am already taking the Eternal Apprentice, I do not think it would bother the cosmic forces overmuch if I were to take one tiny ferret as well.'

I took a deep breath, knowing that Death's words should lead me to despair. But my hope had sprung anew. My ferret had found me much faster than I had thought possible. Perhaps I was not as far away from my other companions as I had imagined.

'But quickly, now,' Death intoned. 'I have other deaths to attend to.'

His bony fingers leapt at me with astonishing speed. I reacted with a yell, lost my balance, and fell to the forest floor. Death's fingers closed above me.

'Come!' Death commanded. 'This is childish! You are delaying the –'

For one brief instant the night around me was turned to day.

'There you are!' sang a voice from above.

I would recognize that raspy baritone anywhere. The light in the sky was Hubert's dragon fire! I saw the great wings spread wide as Hubert circled for a landing.

Death screamed the agonies of a thousand souls. 'I will not be thwarted again! I will have you *now*! Though it may threaten the cosmic balance, I shall take ferret, and dragon, and apprentice, too!' One hand still reached for me. With the other, he pointed to Hubert. 'Come now. In an instant it shall be done.'

'What's going on here?' the dragon asked as he landed. 'It certainly looks dramatic.'

'Dragon! Ferret! Apprentice!' Death opened his jaw to shout: 'I TAKE YOU N –'

'There you are!' half a dozen voices shouted at once. And all about me, stepping out of the woods, were my companions, with Norei at their center!

Something that felt like the north wind but sounded like a scream of rage stopped everyone where they stood. Then the gale was over as suddenly as it had begun. I turned around and Death was gone.

Hubert was the first to break the silence.

'Yes,' the dragon whispered. 'That certainly *was* dramatic.'

'Indeed,' I replied, somewhat shaken by the incident

myself. I looked to the others, half expecting Alea and the unicorn to rush me at any moment with new protestations of affection. And what of Norei?

'Hello, Wuntvor,' Norei said as she walked towards me. All the others, Alea and the unicorn included, kept their distance. 'We were rather worried about you.'

'Indeed?' I replied 'Um . . .'

'It all started,' Norei continued when it became evident that I could not finish my thought, 'when I detected some errant magic in the area. I'm still not sure exactly what it was – well, it might have been an airborne love potion; either that or something to do with animal husbandry. At least that's what I think the spell was. Frankly, it was so awkward and diffuse that it was hard to tell. Somehow, though, the spell reminded me of you.' She laid a reassuring hand upon my shoulder. 'Not that I think of you as awkward' – she paused, then smiled – 'except perhaps in an endearing sort of way.'

I did not know what to say. Norei was speaking to me again!'

'Indeed,' I whispered hoarsely.

'And it's lucky I came along when I did,' Norei added. 'Can you imagine, not only had you been spirited away by a giant, but it did turn out to be a love potion after all, and all these around us had been affected! Well, the spell was so clumsy that it was simplicity itself to remove it, but then we had to rescue you as well.'

'Doom,' Hendrek interjected. 'Luckily, something seemed to happen to the giant's sense of direction. We spotted him soon after we set about our search, stumbling about, back towards our camp. But you no longer seemed to be with him. Hubert went on ahead, to see if he could spot you.'

'Which I did within a matter of moments,' Hubert remarked proudly. 'It's my theater-trained senses, you know. I can always smell out an audience.'

'Indeed,' I said at last. 'I thank you all.'

'I should say you should thank us!' Nasty sneered.

'Why do we always have to be the ones to go and rescue people?' Touchy demanded.

Sickly coughed. Noisy dropped something. So Norei really had counteracted my spell. Things, apparently, were back to normal.

'But how have you fared in finding Mother Duck?' Norei asked.

'Indeed,' I replied, grinning at Norei. I could not take my eyes off her! 'We are very close.' How welcome a sight was her fire-tinged hair, her eyes of deepest green. 'The dwarves assure me of that.' How many times had I longed for this vision! 'Um, could we talk alone for a minute?'

'Well, I suppose so, if you insist.' Norei's smile broadened as she spoke.

I insisted, and told the others Norei and I needed a few minutes for a conference. The two of us walked through the trees until we were out of sight of our numerous companions.

'Norei,' I whispered. I took her hand and drew her to me. It had been ever so long!

'Is this, perhaps, a new definition of the word conference?' she began sternly. But then she laughed. 'I have missed you, too, Wunt –'

The quake came before she had time to finish her sentence.

'Oh, no!' I cried. ''Tis the Netherhells!'

But it was much more than that, for at that moment there

came a great crashing from the bushes. Were my companions rushing to join me?

And then there was a knife at my throat.

Grott and Slag stepped out from behind the knife-wielding Vermin.

'Ah,' Grott sneered. 'We are so happy that you have found a quiet spot at last. We hope the young lady doesn't mind if we have a little talk?'

'Indeed,' I replied. 'This young lady is a witch.'

Grott and Slag got a good laugh out of that one.

'Yeah,' Grott added. 'And I'm the great wizard Ebenezum!'

'Yeah,' Slag remarked. 'Great.'

There was another quake beneath our feet, much worse than the last.

'Indeed,' I said when the quake had run its course. 'And do you realize that we are about to be attacked by the Netherhells?'

Slag and Grott thought that that particular comment was even more hilarious.

'Look,' Grott said, wiping the tears from his eyes. 'Your pitiful attempts at distracting us are too funny for words. What are you going to tell us next, that our shoes are untied?'

'Yeah.' Slag glanced hastily at his feet. 'Shoes.'

Grott frowned. 'Well, perhaps that was a bad example. Anyway, all this talk is distracting us from our real purpose. We've come to collect the seventeen hundred pieces of gold you owe us.'

'Seventeen hundred?' I exclaimed.

'And twenty-five,' Grott added. 'That's right. Seventeen hundred and twenty-five pieces of gold. Unless, of course, you've come up with a cure for our masters?'

'Wuntvor?' Norei turned to me. 'Who *are* these people?'

That's when the earth tremors *really* started. Vermin fell to the ground, almost losing his knife. The rest of us soon followed.

When the dust cleared, we saw a table, behind which sat five demons.

'Oh, my,' Grott commented. 'You weren't kidding about a Netherhells attack, were you?'

'Point of order!' The small, somewhat undernourished demon at the far end of the table turned to regard the larger fellow who held the gavel. 'Exactly where *are* we?'

The larger demon pounded his gavel. 'We are in the presence of magic!'

'Where?' his undernourished comrade barked. 'All this time you've been saying "I know where Vushta is!" But have you been able to get us there?'

Grott stepped rapidly to my side. 'Uh, about those seventeen hundred and fifty pieces of gold – I suppose we could negotiate.'

The other three demons behind the table were becoming restive as well, grumbling as their two fellows continued their argument.

'I tell you,' the gavel demon insisted, 'I came here because I was following a spell.'

'Of course!' the undernourished fiend shouted, shaking a finger at the other's gavel. 'You don't mention it was the only spell you managed to find since we started looking. You also didn't mention that, of all things, it was a love-potion spell!'

'Not necessarily,' the gavel demon said defensively. 'The spell could have had something to do with animal husbandry.'

Grott tore his gaze away from the fighting demons long

enough to glance at Norei. His pale complexion became paler still. 'Uh . . .' he began hesitantly, 'Wuntvor, old comrade, you were joking when you mentioned Norei was a witch?'

'Indeed,' I answered, 'no.'

'Indeed?' Grott replied. 'Well, about those eighteen hundred and fifty pieces of gold . . . Perhaps we can agree on some sort of time-payment scheme.'

'Wuntvor?' Norei asked. 'What do you want me to do with these, uh . . . people?'

Before I was able to reply, I was interrupted by a particularly loud quarrel among two of the demons. After a moment the three other fiends managed to pull them apart.

'Hey,' one of the noncombatants asked, 'why are we fighting each other? There are humans over there!'

'That's right!' another demon wearing a flowered hat added. 'And some of them probably know the way to Vushta!'

'Does that mean we can't eat them?' asked the only demon who hadn't spoken.

'Of course not,' the flower-hatted fiend replied. 'We have to find out where Vushta is. Then we can eat them.'

'Let's just say you owe us nineteen hundred pieces of gold,' Grott said hastily. 'We'll discuss the exact terms when we're back in Vushta. Slag? Vermin?'

Unfortunately, Vermin took the mention of his name as a signal that it was once again time to take a memento from somewhere in the vicinity of my nose. He leapt for me with his knife as Norei barked a short, guttural spell. A tiny whirlwind sprang up around the three apprentices, spinning them away.

'Wuntvor!' Grott screamed above the wind. 'That's nineteen hundred and twenty-five you owe –'

They spun into the arms of the committee.

'Do you think these three will do?' the flower-hatted demon asked as they grabbed the Vushtans.

The undernourished demon chewed and swallowed Vermin's knife. 'Umm. Tasty.'

'Fine,' the gavel demon ordered. 'Toss them into the hole.'

Grott wrenched his head around to give me a final glance as he was pushed into the pit.

'Remember, Wuntvor, two thousand and fifty –' Then his voice was lost in the distance. Slag and Vermin quickly followed.

'Now,' the gavel demon continued, 'I think it's time we got down to some serious blood boiling.'

'What's going on here?' a voice called out of the woods behind us. It was a woman's voice, as full of authority as that of my master. I knew who that voice belonged to even before I saw the bonnet and the high-buttoned shoes.

It was Mother Duck. She was a woman of middle age, rather tall, almost my size, and imposingly built as well. Everything about her, from the way she surveyed the crowd before her to the bold way she marched among us, said that she was a woman used to command.

The rest of my companions and the Seven Other Dwarves all rushed to join us.

'Doom,' Hendrek remarked. ''Tis the Netherhells.'

'Yeah,' Snarks added. 'Don't you guys know when to quit?'

'I think we should boil that demon's blood first.' The undernourished fiend pointed at Snarks.

Snarks started to shake as the Netherhells committee concentrated.

'Buckles and laces!' Tap exclaimed. 'Could this get any worse?'

There was an explosion in our midst. Tap moaned.

'It's . . .' he managed weakly after a moment, 'it's his Brownieship!'

'No thanks to you,' his Brownieship stated darkly.

'Excuse me,' Norei mentioned, 'but certainly we should consider helping Snarks before the demons boil his blood?'

Norei had a point. Things had been happening so fast in the past few moments that I hadn't had time to react the way a leader should.

'Companions!' I called to those around me. 'Forward! We must save Snarks from the committee!'

Hubert asked if I was absolutely sure about that, but even he joined the fray. The demons were badly outnumbered, what with Hendrek and his club, Guxx and his claws, Hubert and his dragon fire, not to mention Brax and any number of previously owned weapons. Then Norei joined in with her magic while Alea and the dwarves threw rocks to distract the fiends. It was time for me to talk quickly with Mother Duck.

'Indeed!' I called to the gray-haired lady. 'I have traveled from far Vushta to seek your help.'

'But wait!' his Brownieship interrupted. 'You have not heard my urgent message!'

'I am sorry,' I replied, 'but there is no time just now. Mother Duck –'

I was interrupted by the descent of a giant shoe, crushing at least a dozen trees.

'Oops,' the giant remarked.

'Richard!' Mother Duck looked up at the large fellow. 'I'm glad you finally found us. Is this the one?'

Richard the giant peered down at me. 'The one with the

toothpick? Yes.' He kicked his foot petulantly. Another two dozen trees met their untimely end. 'Pumpernickel and whole wheat are too good for him. I think we should make him raisin toast!'

'Now, now, Richard,' Mother Duck chided. 'I have other plans.'

'Are you sure you don't want to hear my pronouncement?' his Brownieship inquired.

'Oh, listen to him!' Tap entreated. 'Please listen to him!'

His Brownieship glared at Tap. 'I used to know a Brownie once who looked a lot like you. Of course, he would have waited in Vushta for me.'

Tap moaned something about his eyelets being lost forever. I couldn't stand to see the little fellow in such pain. I would let his Brownieship make his pronouncement as soon as I introduced myself to Mother Duck.

'I will be with you in one second,' I assured the Brownies.

'Indeed,' I continued. 'Mother Duck, as I was saying, I have come here from far-distant Vushta to seek your aid on behalf of my master, Ebenezum, and all the other magicians at the great Wizards College.'

'Aid?' Mother Duck asked. 'What sort of aid?'

I explained to her about the Netherhells plans to take over the surface world, culminating with the attack going on behind us even as we spoke.

'That?' Mother Duck shook her head curtly. 'I can take care of that.' She marched smartly off in the direction of the fighting.

I looked back to his Brownieship. 'Now,' I said, 'I can hear your pronouncement.'

'Wha –' His Brownieship tore his gaze away from the giant's enormous shoe. 'Sorry. What wonders one finds in the outside world. Nice stitching, too.' He reached inside his jerkin to retrieve a small roll of parchment, then glanced up at me and cleared his throat.

'A Brownie Pronouncement.'

His Brownieship unrolled the scroll and read:

'To Whom It May Concern: Be it known that through certain arcane and difficult procedures known only to the ancient and revered society of Brownies, we have determined a fact of utmost importance that we believe has great impact on whatever quests are currently in progress. To be more specific, we have uncovered certain facts regarding Mother Duck. To be even more specific, these facts concern Mother Duck and the recent treaty she has signed with the forces of the Netherhells, dividing the soon-to-be conquered surface world into two kingdoms, one ruled by demons, the other by Mother Duck. For this reason, your proposed overtures to Mother Duck would seem . . .'

The Brownie's voice died as Mother Duck returned.

'It's been taken care of,' she remarked dryly. 'Even demons know that if anything happens in the Eastern Kingdoms, it is done by me.'

'Oh, most certainly, Mother Duck,' Smarmy agreed as he ran after her. 'Anything you want us to do, Mother Duck?'

'I was going to ask her that!' Touchy blurted.

'If anyone should be asking things of Mother Duck –' Snooty began.

'Of course!' Mother Duck interrupted her dwarves with a smile. 'Mother Duck has things for everyone to do. Now, why don't you be good little dwarves and gather together all the other intruders. They are now our prisoners!'

'Certainly, Mother Duck!' the dwarves shouted more or less together before they ran off to capture my companions. But then we would be prisoners of allies of the Netherhells! What could I do?'

'Indeed,' I began, 'perhaps you did not –'

The woman turned to regard me with her penetrating blue eyes, as clear as a bright winter sky. 'Mother Duck has things for everyone to do,' she repeated.

'Indeed,' I tried again, 'but if you would only listen –'

'Mother Duck wants you to be quiet,' she interrupted again. 'Richard, if you would?'

The giant's hand scooped me up from behind, knocking my legs out from under me. I found myself once again in the giant's palm, a hundred feet above the earth.

'Where do I take him?' Richard rumbled. 'To the bakery?'

'Oh, no, no,' Mother Duck chortled happily. 'You'll have to do without your bread, at least for a little while. Once I found out that this fellow was the Eternal Apprentice, why, my plans for him changed ever so much.' She clapped her hands gleefully. 'Oh, my. Mother Duck is going to have such fun!'

'To the Storybook, then?' Richard asked.

'Oh, yes, the Storybook!' She laughed brightly. 'Take him there at once, my lovely giant and my energetic dwarves!'

'To the Storybook,' Richard repeated, stepping carefully away from Mother Duck, heading, I assumed, deeper into the Eastern Kingdoms. We were soon out of sight of all the others.

'Indeed!' I called up to the giant. 'What is this Storybook?'

The giant shrugged his massive shoulders. 'You probably would have preferred the bakery,' is all he would say. And he continued to carry me off into the night.

I sat back down in the giant's palm, helpless, at least for the moment, to alter my fate. There were so many questions: Would I see my companions again? Would I get a chance to talk to Mother Duck and somehow show her the error of her ways? Would I even live long enough to see tomorrow's sunrise?

'And what,' I whispered aloud, 'about Norei?'

Yet as dramatic as all these queries were, they paled bef the one question that would not leave my head:

This time, had I failed my master forever?